Devil AND THE Bluebird

Devil AND THE Bluebird

JENNIFER MASON-BLACK

Amulet Books
New York

Library of Congress Cataloging-in-Publication Data

Names: Mason-Black, Jennifer, author.
Title: Devil and the bluebird / by Jennifer Mason-Black.
Description: New York : Amulet Books, 2016. | Summary: Armed with her mother's guitar, a knapsack of cherished mementos, and a pair of magical boots, Blue journeys west in search of her sister Cass, but when the devil she met at the town's crossroads changes the terms of their deal, Blue must reevaluate her understanding of good and evil.
Identifiers: LCCN 2015045546 (print) | LCCN 2015048484 (ebook) | ISBN 9781419720000 (hardback) | ISBN 9781613128961 (ebook)
Subjects: | CYAC: Demonology—Fiction. | Sisters—Fiction. | Magic—Fiction.| Music—Fiction. | Mothers and daughters—Fiction. | Voyages and travels—Fiction. | Good and evil—Fiction. | BISAC: JUVENILE FICTION / Family / Siblings. | JUVENILE FICTION / Fantasy & Magic. | JUVENILE FICTION / Action & Adventure / General. | JUVENILE FICTION / Performing Arts / Music.
Classification: LCC PZ7.1.M3764 De 2016 (print) | LCC PZ7.1.M3764 (ebook) | DDC [Fic]—dc23
LC record available at http://lccn.loc.gov/2015045546

Text copyright © 2016 Jennifer Mason-Black
Book design by Alyssa Nassner

Printed and bound in U.S.A.
10 9 8 7 6 5 4 3 2 1

ABRAMS
THE ART OF BOOKS SINCE 1949

115 West 18th Street
New York, NY 10011
www.abramsbooks.com

To Jonathan,
who has always believed

THE GUITAR RESTED AGAINST HER BACK THE WAY HER mother's hand had when she was small and afraid. She pulled her fingers into the sleeves of her canvas barn coat, searching for warmth there. Above her, the stars burned cold; everything else was black and silent. No moon out to keep her company, to turn the dust of the crossroads silver where it speckled her hiking boots.

She shivered. She didn't know how long to wait, or whether waiting would even work. Old stories meant nothing or everything, depending on whom you asked. Her mother would have said that a story could change anything—the world, time, the future—but stories hadn't changed her mother's cancer. Hadn't changed the way she'd been eaten up from the inside, only a husk left by the end.

A breeze sprang up, tugging at her hair, and she tucked her chin into her collar. Clouds stretched like fingers across the stars, shuttering their lights one by one. She held up one hand. Her fingers showed as just one more shade of dark. She reached into her pocket for her phone to check the time.

"No need." A voice like wisps of stream rolling across water stayed her.

She fumbled for the switch on her flashlight. The light sputtered, then dimmed; and she hit it hard. For a moment, it caught, cast a stark white light across the dirt road. A woman stood before her, tall and long-limbed, in a red dress that dripped off her hips and blew loose around her calves. Her straight black hair blew as well, a rippling veil around her face. Eyes so dark they disappeared into the night; bare feet; a pair of red high heels dangling from one hand. No sign the cold bothered her at all.

The flashlight died again. The woman sounded closer—soft rustles, the slip of feet in the dirt. Suddenly, running seemed a reasonable option.

"I thought you'd be a man." The words limped out, tiny and lifeless. She cleared her throat and tried again. "If, you know, you're who I'm looking for."

So close now that she could feel the woman's breath hot on the side of her face. "Oh, I'm the one you're looking for. Question is, should you be, Blue Riley?"

Blue stood up a little taller. Something glowed between them like candle flame, only cold. The woman fingered the top button of Blue's coat, one red nail tapping against it.

"I came at the right time," Blue said. "The right place, too."

"Child, you did everything right, and that's a start. Most people have no respect for the right way of doing things these days. You even came prepared." The woman's hand moved to the neck of the guitar perched above Blue's shoulder. She could feel the wood begin to heat under the stranger's touch. More than heat—it vibrated, as if it were ready to play on its own.

The woman sighed. "She's been in more hands than yours, Bluebird."

It wasn't the wind that brought tears to her eyes. "That's private, that name."

"There's nothing private when you wait for me at midnight at the crossroads, little girl. Your history isn't more than a speck of dust on this here road. Can you play?"

She clenched her numb fingers, brought them to her face to blow on them. "I just need a minute—" she began.

The woman took Blue's hands in her own. Heat ran like water over and under her skin. Blue pulled away and unslung the guitar from her back. One strum. She winced.

"I just gotta tune it. The cold . . . It'll just take a minute."

"Listen, baby, you think I got all the time in the world? Hand it here."

"I got it." She bit down on the tip of her tongue and listened as she plucked the first string. Cass would have been finished already. Cass made everything into a show when she tuned and played, while under the eyes of others Blue felt like random pieces: hands, fingers, ears. A turn of the peg, another strum. She shivered as the breeze picked up a little.

"I expected a man," she said again, trying to fill the empty space.

"I call bullshit on that one." The woman leaned in closer. She smelled like . . . like honey cooked hot on the stove and oranges about to turn to badness—and something more, the faintest whiff of something familiar and forgotten. "I think I'm exactly what you expected."

Her hair blew across Blue's face. Blue's eyelashes fluttered against it as she turned the third peg. She strummed again, straining to hear whether she'd got it right.

"It's the cold, you know?"

The woman laughed. "Yeah, I know."

"I'm ready." She looked down at her fingers on the neck of the guitar, trying to count a beat in her head, slow and steady. She only made it to two before she jumped in, anxious hands rushing the start like a spooked racehorse. Her voice stumbled over the first verse. She struggled to remember the way the words rippled and rolled, irresistible as a river, when Mama had sung the song. She sounded tinny by comparison.

The second verse was better. By the third, the memories had fled, leaving her with her own voice, her own fingers that no longer tripped over all the strings. Sweat was dripping down her back by the time she reached the final chorus, and her bangs were damp on her forehead.

The woman said nothing for a minute. A long slow minute, just the night and the wind and the shifting speckles of stars to mark the time.

"Used to be I met real musicians here." *Used to be.* She'd tried. She'd failed. Was it relief that rumbled through her? "Used to be they understood their instruments better than anything else in the whole world. They'd die for a few pieces of wood and string. They weren't the best, not when they met me, but they burned to be."

A faint glow, like what embers gave off, lit the air. "You, little girl, you love that guitar of yours, but only for what it's already done, not for what it could do. You're after something else tonight. Give it here."

The woman's words ran like cold water over Blue, goose bumps rising on Blue's skin. She shook her head, tightened her grip on the neck.

"No fear. I'm not taking or giving at the moment. Just hand it to me."

She did. Without it, she felt smaller, colder. She'd lost. Nothing would change, the same faces, the same mistakes waiting for her Monday morning. Teena, Beck, looking past her, through her, no one there to take their places. Weightless as a scrap of paper, a plastic bag, no meaning to her at all.

The woman tuned it again, faster than Blue had. She began to play, a pick pulled from who knew where. The song she launched into was one Blue'd heard a thousand times, a traditional tune that Mama and Tish had finished every concert with.

> *I'm a maid of constant sorrow*
> *I seen trouble all my days . . .*

The tears ran loose across her cheeks. It wasn't the song that moved her; it was her mother's voice. Everything: the tone, the places where she dragged out a word an extra beat, where the sad showed through like sunlight between the drapes. All coming from the woman in the red dress, nothing like Mama, her shag of brown hair, her speckled eyes and unpainted nails.

The woman had lied. She was giving and taking, right there, right then.

"You tricked me," Blue said, wiping her face, the wind stinging the damp skin.

"Don't you know what instruments do?" the woman asked. "They suck people in and continue to echo them out forever once they're gone. Didn't you ever wonder why some dusty old violin has so much power?"

Blue shook her head.

"I haven't done anything but let a bit of that echo out." The woman handed the guitar back. It was hot, almost too hot to hold. Blue ducked her head under the strap, returned the guitar to her back.

"Here's the thing, little girl. You know your chords, and your voice, it's . . ." A breath in, like a smoker taking one last drag. "That's not why you're here, though. You came looking for something else. Tell me."

She squared her shoulders. No wavering, not even to ask what the woman meant about her voice. The woman had already confirmed it, hadn't she? People came here when they burned to be the best. "I think you've been here before."

Another laugh, a little surprised. "Maybe. Maybe not. There's plenty of crossroads in this world. You think I remember every one?"

"I think you were here two years ago. You met Cass. My older sister." The salty taste of loss rested on Blue's tongue. "She was looking for something. I think she asked to trade with you."

The woman came closer, her scent changing to heat. Not smoke, not wood fire, just raw heat. "Might be. Lots of people do."

"She was seventeen then. I'm seventeen now. I haven't seen her for two years. She called four times, but nothing—" She stopped before the rest: *But not when she should have. Three days ago.*

"Kid, she could be doing anything. She's moved on. Probably a waitress somewhere. Not as though there's much to hold anyone here."

There's me, Blue thought. But she couldn't say that. She hadn't kept Cass, after all. "She isn't like that. She wanted something."

"Everyone wants something. That doesn't make her special." An owl called from far away, a distant *Who cooks for you all.* "She could have been picked up by someone. She could be dead."

"She's not." Because she had to believe that. Because being the girl who'd lost her mother was one thing, being the girl who'd lost her mother and sister something else entirely.

There was the promise, though, made seven years ago, their

hands tightly clasped as they stared at each other in Halloween makeup, Cass with pointy ears and whiskers drawn in black pencil, tears erasing Blue's clown face.

"Don't go without me. Don't go at all. Please, Cassie. Not now."

Cass could have said anything. For a moment, Blue thought she would say, *It's Halloween*, ignore the rest—that it was also Mama's birthday, the first without her there.

Instead, "It's okay. We'll stay together. We need to fix your makeup first."

Incomplete relief. "Not just today." She couldn't ask too much, not from her quicksilver sister. "Every year, for Mama's birthday. Always. Even when we're old." She gripped Cass's hands more tightly.

A crack, tears pooling, unshed, in Cass's eyes. "Okay. I promise."

Last year on Halloween, a phone call, one she missed, and a voice mail left behind. Cass, saying nothing much. *Happy Halloween, happy birthday, Mama, remember, I promised.* This year? Silence.

She couldn't be dead. She just needed finding. "She came here, looking for something." It had been in the note she left. *I walked out as far as the crossroads of Wendell and Burnt Hill roads last night, and I realized I needed to keep going, a lot farther, to get what I want.*

"What if she did? What's it to me?"

Blue closed her eyes. She thought about being little in Mama's lap: Cass on one knee, her on the other. She thought about playing guitar with Cass—Cass using the one she'd bought herself, Blue on Mama's—and how they sang together, and it was like being inside and outside herself at the same time, like being the world.

She thought about missing people until all you had was loneliness inside, and about the things you might try to fill that loneliness with.

"I want to find her and make her safe. My soul for hers. That's my trade." Said aloud, it sounded silly—the sort of thing a little kid might dream up. Yet here she was, saying it. And if she could find a woman in a red dress waiting at the crossroads at midnight, then surely Cass could have, too. They had been raised on the same stories after all, and if anyone burned to be the best, it was Cass.

A soft chuckle. "You think it's that easy? You think I'm swapping baseball cards here? That's not how things work."

"But a brave heart makes the difference." Mama's words, not hers. She raised her chin to look the woman in the eye.

The ember glow brightened. "A brave heart . . . You're living in the wrong time, little girl. Those are mighty big words for this day and age."

"No. It's always true. Like . . ." She scrambled for comparison. "Like water's always H_2O."

Laughing, again, as if she'd made the funniest joke ever. "Well, now. Some things may be constant, that's true. Perhaps the more important constant is that sometimes I get bored. Sometimes I enjoy a game. Do you enjoy games, Blue Riley?"

She trembled. "Sometimes. I like poker and cribbage." Cribbage, the game Mama had taught them in motel rooms using the board her grandfather had made. Burnt holes and blue and red pegs. Cass always handing over the worn cards to Blue to shuffle, because no matter how good she was with other things, Cass couldn't shuffle worth a damn.

"Well, there you go. Let's say you and me have a little game.

You win, your sister comes home, safe and sound. I win, two souls for the price of one."

"What's the game?" Fear and hope wriggled within her until she felt as though her skin must ripple with them.

"Six months, Blue. I'll give you six months to find her."

"But I don't—"

"Uh-uh, listen all the way first. I'll give you . . . let's call it a homing device. Like a bird, you'll know your direction. It'll be up to you to find your way."

"Like a map?"

"No, like instinct. No way to know how far. You just have to go."

"That sounds easy."

"Does it? Perhaps it is. Perhaps I'm feeling kindly toward a brave heart. You find her and reassert the sacred vows of sisters, and you'll both keep your souls."

Cass, safe. Six months. A direction. A chance to keep her soul and reclaim Cassie's. It was better than she'd hoped. "I'll do it."

"Splendid. Six months, Blue Riley. Let's see what you have in you."

"How do I get the homing device thing?"

The woman took Blue's chin in her hand. She moved all the way in, her breasts bumping warm against Blue, her hair tangled between them. She tilted Blue's chin up a little, paused, looking into her eyes. "Every time, little girl. Every single time, they ask . . ."

She kissed her. It was like nothing she'd felt before, not the dry peck of her aunt, or the awkward thrill of fumbling lips. This kiss dove deep, like fire burning away everything, like fear and wildness and want. As if she could lose herself in it and never be found. And at the very end, a pull—something giving way. Breath, maybe. Maybe more.

"Do you feel it?" The woman released her chin. Blue nodded. Like September, when the sunlight began to shift and in the middle of wildflowers she could feel the winter coming. A certainty lodged inside her, down in her feet within the cradle of her boots. Her feet knew where to go.

"Tell me you feel it, Blue."

Blue looked at her. The woman's dark eyes glittered. "I feel—" Blue began.

Nothing came out. She tried again. Again, this time with force. Nothing, not even a whisper.

"You were right," the woman said. "Too easy. This way is more fun. For me, at least. You win the game, you get your sister and your voice back."

She turned, walked a few steps away, and the dark swallowed her whole. Blue stood alone, the crossroad dust swirling around her.

SHE WOKE TO SUNLIGHT ON HER FACE. FROM DOWN THE hall came the roar of the vacuum. Aunt Lynne's Saturday morning scour. Her aunt believed dirt had a place all right—outside her door and well away from her stoop. Saturdays were made for cleaning from top to bottom, Lynne on her knees scrubbing, dusting every crack and corner, polishing everything that could shine, before heading out for groceries.

"It's the only way to live in a small space," she'd told Blue when asked why she didn't sleep late, or at least drink a second cup of coffee and try her hand at the Saturday crossword. "You let things go and you may as well move into Gus Thompson's barn."

Gus's barn smelled of hay and ammonia, and his rooster crowed from sunrise to sundown. That was bad enough, but then there was Gus's tendency to start his chain saw up first thing in the morning on weekends to work on the sculptures of bears and eagles he sold to tourists venturing away from Vacationland's coast. By comparison, Lynne's neat streak ranked as a minor irritation.

Most everything about her aunt counted as a minor irritation. Lynne had fed them and clothed them and made sure they went to school, kept them up-to-date on vaccinations and left presents under the Christmas tree. She wasn't Mama, though. You'd never open a drawer in her house and find an old bird's nest where you expected the silverware to be. Lynne was meant to be the relative you visited at Christmas, not lived with year-round.

Family was Cass, and Cass was gone.

Blue sat up and touched her feet to the floor gingerly. Last night, walking home, they'd ached. Not like when she used to cover for Teena at the diner, before Teena stopped talking to her and started talking *about* her. No, this ache ran deep and strong.

Nothing happened, though, when her arches sank into the soft rug. Just her feet, plain and normal, second toes longer than the first, one big toenail only half grown back from when she'd dropped a brick on it over the summer. The same as always.

If her feet were fine, then . . . She called out to Lynne. Tried to. Her mouth made the right shapes, but only air escaped her lips. No words, no whistle, no nothing. Not fair. No voice meant she should also have the homing device the woman in the red dress had described. Otherwise, it wasn't a game, it was torture.

The noise of the vacuum grew. She jumped back into bed, pulled the covers up to her nose. A few more swipes and Lynne would reach Blue's door. She'd crack it open same as always, to confirm Blue was there. There, yes. Able to talk, no. She closed her eyes and slowed her breathing to sleep speed.

The vacuum turned off. A whiz as the cord retracted, a tap at the door. "Blue, you awake?" A creak as the door opened, the smell of pine soap and lemon.

Two years ago, it must have been the same. Lynne knocking and calling to them, only that time Blue had been asleep. Lynne had shaken her awake to ask if she knew where Cass was. Then they'd found the note. Cass was gone.

A retreat, a gentle click as the door shut behind her. Ten minutes more, and the front door opened and closed, followed by the sound of Lynne's Subaru starting up.

Her voice. What had happened? Last night there'd been the woman in the red dress, and the deal, and the kiss. They couldn't possibly be real. She tried summoning it again, attempting everything from a whisper to a yell. Still nothing came.

She hurried into the bathroom, where she started the shower, washed her hair, and breathed in steam, waiting for her throat to loosen up and her voice to come pouring out. No luck. Clams made more noise than she did.

Showered and dressed, she headed to the front door out of habit. All the way through last summer, Teena would pick her up on Saturdays. They'd shop for groceries for Teena's gram and clean her house. She insisted on giving them a little money in exchange—pocket change—but Blue would have done it for free. Anything for Teena's gram, who smelled of violet perfume, had papery skin through which you could see the bones of her hands, and told stories of feeding hoboes during the Great Depression. Blue's own grandmother had died before she'd been born—the one on her mother's side, at least. On her father's—well, her father's side didn't really exist. Family wasn't part of a sperm donor's donation.

She studied her feet as she sat to put on her boots. Encased in gray wool socks, they looked like feet. No sparks of magic, no weird tingles, nothing more special than bones and muscle and skin waiting to do their job. Her hiking boots rested on the plastic floor protector by the door. She unlaced them, thinking about walking out along the trail through the pines or maybe going all the way back to Somerset Hill and up, away from everyone.

She slipped the first boot on her foot. The feeling came fast, as if she'd stuck her toes in an electrical socket. It was the same aching need from last night: the call to move. Only in the booted foot, though. The other stayed unchanged, just a foot in a sock on a rug.

Last fall she'd gone with Teena to the outlets in Kittery, where they'd picked through the remnants the tourists had turned down. She'd just finished reading a book about a woman hiking the Pacific Crest Trail in California, and she'd longed for something similar. She didn't yearn for Augusta, or Portland, or even Boston, the way Teena did. Used to be that Teena's dreams were hers, too—that she was happy to follow Teena's course for their future. Little by little, things had shifted, and she'd found herself between racks of fleece and flannel and sweaters with moose on the front, asking for a good pair of boots.

"Hiking boots? Whatever," Teena had said, but they'd gone through every shoe section of every store. None of the boots were right—too big, too small, way too expensive—until Teena groaned with frustration and made a U-turn into the Goodwill parking lot. There, on the third shelf from the bottom, perched a pair of red-dish-brown leather hiking boots. Blue's size. No wear marks. Ten bucks.

Blue had worked oil into the leather until they darkened up nice and ripe. She'd gone on day hikes to break them in, until they fit her feet as if they'd been made for them. The extra half inch of height they gave her, the firm way they met the ground—in them she became just shy of invincible. Different, too. The kind of girl who might start dreaming things on her own, whether she wanted to or not.

Thanks to the woman in the red dress, now they'd become something more. With the second one on, the sensation ran like a current straight up both legs and into her heart, telling her it was time to go.

Time to go.

When Cass left, she'd wanted to sweep everything off her sister's dresser, to toss the expensive makeup out the window to be crushed on the gravel drive. It had felt as if every layer Cass had applied was one more coat sealing in her anger. "Our mother," she'd said, sitting on her bed the summer before she'd gone, "could have left us with a lot more than Eliotville, Maine, and Lynne's trailer if she hadn't insisted on playing music no one wanted, with frigging Tish Bellamy as a partner. I'm never going to be that stupid. I deserve more than this."

She'd said it as if she were talking to Blue, sure; but it felt like a conversation Cass was having with herself. As if Tish were the root of everything bad—as if she could have even planted cancer in Mama. Cass—the same girl who could spend forty-five minutes gently unsnarling Blue's hair when winter hats and scarves conspired to tie it in knots—had given herself up inch by inch to fury. All Blue knew how to do was to watch, until that day, when she found what she shouldn't have and showed it to Cass.

Now it was time to fix what she had broken. She pulled out her day pack and started stuffing it. T-shirts, jeans, underwear, a couple of flannel shirts worn soft and cozy. Socks, three pairs of wool ones Lynne had knitted her for Christmas. She put on the oversized Guatemalan sweater she'd impulsively bought last year in a little hippie shop in Portland only to cast it aside, too shy to wear it. It was itchy as hell but warmer than anything. She threw her barn coat on over it. What else? What do you pack when you have no clue where you're going?

She picked up her phone but put it back down. If she brought it, Lynne would call it. It could be used to track her, too, and she didn't want that. The one reason to bring it was in case Cass called it, but Cass had called the house phone every other time. Better to leave it and buy a new one once she was away from Maine.

That left just a few things. Her velvet keepsake bag. Hidden in her dresser, it contained the sorts of treasures only she could appreciate: letters and pictures, comfort and memory. She took out Mama's silver ring with the turquoise detail and slipped it on her finger before placing the bag in her backpack. Mama's guitar, safe within its hard case, came next. A notebook; some pens and pencils. Without a voice, she'd either need to write or become a mime to rival Marcel Marceau.

Lynne's trailer had seemed like a dream when Blue visited it as a little girl, with its shag rugs and vases with silk flowers, every petal free of dust. It was so different from the apartments she and Mama and Cass and Tish had drifted through. Those had been carved out of corners of ramshackle houses—drafty spaces with water stains on the ceilings and mice running along the floorboards at night.

They'd moved in for good the year Blue turned nine, the year being sick had become Mama's full-time job. Mama'd died in Lynne's room, on Lynne's bed, a year later. They'd known the end was coming, and Blue had tried to stay through the hours, days, but Mama had held on so much longer than anyone had thought she would, her harsh breathing slowing and speeding again and again. When the spaces between the breaths began to stretch further and further, Blue felt herself strangling, desperate for air. She'd run from the room, outside, into the pines where she'd hidden behind the biggest one she could find. No one had followed—they couldn't, wouldn't have left Mama—and she'd come back alone to the terrible nothingness left where Mama's breath should have been.

That was the only time she'd seen Lynne cry. Not in the year before, when Mama was sick. Not later, when Cass had left. Lynne had done lots of things then—called the police to report Cass as a runaway, talked to the social services people, questioned Cass's friends herself to see if they knew where she was, continued to change the sheets on Cass's bed once a week—but crying hadn't been one of them. After the first call from Cass, a month after she'd left, Lynne had said that Cass was old enough and smart enough to make her own choices.

"She's not here, Blue," she'd announced, when Blue got home from school that day. "She's not in Maine anymore. She's not a fugitive. She hasn't been kidnapped. She knows she can come home. She's almost eighteen, and she doesn't want to be here anymore." Was that what Mama would have done? No, because Mama wouldn't have let Cass fill up with anger. At least, that was what Blue thought. It was hard to know, with no one to help sort out her real memories of her mother from her imagined.

She opened to a blank sheet of paper in an unused green notebook.

Dear Lynne, she wrote, taking pains to be neat. *I've got to go for a while. I think I know how to find Cass. I'm okay, so you don't need to look for me either. I'll be in touch when I can. Love, Blue*

She meant more: something about thanks for taking care of her, and for the socks Lynne knitted, and for the handful of times she'd driven them out to the ocean to wander along the rocks or taken them to pick blueberries on the hill up past the edge of town. She meant *I'm sorry*, too, because even if Lynne didn't cry, Blue knew she still hurt inside. It was obvious in how she looked at Blue sometimes, or called her by Mama's name when she was tired. They'd each lost a sister; only, Blue had a chance to find Cass now, while Mama was gone for good.

She ripped out the sheet and folded it, wrote "Lynne" on the outside, and left it on the coffee table. Then she shouldered her backpack, grabbed the guitar, and headed out the door.

SHE HAD A LICENSE BUT NO CAR. SHE'D NEVER SEEN THE
need. Teena had had the Beast, a rusted-out old pickup with the
Pats' Flying Elvis painted across the hood. Not "had," past tense.
Teena still had the Beast; only, Blue no longer had her. Not Beck,
either, who drove a full-sized white pickup that he kept spotless
year-round, and who'd always been willing to take her anywhere.

Once she'd had friends. Now she had her feet and almost $900,
saved up from cleaning cabins for Emma Bissonette during hunting season, babysitting, and working the shifts Teena tossed her at
the diner. Road trip money, earmarked to get them to the Rock and
Roll Hall of Fame. Teena had planned it all out for them in junior
high. In seventh grade, it had sounded marginally fun. By tenth,
Blue could imagine a whole long list of things she'd rather use the
money on; but friends did that, right? Stuck with plans they'd made,
didn't change things even when they wanted something else.

Never mind. It was Find Cass Money now.

Money stashed safely in her backpack after stopping at the
bank, Blue hurried out and up the street. Past Teena's aunt's hair
salon, past the Laundromat, past Jayne's Hardware. She hesitated
at the diner, her stomach rumbling. In the window she could see
Teena, paused by a table, a tray in hand. Teena, not even five feet

tall, could party like someone three times her size. She had a Tweety Bird tattoo on her left hip, a brown stain of a birthmark between the thumb and forefinger of her right hand, and a passion for classic rock.

Cass was Blue's sister, but Teena had been her savior when life had shipwrecked her in Eliotville. She'd ridden up to her on a battered boy's bike, looked Blue up and down as she waited by the door of the 7-Eleven, and said, "We got five kittens in the barn. You ever seen kittens in a barn before, city girl?" Then she'd coaxed Blue onto the handlebars of her bike for the ride to her farm, Blue wondering the whole time whether being a city girl was considered good or bad. She'd assumed that it was something she wore that made her stick out. From that point forward, she'd studied how Teena dressed, adjusting her wardrobe piece by piece until her clothes no longer gave her away.

Blue and Teena. And Beck: nice-guy Beck, with his truck, his cautious smile, and his hurry to open doors for her. He was Teena's cousin, son of the local cop, always around if Blue wanted anything. Like a boyfriend. Options were slim in Eliotville when it came to boys.

"Come on, Blue. He's cute and he's totally into you, and you could get married and we'd have the same last name, and I'd be auntie to all your babies." Teena made their relationship sound as inevitable as graduation.

Blue liked Beck. She liked how he looked, and how he smelled when she leaned close to him, and how his hands felt when he helped her out of the back of Teena's truck. She just didn't love him. Making out with him, after the first time, when half the thrill had been wondering whether he would actually kiss her, had slowly begun to feel as exciting as brushing her teeth. She thought maybe that was what happened, maybe she simply wanted more than a few kisses, and so she'd pushed forward, until she realized that no matter how much fooling around they did, she wasn't interested.

She hadn't even planned to break up with him. She had just said no again and again, to everything, until he finally asked her on the last day of school if she didn't like him anymore. For a moment, standing under the sun as the buses pulled away, she wanted to say no, that everything would stay the same forever.

Instead, she'd said, "I'm sorry." That night, she'd told Teena that it wasn't a temporary breakup. Somehow, though, it became bigger than whether she was going out with Beck. It was about her and Teena, and about the Rock and Roll Hall of Fame and how she didn't really want to go, and it was like discovering that what she'd assumed was a mountain was a volcano about to erupt. By the end, Teena had called her a bitch, and Blue had said she didn't care, and they hadn't spoken since.

Now, as Teena glanced out the diner window, Blue raised her hand in a wave. Teena turned away. So much for salvation. Nothing ever lasted.

She left town in a truck full of fish. The woman driving had hair dyed shoe-polish black. She kept a cooler on the seat between them, a bag of unshelled sunflower seeds on top.

"Help yourself," she said, waving a hand in Blue's direction. "Always buy unshelled. Slows you down when you're eating. It's important to watch your calories when you spend your time on the road. The first year I was driving, I put on weight like you wouldn't believe. It got so my knees hurt all the time, you know? Probably not. You're too young to know about it."

Blue nodded. She suspected the woman had forgotten she

couldn't make a sound, and it wouldn't have made a difference if she hadn't. The woman talked as easily as fish swam, before they landed in her truck at least.

"Anyway, unshelled sunflower seeds, unshelled peas, real peas, not those skinny little kind they put in that Chinese food, and celery sticks. Sometimes in the summer, I'd put in some watermelon all cubed up; but then I figured out it made me pee all the time." She lowered her voice on the word *pee*, as if someone might hear.

Blue had met her in the parking lot of the diner. Uncertain, she'd leaned against a truck with a basketful of clams painted on the side until the woman came out and studied her from the far side of the parking lot.

"What you doing, kid?" she called out.

Blue opened her mouth, paused, and closed it again. Voice wasn't something she'd ever thought about before. It was just there, like the sun and the moon and the ocean.

She pulled the notebook out of her back pocket.

Need a ride. Can I come with u?

The woman came near, looking from the paper to Blue's face and back again. After a minute, she pulled a glasses case from her shirt pocket. "Reading glasses." She waved them. "Getting old's a bitch."

She read the note, then looked at Blue again. She examined her, as if something more were written on her face—as if maybe those words were more important than the ones on the page.

"Just you? You're traveling alone?"

Blue nodded and pointed at the bag between her feet, then at the guitar by her side.

"A musician, huh? You know about that, right? You never turn down a musician in need. I learned that from my husband."

Pen to paper again.

Is he driving 2?

The woman shook her head. "Bill was a logger when he wasn't playing the drums."

Was. The word needed no explanation. Her mother was, too. Was funny, was smart, was quick to cry, quick to laugh. Was gone forever.

"Okay, kid. You promise me I'm not gonna find the cops on my tail, I'll give you a lift. First, though, how do you know I'm even going in the right direction?"

Blue blushed. She'd just assumed. The woman could have been headed back up the coast, straight on up to Canada, and Blue knew she didn't want to go there.

"You gonna hitch your way anywhere, you gotta make sure your ride's going the right way."

Once they'd worked things out, Blue had put her bag and the guitar in the cab and hopped in. Lou, the driver, had talked ever since.

As they passed over the bridge and left Maine behind, Lou checked a packet of papers attached to her visor. "I'm going straight into Boston. You want that, or should I let you out before then?"

Blue shrugged, then immediately regretted it. Wrong answer. The right one would have made it seem she had a real destination.

Lou stayed silent for a minute. "Listen, kid. This is the deal. Sometimes when you're hitching, you're gonna meet people who think they know better than you. Some of them do. Some kids don't have any sense at all. They leave homes where people love them and end up in places where people don't give a fig for them.

"Sometimes, though, the people who think they know better

don't. Some kids got real good reasons to leave a place behind, and some self-righteous fool could do them real damage by putting them right back in it."

Blue nodded, not knowing what else to do. She didn't fit either category. Yes, she was leaving Lynne, and Lynne had loved her—or, at least, had given her a good home—but she could always go back. And she was moving toward Cass, so really she was leaving someone who loved her and going to someone who loved her. Total win.

"Another group of folks won't care a bit about where you're going or why. They'll give you a ride if it works for them, usually 'cause they're bored and talking makes the miles go by. Some of 'em will be hoping you'll give them something in exchange, if you get what I'm saying."

She waited until Blue nodded again before continuing. "And once in a while, if you're really unlucky, you meet a monster. They're out there, kid, and you won't know it by looking at them. You gotta learn to trust that little alarm system that lives inside you, right? You know about those alarms? They're what goes off when you're a little kid and you see a dog that's not quite right, and something in you tells you to walk away from it and hide behind your mama's legs. You gotta keep that alarm sharp if you're taking to the roads. When the monsters come calling, it's the only thing there to keep you alive."

One more nod, this one a whole lot less certain. The thought popped into Blue's head that Lou was one of the monsters, that maybe she was going to peel away her face and reveal one made of thorns and pus and teeth. The thought vanished just as fast. If Blue had any kind of alarm system at all, it couldn't be less interested in Lou.

"There's one last group, the kind you hope you get. The people who know all about the good and the bad because they've been there themselves. They're the kind who'll be happy to give a lift to a kid with no voice and a guitar, happy to tell them that if they're thinking of using their money to stay in a motel somewhere, they're better off not going into Boston 'cause the prices are gonna be much higher. Got it?"

Blue gave her a thumbs-up. Lou glanced in the rearview mirror and switched lanes. "Like I was saying, you gotta eat good if you want your body to last you long enough that you can see your grandkids, maybe even great-grandkids . . ."

Lou taught Blue a few more things, too. For one: some motels that said they wouldn't take cash would, as long as you offered them a deposit up front. A straightforward lesson, like the ones Mama had taught Blue and Cass once she knew she wouldn't live.

Not that Mama'd explained them that way. After she was gone, Blue realized the lessons had been part of a long good-bye that started one Sunday morning, both girls just out of bed—Cass wearing a shorty nightgown, Blue in flannels—and snuggled against Mama on the saggy couch in their latest apartment. Tish hadn't been around for a few days, and the house felt emptier without her.

"Here's the thing, girls," Mama'd begun. She often started that way, as if they'd been waiting to hear whatever she was about to share. It could be about anything—homework, or bees, or how to choose guitar strings. Those were sometimes the best times, listening, being close, or sometimes the worst. "I think maybe it's time to stop with the moving for a while. Lynne has space in her house in Maine, and I miss her."

Cass had hissed a little through her teeth. There was something about moving that Cass loved. She was drawn toward instability the way magma's drawn through cracks in the earth. Even at eleven, she had a quality that sucked people in, made the kids at every new school flock around her as if she were an emissary from the Land of Glamour. Her thoughts on settling down, in Maine or anywhere, were written clearly on her face.

"Maine is boring."

"Maine is America's Vacationland," Mama said, grinning. "People save up all year just for the chance to go and stay for a week in the summer."

"On the ocean. Lynne lives in the woods. Nowhere."

Mama wrapped an arm around Blue then. "What about you, Miss Bluebird?"

Blue wasn't like Cass. Every new place came at her like a hurdle over a bar that kept rising. She didn't want to try again. She wanted everything steady and still—places, people, things—and not to have to figure out how to fit in all over again.

But she didn't want Mama to feel no one was on her side, either. "Sure, I guess. Where will Tish stay?"

A frown—thunder and doom—for just a moment. "Tish's going her own way. This adventure's ours. We'll start by skipping school tomorrow to pack. Packing's a skill as important as fractions, don't you think?"

She hadn't told them then. Not a word about it until they were with Lynne, until there was nothing but forest to run to, and more arms to fence them in. The words came then, the ones no one could take back, about stages and options and the fact that lives could be cut down into a measure of months.

Eight years ago, and she could still feel that day burn up

the back of her throat as she lay on the bed in the room Lou had helped her find. "Listen, your money ain't gonna go far if you keep staying in motels," Lou'd said. "Shelters, you're best staying out of them if you can. Each place you come to, you figure out the best option there. Hostels aren't bad if you're only staying a night or two. Don't flash your money around, don't ever leave it alone. Stay clear of any man that comes up to you all friendly in a bus station, train stop, that kind of stuff. When they come on all sweet, you know they're trouble."

She'd paused, looked over the room one last time. "You take care of yourself, kid. If you run into trouble, just trust your gut."

She was halfway out the door when she turned back. "And remember, unshelled sunflower seeds. They keep you eating nice and slow."

THE NEXT MORNING, BLUE STARTED OUT WALKING ALONG
the road. A line from one of Mama's songs kept running through her mind: *November skies, they got me down, / Ain't enough love left to keep me in this town.*

Only it wasn't really one of Mama's songs. Tish had written it, and while Mama sang it beautifully, Tish sang it true. Tish, with her spiky hair, her kohl-dark eyes, and her voice rougher than the rasp of a saw into dry wood. She'd played the fiddle, one half of Dry Gully. Her partnership with Mama had extended beyond the music. Things between them weren't always easy, but they always *were.*

Then she'd left with no explanation when they moved to Maine. Blue had thought it was just another fight and Tish would turn up after a week, a month. She didn't. No cards. No calls, even after Mama had died.

"It's simple," Cass had insisted when Blue asked why. "She was selfish. She found out Mama was sick, and she bailed. You just don't remember her as well as I do."

"I do remember her. You're just being mean," she'd said. She remembered Tish laughing a lot with Mama. She remembered her drinking a lot, too. Maybe "selfish" was the right way to describe her.

Ahead of her, a little white station wagon slowed to a stop, its blinker clicking double time. A man leaned out the driver's side window. "Dude, need a ride?"

Blue froze for a moment. The guy had a soft fuzz of beard around his mouth, and a few brown curls escaped from the Rasta cap he wore. A smile lit his face. He'd said "dude." He thought she was a boy. With the barn coat and her hair tucked up in her watch cap, she supposed she did look like one. She took out her notebook and walked forward.

I guess so.

"Can't talk?"

She flipped back a page, circled *laryngitis*.

"Bummer. I'm headed to Albany. Where you going?"

The answer was in the way her boots had felt as she'd walked.

West.

"Hop in. You can fit the guitar in back. Just push stuff around."

She opened the hatch to find amps, a guitar case, wires and plugs. Her guitar just fit. Up front, the car smelled of pot and boy sweat. The black vinyl of the passenger seat was cut in a few places and burned in one or two more. A patchwork of silver duct tape crossed its surface. She didn't recognize the music playing, but it was the sort of college jam band Teena would have loved.

"Headed to a gig?"

She held out the notebook and tapped it.

"Right. I guess the talking's up to me." He didn't look more than twenty-one or so. Around his left wrist he wore a braided bracelet, purple and gold.

"I'm Jed. I'm headed to Albany. My band's got a gig tonight. Mr. Chicken."

She gave him a look.

"That's the name of the band: Mr. Chicken. My girlfriend, Bet, she had a rooster as a kid and she called it Mr. Chicken. You know how it goes."

Not really. Teena's family had had a revolving cast of roosters, and every single one ended up as dinner. If they were called anything, it was usually Evil Bastard, or Good-for-Nothing. Blue hadn't understood the names until the day she saw Teena's little brother come in from collecting eggs with blood running down his leg.

Jed reached his hand into the crack between his seat and hers, pulled out a piece of green paper, and handed it to her. "Check it out. This is going to be our year. We're really getting some traction, you know?"

This she did know about. She knew all about traction and friction, and about what happened when one person thought they were gaining ground and one didn't. She could remember the shouting: Tish getting loud, Mama getting low.

The flyer boasted a black-and-white sketch of a rooster front and center, his long tail trailing around his feet like the train of a wedding dress. Whoever had drawn him had a good eye.

She gave Jed a thumbs-up.

"What kind of music do you play?" He clapped his hand over his mouth. "Shit, I'm no good at this. Tell you what, you just give me a signal when I guess right."

She nodded.

"Okay, let's see. I'm gonna guess . . . folk. Total folkie, right?"

Blue shook her head. Pretending, that's all she was doing. The guitar wasn't hers, after all. Neither was the music. Mama and Cass, they were the ones who loved to play for people, who sounded polished and perfect. The only time she sounded good was when she sang with Cass, their voices finding harmonies as weird and wild and wonderful as a hermit thrush's song.

The guitar was Mama's. The music was hers, too.

"Not folk? Okay, well, you're carrying acoustic. Some kind of old-timey country?"

She shook her hand side to side.

"Sort of like that? More country? Like bluegrass?"

Again, her hand, only this time she drew her fingers in a little. Pulling, coaxing.

"Something like bluegrass. How old are you again?" He shot her a look, did a double take. "Holy crap, you're a girl!"

She nodded, less interested in that than in the game.

"If you're a girl, you're older than I thought. You can't be the singer, not unless you're heading away from a gig. Or you're saving your voice."

Blue shook her head, trying to force something through her lips. Only the sound of air escaped.

"Okay, not the singer. Not the backup to someone doing folk. Something like bluegrass, only not. Is it some weird mash-up kind of thing?"

She clapped.

He groaned. "So there's no way in hell I'm going to get it?"

She shook her head, smiled. Alt country, that was the category Dry Gully had been placed in back in their heyday, but it never really fit. The way Mama looked with her shaggy brown hair and silver bangles and peasant blouses made people want her to fit in "folk." But Dry Gully was Tish, too; and Tish played her fiddle as if it were the line between herself and Armageddon. She wore black tees and black jeans and a silver skull on her middle finger. When she and Mama sang together, it wasn't angelic, it was unholy.

There wasn't a lot available of Dry Gully online. A song here, a set there, mostly taped at summer festivals. Blue had watched them all over and over, always ending in the same place. Mama, front and center, Tish playing gentle, the melody of birdsong rising and falling.

> I've got a bluebird, sings by my door,
> I've got a bluebird, rides out every storm,
> Just a little bird, feathers, hope, and wings,
> Reminding me of how small the space
> Between life and loss can be.
>
> The color of the morning sky,
> The color of my baby's eyes,
> Pauses in the lilac bush,
> While I drink my tea.

"Know what I mean?"

Jed's voice took her by surprise. She brushed at her face and felt the dampness there.

"I just think marketing is deadly to music. Bet'll talk your ear off about it, if you come tonight. Real art just flows over everything. It doesn't live in boxes."

Another thumbs-up. It sounded like Bet would have gotten along well with Tish.

"Listen, I need something to eat. There's a good co-op here. Come in and find something, too?"

She nodded. Off the highway they went, along a wide main street edged with local stores and social services. Jed parked in a municipal lot on a side street and fed a quarter into the meter.

He double-checked the locks on the doors. "Okay. Now that I have my eyes free, tell me your name."

She considered making something up in case the police came looking for her. It wasn't likely—they hadn't gone after Cass, after all.

Blue Riley. Sapphire Blue 4 real. Weird mom. ☺

"Well, Sapphire Blue, let's get something to eat." He grinned at her and pointed toward the door.

The co-op smelled like every other one she'd ever been in, like cumin and curry and chamomile. The bulk food bins by the door reminded Blue of Saturday afternoon grocery shopping with Mama and Tish, Tish complaining that Mama bought food for birds, not humans. This co-op was bigger than most, with a loft full of people eating lunch—dreadlocked mothers with nursing babies, bearded men in meandering conversations.

It was all so familiar. She'd arrived in Maine knowing all about couscous and falafel and marinated tempeh. The first time she'd seen a dead deer hanging from a maple in a front yard, though, she'd been horrified. Teena had laughed when she said something about it.

"Yeah, it's not quite in season; but Jimmy Ballston usually looks the other way when it comes to Meggy's pop. They need it, you know?"

She hadn't known. It had come as a total shock to discover that there were people who counted on those deer, along with everything else their families shot, grew, or scavenged from the land, to feed them through the year. She'd thought she knew what poor looked like, but she learned pretty quickly that there was more to it than what she'd seen in the cities and college towns Mama had set them down in.

She wasn't going to find venison on the co-op lunch board—just locally raised pork, free-range chicken, and winter greens from "extended season" farms. She settled for a cup of mushroom-barley soup and a roll studded with wheat berries.

She was fumbling in her pocket when her turn came at the register. A faint scent—something sweet and bad and familiar—teased her nose. She looked up, into the pale blue eyes of the cashier. The woman's long brown hair was separated into three braids and held away from her face with a red bandanna. A silver stud pierced her nose, silver rings garnished her fingers, and silver chains draped around her neck. She raised one eyebrow.

The bills drifted from Blue's hand to the floor as shock loosened her muscles. Her soup steamed on her tray, the plastic making a slight chattering sound as it shivered under her touch. She reached for her notebook.

"No need." The woman's voice carried smoke in it. Tails and curls spun out along the air. "Remember this, Bluebird Riley: you have just three days with any person who knows your name. Three weeks if you keep your true self hidden. If you stay with anyone longer than that, you'll invite suffering upon them."

Blue looked around her. No one seemed alarmed. Either they couldn't hear the woman, or evil cashiers were part of the scene here. Blue wrote quickly.

That's not the deal. You didn't say anything about that!!!

The woman drew her finger over the words. The paper darkened, the edges curling up as she passed over it. Again Blue looked, and again she saw no reaction from the people around her. "Terms and restrictions, the fine print. Never accept a deal without knowing everything. Once you give away your voice, Bluebird, you give away your rights." Her eyes flicked back, toward where

Jed balanced an apple on a paper-wrapped sandwich. "Besides, a resourceful girl like you shouldn't need others to do her work for her."

The noise of another tray against the metal counter behind her. "That'll be $6.15, please."

Blue bent down and grabbed her money off the floor. She pulled out a ten and waited for her change. The woman smiled, dimples dotting her round cheeks. "Thanks so much, and you have a nice day."

SHE DIDN'T FEEL HUNGRY AS SHE FOLLOWED JED OUT,
just kind of sick, as if she'd bitten into something moldy. How could
it be a game if the rules kept changing? No one ever stopped play
in a soccer match to tell the players they had to run in the stands
instead of on the field.

She couldn't talk, her feet ached every time she settled in a spot
for more than fifteen minutes, and she didn't really know where
she was going. And now she couldn't even give anyone her name.
Except for Jed, who already had it, so she had three days to leave him
or risk something bad happening.

What would happen if she stayed? Not that she would, because
the point of everything was to find Cass, not to become a groupie to
some band called Mr. Chicken.

Was it possible she was imagining everything? After all, if the
devil was working as a cashier in the co-op, there should have been
more suffering there.

She tried a spoonful of soup. It was better than she expected,
and she ate slowly, dipping the bread into the cup and taking small
bites to make it last.

"So, you should totally come tonight. Bet'll think it's fun to have
you along, and you can crash with us. She's taking care of her aunt's

place while she's away, and there's tons of room. How many days have you got, to get where you're going?"

She held up three fingers. It made sense to go with Jed to Albany, and it couldn't hurt anything to crash one night there and skip paying for a motel room.

"What do you say, then?"

She gave another thumbs-up. Her voice had been gone less than two days and already she hated the gesture. She needed a reversible sign: yes on one side, no on the other.

"Cool. I'm excited for you to see us play."

He turned the music back on, and the miles rolled away.

Bet's aunt lived outside of Albany, in an old farmhouse surrounded by trees stripped bare for the coming winter. Blue shutters flanked its windows, and flower beds full of dry brown stems followed the winding driveway. As they pulled in, the door of the side porch flew open and a woman came running out.

Bet laughed breathlessly as Jed picked her up and spun her around. She was small and curvy, like a snowwoman with curly brown hair and glasses. She was a good six inches shorter than Jed, and when they kissed, she stood up on her toes and leaned against him, his hands on her hips.

Blue looked away. She always noticed details even when she felt she shouldn't. Big Eyes, Cass had always called her, circling her own eyes with her fingers. "You're like an owl, always watching." And Blue would raise her shoulders as if fluffing her feathers, until Cass would laugh and call her a freak.

"The guys aren't here yet?" Jed took a step back from Bet, hands still on her hips.

"Vik said they'd be here by five. We've got the place to ourselves."

She put a hand on the flat of his stomach. He took another step back.

"Bet, this is, uh—" He waved a hand at Blue and she emerged hesitantly from the car. "This is Blue. I picked her up near Boston. She was hitching with a guitar, and she's got laryngitis, so she can't talk. I told her she could crash here, that you'd be totally into it."

For a moment, the look in Bet's eyes was anything but inviting. It passed quickly, though, and she smiled. "Totally. That's cool. Blue, right? I love your name. You really can't talk at all?"

Blue pulled out her notebook.

Sorry! You really OK with me staying? ☺

"You kidding? It'll be fun to have company. Have you heard their music? They're so good."

In the car. They're great!

"Great" might have been an overstatement. Mr. Chicken sounded good in a forgettable way, everything clean and lacking in what Mama would have called a beating heart. "Someone really good," she'd always said, "someone who's making art, not making noise, you can hear the rhythm of their heartbeat under the music. They leave something of themselves in the lines, enough that you have to open yourself up to hear it."

What Jed had played for her had been smart and catchy, but it hadn't caught hold of her and demanded that she listen. Not that she'd ever say that to a musician, especially not before a gig.

"I think they're about to break through. Really." Bet's eyes shone. "They so deserve it."

Deserve. Whatever it took to make it big, Blue didn't know that deserving played a part.

I hope so! I ♥ them.

Interesting how much easier it was to lie on paper than it was to lie out loud.

Bet set her up in a guest room with a single bed covered by a white cotton spread. There was a print of a Wyeth painting on the far wall, and a braided rug on the floor.

"This is the quietest room in the house, in case you want to sleep before four in the morning. They get pretty buzzed after a show." She paused, ran her hand over the nubbly bedspread. "But maybe you know what that's like."

She'd fallen asleep more nights than she could remember with Mama still awake and talking with Tish, her feet propped on the old lobster trap that served as one of their few pieces of furniture. "Takes a while to come down, if you do your show right," Mama had said. The coming down, Blue had loved it. It hadn't mattered where they were; it just felt like home.

You don't play? Sing?

Bet smiled, as if at a joke. "Me, up onstage? No way. They'd laugh."

Just 4 fun?

"Nah. I don't have anything when it comes to music." There was another pause and the sound of a door creaking open in the space between them. Blue thought of the flyer, of Jed's summary of Bet's thoughts on art and categories.

You drew the rooster? ☺

A wide smile, a pair of dimples deepening in her cheeks. "Did Jed say something?"

She wanted to say yes. Jed had said plenty of things about Bet, just not that one.

It looks like you. Not that you look like a rooster! Just like something you'd draw. Make sense?

"Cool." She looked a little sad, but mostly happy. "Mr. Chicken really did look like that. He had this long green tail. He was a hero. He died trying to save the hens from a couple of dogs running loose."

So good! Do any other stuff?

At the sound of a car on the gravel drive, Bet slipped away to the door. "That'll be the rest. I should go see them."

Blue didn't follow her out. She heard whooping, the thud of doors closing, and a drumroll of skin on metal as someone played the hood with her hands. Her window looked out over the backyard, though, and she was content to watch the stretch of shadows across the lawn.

After a while, Blue went looking for everyone. She counted five newcomers in the living room. The three guys blended together, and in her head she labeled them by their instruments rather than their names.

The backup singer, Jill, was striking—tall, with high cheekbones, and long silver earrings; her straight black hair looped back from her forehead in a pair of thin braids. She sat between Bet and the lead guitarist's sister, Meena.

Meena wore her thick black hair loose and smoked one cigarette after another. "You a cheerleader tonight?" she asked Blue, knocking ash into a plastic cup filled with water.

"She can't talk. She's got a sore throat," Bet filled in for her.

"Well, you can be the one that does tumbling instead of cheers," Meena said.

"Tonight. You. Me. Right?" The drummer pointed at Meena with a drumstick.

She blew smoke out in a long, steady stream. "Jesus, not as long as there's breath left in my body."

Jill rose. "I'm going outside. Too much crap in the air in here. Want to come, Bet?"

Bet hesitated, then shook her head. Blue followed Jill out onto the back deck instead.

Jill lay back in a lounge chair, one long jean-clad leg crossed over the other. "Chris is an ass, and his drumming sucks. Jed only keeps him around because they went to high school together. You know how those things go." She waved her hand in front of her face. "You really can't talk?"

Blue shook her head and pulled out her notebook.

Just a temp thing. ☹

Jill studied her. "You must be a singer if you're that protective of your voice. Most people would whisper anyway."

She shook her head again, then touched her hand to her throat. She imagined the emptiness beneath her fingers and suddenly longed to sing. Jill reached out and took Blue's hand, turning it over to look at her ring. "That's pretty."

Tx! It was my mom's.

"Jed said you were a musician. What do you play?"

Guitar.

"What kind?" Jill kept her pale blue eyes focused on Blue's face.

Guild.

With that, she'd passed some test. Jill nodded. "Nice. Year?"

1968.

"These guys ... Jed has real talent. The others ..." She shrugged. "I deserve something better than backup for them, but it's tough for a woman singer, unless you're lucky. You know all this shit, right?"

Jill didn't watch for an answer—just leaned her head against the cushion, her eyes on the sky as it deepened to purplish blue.

MR. CHICKEN WAS THE SECOND BAND OUT THAT NIGHT.
The first, Ask Rosie, had an enthusiastic group of followers; but
they played a stale mix of covers and uninspired originals. The bar
pushed to overflowing as Mr. Chicken's time drew near. The crowd
was a bit older and a lot hipper. The increasing energy in the room
lifted her with it.

The real shock came when they took the stage. Presence—Blue
had come to understand it watching the old footage of Dry Gully.
Lots of decent musicians didn't have an ounce of it. They could
play something with feeling, but they couldn't translate it into commanding a crowd.

Jed could. He was perfect, from the moment he stepped onto
the stage to the last motion of his hand as he left. The crowd would
have held its breath indefinitely, had he asked it to. Jill, her voice
rising over his in effortless harmony, was far more than backup.
Her voice was the current that electrified them.

When they left the stage after their final encore, Bet pushed her
way out toward the back. Meena followed, and Blue moved to join
them.

A scent—unpleasant, charred, hot—stopped her. There was
no sign of fire or smoke, and no one else looked concerned. The

woman in the red dress had given off a similar scent . . . But this had an unfamiliar bitterness. She drew a deep breath, trying to track the seared odor. It took a while to push her way through the bodies, the smell growing stronger with each step. In the far back corner, where it filled the air, she found a man seated alone.

He had dark brown hair in a nondescript short cut, and he wore a blue cotton dress shirt, unbuttoned at the neck. His face was the kind some girls would find attractive, though Blue found it bland. He didn't at all resemble the woman in the red dress; and yet she didn't know anyone else drenched in Eau de Flame.

The man glanced at her, then returned to the papers in his hand. She walked up to him and ripped a piece of paper out of her notebook.

Why are you here?!

If the devil could steal someone's voice with a kiss, surely it could look like a man or a woman. Except . . . the face of the woman in the red dress—and the woman in the co-op—had been real. Lived-in.

Her uncertainty rose as the man looked at her note without interest. "I beg your pardon?"

Changing the rules again? What now?

"I don't believe we've met, and I don't have a clue which rules you're referring to. If you auditioned at some point and didn't get in—well, I'm sorry, but we have very few spots. Keep practicing. Hard work makes stars."

She'd been ready to walk away. But a metallic sparkle shimmered in his eyes, a flash of undiluted glee. Her heartbeat quickened.

It's not me, is it? Who called you then?

"Called me? Really, I think you have things confused. We look for talent, we're not called by it." Around them the crowd had begun to thin, the staff wiping tables and stacking chairs. They clearly didn't smell him. Could they not see him, either?

She heard Jed's voice behind her, and the man stood, holding out his hand. Blue's pencil dropped from her fingers. So he wasn't invisible.

"Good of you to see me. I'm John Rathburn." The man held out a business card. Jed took it without a glance. "We're very impressed with what we've seen of Mr. Chicken. As I mentioned to you over the phone, Vineyard Productions is in charge of casting for a number of high-quality, reality-based network shows. We think you'd be perfect for *Major Chord*. We've chosen nine acts to date. We'd very much like for you to be the tenth and final one."

No one spoke for a moment. In the silence, Blue searched for her pencil, to no avail. Then Jed shouted across the room to the others. All around them the burnt odor filled the air, but no one else seemed to notice, or to care. More and more she felt crazy, seeing things no one else did, believing things that made no sense. She had to be wrong about this.

She walked away. First to the bathroom, where she waited at the end of a long line. Then, passing through a room almost emptied of people, she headed outside. Above her, the stars shone brilliantly. Few cars remained in the parking lot. The bartender and a couple of waiters leaned against a beat-up sedan, red glowing under their cupped fingers from time to time as they smoked. Jill stood with them, taking in the sky.

The bartender grinned at Blue and offered his cigarette. She shook her head. He shrugged. "You with the band?"

She nodded, felt for the missing pencil again. Her hands still trembled from before.

"Blue's got a sore throat." Jill moved close, linked an arm

through hers. The way Teena used to. "Either of you have something she can write with?"

The bartender shrugged, looked at the waiters. "Talia, you got a pen in your shit heap of a car?" The woman beside him, her pale hair slicked back in a ponytail, stretched lazily. A warm, sweet scent drifted off her as she reached into the front pocket of her black pants and pulled out a stubby, zebra-striped pencil.

Tx! ☺

"Jesus, you were hot tonight," the woman said.

Jill pulled Blue's arm a little closer. "Some nights, you know? Some fucking nights, the world is yours."

The bar door opened and Jed and Bet came out. Bet looked upset. Jed leaned down to whisper to her, something that brought a smile to her face but didn't ease whatever made her cross her arms in front of her.

He looked up and saw them. "Jill." He ran over, Bet following at a walk. "We did it!" Jed's jubilance skipped across the cars, rang out into the endless sky. "Tomorrow afternoon we sign a contract to appear in *Major Chord*. Big time, Jill. That's where we're going."

The bartender gave a wolf whistle as the waitress clapped. Blue just stared as her anxiety returned. If the man in the blue shirt was the same as the woman in the red dress, what would it mean for the band if they signed a contract with him? Were they doing the same thing she had—making a trade—and if so, did they understand the rules?

Jill gave Jed a disbelieving look. "Are you serious?"

"There's a few little things to work out, but starting next week we'll have free food and housing, free lessons with pros, free exposure on national TV—"

"And a one-in-ten shot at winning a contract and a million

dollars," the drummer, appearing from nowhere, broke in. "Big fucking time, baby."

"What kind of little things?" Jill's eyes flicked toward Bet, who looked even more miserable.

"Um, stupid things. Just little made-up things to make it flashier."

"Like?"

A deal. Blue could feel it in the air. What would they lose?

"They think we need a little more of a hook, so . . . It would just be pretend."

"You and Jed, all boyfriend and girlfriend," the drummer said. "All romantic and shit."

"You serious?" Jill kept looking at Bet—only, Bet looked away. If Blue could see the hurt there, surely Jill could, too.

Time dripped, one single perfect drop, the glow of the cigarette in the dark, the flicker of streetlight, silence where Jed's breath should have been, had he not been holding it. Hush, the kind of hush that must have surrounded her at the crossroads as well.

Then Jill stopped looking at Bet. "A million bucks and a record contract? I'll pretend to be anyone's girl for that."

A whoop from Jed as he leaped forward, spun Jill in the air, her hair a shower of black. The drummer playing air guitar, everyone dancing.

Almost everyone. Blue watched Bet as she tried to shape a smile. The man in the blue shirt was no good. Blue was sure of it. He'd promised them what they wanted, but she'd bet anything they didn't know what they'd be giving away.

THEY STAYED UP ALL NIGHT. BLUE HUNG OUT ON THE DECK
with Jill, watching her drink vodka and cranberry juice, and
counted the stars.

"I'm twenty-seven, you know," Jill said finally. "Time to make
something happen. I'm pretending to be his girl on TV—big deal.
It's not like I'm marrying him or anything."

Blue nodded. The noise from inside had died back a bit, the
spaces of quiet filled with the low thrum of the bass. It had been
three months since she'd last spoken with Teena, seven months
since Cass. Here, listening to Jill, being close, felt like standing in
the sun on the first warm day after winter.

"It's mostly Bet that I feel bad about. I love her, she's great,
but . . ." Jill swirled her drink. "She feels a little left out of the
whole scene with the band. And she hears all that shit that Chris,
the drummer, talks, and . . . It makes things seem different than
they are. I told her I'd never sleep with Jed. It's true, I wouldn't.
This thing for the TV, it's just for show. Who cares what people
see on the outside, right? It doesn't matter.

"The thing is . . . she gave up going to Italy on an art scholarship this year to be with Jed. They made a deal they'd go together
instead. They're supposed to leave in three weeks. She's got to

know a chance like this is more important. It's not like Italy's going to vanish."

Blue followed Jill's gaze through the window, to where Bet sat next to Meena. Jed was talking, and as Bet watched him, something close to despair flashed across her face, to be replaced with a smile as soon as he turned toward her.

Did Jed not see the hurt, or did he not care? Had he even stopped to ask Bet how she felt about it?

Cass had done the same thing. *I'm not making the same mistake Mama made. I've got talent, and I'll do whatever I need to make people see it,* her note had said. Including, apparently, leaving Blue behind, giving her nothing but four phone calls to hold on to.

"Come on." Jill took Blue's hand and led her through the garden. Her boots kept her feet dry and warm as they passed through the remnants of the flower beds, but her feet ached with something akin to hunger. "You'll like this."

At the far end of the garden was what she had assumed was a shed. Up close, she realized it was much too fancy to store tools in. The front door had doves painted on it, and it opened into a room lit with the soft glow of paper lanterns. Jill made her way to the back wall, where she tugged a chain and lit a silver floor lamp. It shone on a red velvet couch with carved wooden legs. The walls and floor were dark-paneled. In one corner stood a stereo system; one whole wall was filled with shelves of old records.

"Bet's aunt used to review music. She's got a ton of great stuff, stuff I'd never heard of until we started coming here. Lie on the couch and close your eyes. I'll pick something out."

Blue sat down, unlaced her boots, and slipped them off. Exposed, her feet felt normal, same old skin and toes. She wiggled them as she lay back, hands behind her head, and closed her eyes.

A hiss filled the room, the soft sizzle of a record in the seconds before the music started. It was followed by the first few bars from a guitar she knew far too well. The fiddle trailed behind, melancholy, her mother's voice matching its mournful timbre.

This road I know far too well,
The one between your door and mine,
More holes than tar, more lost than found,
Avenue A through my private hell.

Tish's words, her mother's music. She remembered the smell of Tish now—cigarettes and leather and peppermint and whiskey. A tattoo of vines and thorns circling her wrist. Another of a blue eye at the base of her neck. Her raspy voice in response to Mama: "For fuck's sake, Clary, you gotta want more than this."

"What do you think?" Jill's long hair tickled Blue's nose as she leaned over her. She smelled sweet, like hay and fruit. "Good stuff, huh?"

Blue opened her eyes. Patterns of dark and light shimmered, the night gentle against the windows as the world started its slow shift toward morning. She took out her notebook, thought for a moment. *It's my mom,* she should say. *She and Tish made that record, and I thought it would change everything, but it didn't. They never got their big break. Mama died, and people forgot that Dry Gully ever existed, and I forget little bits of her every day. She told me that the important part was making music, that all the songs, even the forgotten ones, swirl in the air, become part of what's to come. That musicians play in the midst of ghosts every day. I think she would have told you not to do what you're doing, because maybe you're giving away more than you know for less than you think.*

She should have said it all, but maybe she was wrong, just a messed-up kid running away from home. Instead, she wrote just three words.

Yeah, good stuff.

Rosy fingertips of light stroked the sky by the time they slipped back into the house. The drummer was sprawled on the downstairs couch, a line of drool slick at the corner of his mouth, a baby's softness to his face. Beer bottles lay along the edges of the rug, clinking softly as Blue tiptoed past them. She followed Jill up to the bedrooms, Jill keeping one finger to her own lips, giggling as the floor creaked beneath their feet.

"Beauty sleep," she whispered. "Gonna be superstars, you know."

Blue caught her hand as she turned to enter her bedroom. Jill paused, and Blue hunted for her pencil. A pink flush had colored Jill's face, optimistic as the rising sun. Happy, she looked happy. Maybe everything else was a dream. Good things happened. Bands got gigs just because they played well, got contracts and became famous without losing everything. Who was she to say otherwise?

She had to try.

"What?" Jill, waiting, smiling, tired.

You sure Major Chord is worth it? Pretending to be Jed's gf? Esp w/ Bet . . .

Jill shook her head slightly, her long hair falling in a wave over her shoulder. "Worth it? If it gets someone to see me as lead, then pretending for a little while is totally worth it. I've just got to play along until I've found my way in. That's all. Bet'll understand."

Did you meet him? The one with the contract?

"Rathburn? For a minute. Why?"

There was no way to ask that didn't sound funny.

He smell weird to you?

Jill giggled again. "Yeah, like money, goofball." She touched the heel of her hand to Blue's forehead, pressed it there for a moment. "Good night, Blue Riley. See you in the morning, um, afternoon. Maybe we can talk about you coming with us." She closed her door behind her.

Sleep felt like another country, one that came with a lock and key and a three-headed dog as gatekeeper. Blue gave up quickly and crept back down the stairs, spacing her steps to skip the creaks. It didn't seem to matter. The drummer was just as out of it when she passed as he had been earlier.

Kitchens all sounded the same, she decided as she searched the cupboards for something to eat. The clang of a radiator heating up, the whir of the refrigerator fan, the tick of a plain white clock hanging over the sink. They didn't all smell the same, though, and behind the scent of dish soap and last night's pizza lurked something more. Something she couldn't quite label, sharp and worrying. She sniffed her way through the cupboards without locating it, then stopped and stood in the middle of the room.

The odor came in short wafts. She paced back and forth until it intensified by a wooden door. She'd assumed the door led to a closet, but when she opened it, she found a set of stairs leading down. Of course, the basement. Down the steps, cautiously. The smell was much stronger now, joined by a sporadic click and crackle.

The answer came in a spray of white-hot sparks. A girl her own age sat on an old chest freezer. In her hands she held the two ends of a frayed wire, and she swung them back and forth as if she were playing jump rope, just as casual. The wires sparked and smoked, the light falling between her knees and onto a pile of rags on the floor.

"Stop!" Blue shrieked, or tried to. Nothing came out.

"Remember the deal?" The girl held one end of the wire to her lips, sucked on it like a lollipop, her cheeks glowing red.

Blue wrote feverishly, the shaking of her hands turning her words to scrawl.

The deal?! You said—

What had she said? Three days. She couldn't stay more than three days if they knew her name, and it had been . . .

"Two days. Turn of the calendar, Bluebird, not twenty-four hours."

2 days? Not 3? You said I had 3 days!

The girl hopped off the freezer. She stood a few inches shorter than Blue, her silvery hair in a neat braid down her back, her tartan skirt and white shirt crisply ironed. She moved the wires to one hand, the ends completely covered by her grip. The sound of their sizzle, the smell of their heat, filled the room. The girl paid it no mind.

"I'm being nice. I'm reminding you that bad things happen if you overstay your welcome. That's all. Just a reminder. I'd hate to have you wake up at 12:01 tomorrow morning and find yourself surrounded by death. That would suck, don't you think?" She twirled the end of her braid in her free hand.

OK, I'll go. After I get my things.

Blue turned away; turned back almost immediately.

But why them? Is it just because of me?

"Why them what?" The girl watched her with expressionless eyes.

Why are you doing it? Making that deal?

Nothing. Blankness. Then a flash, like the slip of a fish underwater. "You and I've got our own thing. They've got theirs."

The girl clenched her fist tightly. It glowed red-hot for an instant. When she opened it, the wire lay there, smooth and whole. "Go on. Fly away, Bluebird. Things will be over before you know it."

She walked away, into the corner of the basement, and vanished into the brick wall, only a faint phosphorescence left behind. Blue ran back up the steps.

SHE HIKED THE LENGTH OF THE DIRT ROAD, DAY PACK ON
her back, guitar in hand. By the time she reached pavement, she
could hear church bells ringing in the distance. Back in Eliotville,
Lynne would be waking up for the second morning with her gone.
Was Lynne sad? Or was she busy emptying drawers, packing
things away, at least a little relieved?

Did she miss Blue? Did Blue miss her?

A pickup slowed to a stop beside her. Inside was a middle-aged
man, with a curly-haired little boy in the passenger seat. "That's a
lot of stuff to be carrying. You need a lift?" She nodded, hopped in.

He gave her a ride as far as town. Not Albany, someplace
smaller, but big enough to catch a bus in. The bus tickets were
sold in a bookstore next to the stop, full of the smell of old books
and dust. The woman behind the counter hadn't showed any interest when Blue slid her note across to her, just took her money and
handed her a ticket.

She'd guessed about a destination. Rochester, a city-sized blot
on the map of upstate New York, seemed like the right direction.
Not that she had much to go by, beyond the boots, but there was
a little.

There had been four phone calls from Cass over two years,

each from a blocked number. The first to tell Lynne she was okay. The second call, three months after she'd gone, came on a Saturday. Blue had been at Teena's. Just a "Hi, I'm doing fine," left on the machine. The third call arrived almost a full year after she'd left—her Halloween message for Blue.

The fourth, eighteen months after Cass had gone, Blue had answered, heard Cass's voice, felt her heart rush into a gallop as she gripped the receiver tight. "Where are you? Are you coming home? I miss you." As if she were six, as if Cass were away on business, as if her return were guaranteed. What she heard in response was distance. The sound of traffic, voices on a city street, a muted siren. "Blue," Cass had said, as if eighteen months translated to endless miles and sisterhood amounted to geography, not soul. "That's not home. Not for me."

A slap, the sting following the blow. "What are you doing?"

"Looking for what's mine."

"But where are you?" *Give me a map, show me how to find you. Don't leave me alone.*

The blast of a car horn through the receiver. She jumped, as if she were on the street with Cass, not standing by the kitchen bar, a half-eaten peanut butter sandwich in her hand.

"I'm following a trail. You know the one." A laugh, sharing something, but Blue didn't know what. "Listen, I'm fine, tell Lynne. I have to go."

No good-bye. Just a click, silence. Cass, there and gone.

She hadn't had a clue what Cass was talking about at first. She didn't know any trails outside of Maine, at least not any with names. But two nights later, lying on Cass's bed next to Mama's guitar, she'd gotten it. Mama had left Maine two years into college. She said she hadn't been sure where she was going, just that it was time to go, time to make music. Tish said she'd woken up one morning on her family's ranch, looked out at the land that would soon be covered in snow, and decided high school wasn't something she needed to finish. Instead, she'd taken her fiddle and a bag and headed up "toward the music." The Gully, she and Mama had named the path they took toward each other, made it sound as if Mama's guitar and Tish's fiddle had called to each other until they'd finally met up.

The trouble was, Blue didn't remember anything about the stops along their journey. She'd been little when she listened, and they'd always told it as if it had been a fairy tale, not a tour map. Tish had grown up somewhere in Wyoming, she knew that much. If Cass was following the Gully, she'd be headed that direction. Northwest. The boots had agreed so far. Rochester was on the way.

While she waited, she paced. Back and forth, back and forth. Not much in the way of traffic, all of it passing quickly until a silver sedan slowed. The driver looked out at her. An older guy, graying hair cut military short, eyes hidden behind sunglasses. Slower, slower, one hand rising as if to wave. A chill creeping along her spine.

A roar, a rush of air, and the bus pulled into the stop. She grabbed her guitar, ticket in her free hand, and fell in behind the old woman. By the time she'd boarded the bus, the car had vanished. He'd probably been looking for directions. Shouldn't have been scary.

Still . . . She settled into her seat, happy to not be standing on the side of the road.

By the time the bus reached Rochester, Blue could have eaten her own hand. Not in a vague, metaphorical way, but in an I-haven't-eaten-for-too-long way, because gnawing at herself began to seem better than going without. Stepping out into the cold air only made it worse. The light was fading fast, and she stood outside the station and looked up and down the street for somewhere to eat.

She saw nothing. A busy road, traffic shooting past, the station set off by itself. More roads, and some run-down buildings farther along. She gripped her guitar a little more tightly. Again, the empty space where speech should have lived surrounded her. No calling after the people walking away from the bus, the little woman with the plastic bags. The bus driver, quick to disappear into the building.

She was alone. Almost. A woman, a little shorter than Blue, a little stout, dressed in a blue fleece jacket and a bright green fleece hat, watched her. When their eyes met, the woman smiled.

"Traveling? You look like a traveler."

Blue nodded.

"I knew it." The woman smiled like Blue's guidance counselor, phony through and through. "Not that you look much different from the Eastman students, but I just knew. In my heart, you know?" She pressed her hands to her chest.

Your heart, my ass. Not really the sort of thing she'd say out loud, even if she could, but it didn't mean it wasn't there. She hoped her smile was sweeter than her thoughts.

If it wasn't, that made no difference to the woman. "You're so lucky. Out here, meeting people, learning about the world. The opportunity for growth gives me goose bumps."

Shrinking's more likely if I don't get some food. This close, the carved rings the woman wore—not too expensive, but not cheap, either—and the opals in her ears shimmered as she moved. Someone who dressed her money down.

Blue scribbled quickly.

Yeah, it's cool. Just got into town, looking for a place to crash. ☺

A tinny burst of sitars sounded. The woman rummaged through her patchwork purse, held up one finger as she answered the phone. Blue studied her. Black leggings stretched over short legs; a woven scarf, Mexican maybe, around her neck. An expensive smell—sandalwood softened with something sweet—wafted from her.

The conversation sounded private, but the woman stayed put, as if Blue were a tree instead of a girl. "I know," and "I miss you, too," and "We should never have tried that to begin with, but you know how these things are." Blue's stomach twisted with hunger. She checked her watch. The screen was blank. She tapped it with one finger, shook her wrist, but the blankness stayed.

She began to wonder whether the raised finger had been for her or was just some reflex associated with the phone. Standing on the sidewalk wasn't getting her any closer to eating. She picked up her guitar from where she'd set it and started down the street. She made it twenty feet before the woman yelled behind her.

"You, wait a minute, come back."

She turned back, pointed a finger at her chest. The woman nodded and returned to her conversation.

Exactly how long was she supposed to wait? And why? So they could talk about how cool it was to be wondering where she would spend the night? If she'd known where to go, she wouldn't have waited, but nothing looked promising along the road. She stood a few more minutes, the ache from her boots traveling up her legs, her frustration traveling down until they met somewhere around her waist.

She couldn't put her finger on what it was about the woman.

Didn't matter. The woman was annoying, and Blue's stomach had swallowed her patience and dissolved it completely. She picked up her guitar again.

"I'll be home soon. You should call me later tonight. No, *you* should call. I won't remember. We can make real plans then." The woman tucked the phone back into her bag.

"You know how it is when you're thinking about someone and then they call you, just like the universe recognizes that energy and opens right up for you? I knew she needed me, and I opened myself, and there she was. Just like with you. That's just how things are for me. It's a gift, though it can be hard sometimes."

Blue waited, one foot cocked. The sinews in her ankles, her knees, felt stretched to their limits, as if they might tear at any minute, letting her legs walk away without her. Finally, she wrote.

Well, gotta go. Need to find food and a place.

"Oh, no, come stay with us," the woman said, with a patient smile. "It'll be a blessing for us. Travelers are considered magical in so many cultures, you know. We could always use a bit of luck." She gave a little laugh, as if luck were the punch line to a private joke.

You are off your rocker, lady. Not that Blue considered herself very threatening—average height, average build, curly brown hair, no ink, just a couple of loops in her ears—but still. She could have had Beck's bowie knife in her backpack, could have been pretending not to talk because it made her look harmless.

"Come on, I'm parked over there." The woman pointed out a black SUV.

Blue hesitated, but only for a moment. Truck-driving Lou had said to trust her gut about people. This woman, this nameless woman who did nothing but talk, didn't make her nervous.

Annoyed, yes, bored, maybe, but she didn't make Blue's skin crawl the way a dangerous person would.

Besides, she needed food, and a place to sleep, and this beat wandering around in the cold and using up her cash. The wad of bills had seemed like a lot when she got it out of the bank, but the motel on the first night had cost more than she'd expected, and she didn't know how many nights she'd need a place to stay.

She hurried down the street after the woman.

AT FIRST GLANCE, THE HOUSE LOOKED AS IF IT HAD BEEN
built of bones. Dry white stretches, long walls, sharp angles, stark
light shining from jagged windows.

"It's completely earth-friendly," the woman said.

It might have been earth-friendly, but it didn't look people-
friendly. The ride had been long, the driveway endless. As Blue
stepped out of the car, she could see trees and stars emerging overhead. She could hear the sounds of distant roads. No other house
lights shining through the woods. Just like a horror movie: no one
around to hear her scream. She drew a quick breath as the hairs
rose on the back of her neck.

The woman had introduced herself as Amy just before letting
herself into the car. Blue had gotten as far as *B* in writing her own
name before remembering the girl in the basement with the spark-
ing wire. *Bess Andrews*, she'd written.

"Bess? That's very retro, isn't it? My mother had a friend named
Bess, I think, or Betsy . . . maybe Betsy. You would never believe
what she was like—" And Amy launched into another long string of
words that didn't end until they stepped out onto the gravel drive in
front of the unfriendly house.

"We thought about going a bit bigger," Amy said, switching

tracks. "But we decided we could make do. Every little bit for the environment, right?"

From what Blue could see through the windows, Lynne's trailer would have fit inside, along with a host of others. Teena's family had a big house, but Teena's family had five kids, plus two uncles and one set of grandparents living in the additions tacked on later in bits and pieces.

Not this house. The entry led into an open empty space. A fan slowly rotated beneath the high ceiling, its long cord twirling slightly with the motion. The chrome-and-white furniture had been arranged to face a glass wall. The kitchen, tucked in one corner, was occupied by stainless-steel appliances. Nothing hung on the refrigerator door except a single white square with a quote centered on it about the beauty of each and every soul. It looked like the kind of place where you might find petri dishes and microscopes, not a family.

"My husband, Todd, won't be home until late. He's with clients. My younger son, Yoshi, is at a friend's house for the night. It's just us girls and Marcos."

Marcos? She'd tuned out during the ride, focused on her feet and her empty stomach. The names Yoshi and Marcos didn't fit with the smiling white woman in front of her.

"Marcos," Amy trilled. No response. She walked to the staircase at the far side of the room, the wide open steps leading to an equally open landing. "Come down, Marcos."

The sound of a door opening somewhere far away. Footsteps followed, a teenage boy appearing on the landing. He was tall, thin, the kind of boy that black trench coats were designed for, and cigarettes, and late-night coffees at diners. His dark hair shot in all directions, as if he'd come straight from bed.

"What?"

He even sounded the way Blue expected: a bit bored, a bit tired, a lot irritated.

"This is Betsy Andrews. She's traveling, and I found her on a street corner looking for help. Of course I told her to stay with us tonight."

If Blue had a voice of her own, she would have sounded just as irritated as Marcos looked. Not that the name "Betsy" really made a difference. One fake name was the same as another; but she still pulled out her notebook and underlined "Bess."

"Bess. That's what I said, sweetheart. You just didn't hear me right." Amy gave her a thin-lipped smile. "Bess can't speak. Can you imagine how lucky she is to have run into me tonight?"

The boy slunk down the stairs. He sized her up just as she had him, practiced and quick. "*Bess*, huh?" he said, with a touch of a smirk. Smarter than she'd thought, then.

"Marcos, did Paulina leave food? Paulina cooks for us," Amy added. "She's lovely, thoughtful, so willing to try things differently from what she's used to. We used to use a chef some friends recommended, but he, well, we prefer to help people, you know. Paulina needed the work more than he did. Things have been hard for her."

The boy gave a quick twitch of his head, rubbed his fingers together. Money. Paulina cost less.

"It may not be what you're used to, Betsy. We follow the Dalapur diet, and we only use fresh local ingredients. It's made such a difference for us. We're so much healthier now. I'm giving a talk on it on Friday in my women's group."

Betsy again. It felt like being poked by a blunt pencil point, over and over. Blue shrugged.

Amy pursed her lips. "Betsy, I'm putting you up in my home,

and feeding you, and treating you like part of my family. The least you can do is show me respect."

Marcos smirked. Blue forced her mouth closed, held her notebook against her thigh to write.

Sorry, it sounds great! ☺

It didn't make a difference to Amy. "It was rude of you to just stand there and shrug. Even if you can't speak, you're perfectly capable of responding."

Blue started to write more, but Amy held up her hand. "No, it's past. I'm very sensitive. It's who I am in this life—very sensitive so that I can feel the world's pain and teach others about it. I . . . I just need to go and sit and find my center. You two can wait for dinner." She left, exiting through a hallway beneath the stairs.

Blue gritted her teeth. At least back in the city she'd had the chance of finding food, even if it cost her money. Here . . .

She wrote quickly—*Food?*—and flashed the page at Marcos.

"She's being a bitch. It's not like she cooks, anyway. That takes too much time away from her full-time job of being *that*." He gestured in the direction Amy had gone. "Come on, I've got food in my room."

She followed him up the stairs, guitar in one hand, backpack in the other. Everything shone and smelled empty—not of polish, like Lynne's house; or of dogs, like Teena's; or even of people. The air smelled of nothing, just empty space—at least until Marcos opened the door to his room.

There it smelled of incense and pizza. The room was designed to be as sparse as the rest of the house, with a loft bed, white walls, and a huge bank of windows. The loft had blankets hanging off it, though, and grayish smudges marred the walls here and there. On one wall hung a poster of a burnt tree standing in the midst of a snowy field. An incense burner waited on the desk, dust streaks beneath it. A laptop sat beside it, the screen covered in bouncing polka dots.

And beside that was an open pizza box. Blue pounced. Cheese, pepperoni, sausage . . . more or less a whole pig on a greasy crust. At home, she would have picked the meat off. Here, she wolfed down two pieces while Marcos watched.

"Hungry much?" He sat in his desk chair swiveling back and forth. He had an odd energy, one she recognized reluctantly. Teena's cousin Rob had had the same as he clock-watched his way through a class. She'd seen it in other people, too, during the Dry Gully days—that glitter in the eyes, that restlessness, things she hadn't had the words for at four, six, eight.

She wasn't a little girl anymore. There was a word, and it was *junkie*.

"You play that thing?" He touched the guitar case with his toe.

She wiped her hands on her pants. The pizza settled into a heavy lump inside her.

Yeah, I play.

How was she supposed to answer? She'd watched real musicians all through her childhood. Their playing seemed effortless, as if the guitar strings had dreamed their fingers into being. She felt like a poseur by comparison.

If she was honest, though, she played better than almost everyone else she knew since moving to Eliotville. It was just . . . She wasn't sure what it was. She wasn't the one who stood up in front of people and played. She was the one who watched.

She picked one of Dry Gully's songs for Marcos, her inattentive audience of one. More than playing, she wanted to sing, even if she wasn't the best. When Mama sang, the words were rich as chocolate. Cass sang sultry, older than she was, like an invitation to a private party. Blue didn't sound like either of them. She had funny pauses and breathless bits.

She still loved it. It was something like flying—like birds, not planes, a sensation of soaring around the notes of the guitar. It was escape, reaching a place where what mattered was the song, nothing more.

"Nice," Marcos said when she finished, though she wasn't sure he meant it. His attention drifted—the clock, the drawer, the door.

Marcos? + Yoshi?

She held her notebook up.

"It's part of this 'we're one big happy world' shit. At least Marcos sounds cool. I'm luckier than Yosh."

Don't you like your mom?

He pulled at the drawer. Half inch open, then back to closed. "Would you? I mean, she has her moments, but . . . moments, you know? She doesn't get it."

Get what?

"Anything. That she's a fake. That people can't stand her. That my dad can't even stand her. That . . ." He tugged the drawer open far enough that she could see a plastic bag peeking out, then closed it partway.

He didn't want her there. Or maybe he did; maybe he was convincing himself he didn't need what was in the bag. It wouldn't work, though. It never had, not with Rob, who'd chosen the contents of the bag over school, home, everything.

"They get hooked," Mama'd said once on the phone, to someone else, not knowing Blue was there. "Then there's nothing you can do to pull them back. It's up to them to choose to do the work.

All you can do is leave a bread-crumb trail of love and keep on with your life."

Bathroom?

He pointed her down the hall. She paused on the threshold. Would it make a difference if she stayed? Didn't matter. She was just passing through.

BLUE TOOK HER TIME, WASHING HER HANDS AND FACE
and neck. She'd ask to take a shower before she left in the morning.
Sleep in a bed for free, get cleaned up, and leave. They wouldn't
even be in danger, since she hadn't given them her real name.

Wouldn't be in danger from her, at least. Marcos's problems
belonged to him. Parents were stupid. Teena's aunt and uncle had
been clueless about Rob, right up until they couldn't be any longer.
They only loved the perfect, imaginary him, leaving the real him
invisible.

Back in Marcos's room, the incense was lit, heady smoke spin-
ning threads as the air moved with the closing of the door. His face
was on his desk, and a strand of drool trickled from the corner of
his mouth.

She shook him gently. He moved his head, too lazy even to
smile. He was alive. He was okay. Now she could be irritated.

She'd go back downstairs and wait for Amy to come out of her
sulk and tell her where to sleep. She grabbed her guitar, then her
backpack. She noticed that the front pocket had come open. If she
wasn't more careful about that, she'd lose her wallet on the street.
She zipped it up.

The door swung open. Amy stood there, and for an instant Blue believed everything would be fine. Amy would see what Marcos had been doing and take care of him. That's what mothers did.

Or not. She glanced around the room, at Blue holding her things, at Marcos slumped at the desk, at the candle and the bag of powder. Anger spilled from her mouth like blood from an artery.

"I invite you into my home, I put all my goodness and trust in your hands, and you do this . . . to *me*. How could you? You prey on goodness, come here, and give my son poison." Flecks of spit flew from her mouth. Marcos shifted slightly, looked up at her, said something that was buried beneath her fury.

"You destroy everything, you and people like you. I know, I know all about your ugliness."

Blue crouched, frozen. Let Amy shout. Words couldn't destroy her. That was something Tish had taught her, not long before she'd vanished.

"Some people need someone to blame." Tish had paused, taken a swig from the beer she was holding. One of many, if the bottles on the counter told the truth. "It's the only way for them to make sense out of things. Doesn't matter who you are; if you fit what they need for a villain, you're it. It's all about them, not you."

The screaming wasn't about taking care of Marcos. It wasn't Amy being a mom. It was about who Amy saw in the mirror, about what she wanted others to see when they looked at her house. Outsides, not insides. She wanted someone to blame for Marcos. Someone who couldn't argue back.

Blue grabbed her bag and her guitar. The toxic flood of words continued as Blue pushed past her, hurried down the stairs, her socks slipping on the buffed floor.

"Get out, get out, *get out!*" Now Blue ran, Amy's voice growing louder and closer behind her. Her boots . . . They were back in

Marcos's room; but she was already at the door, then out, running across the wooden deck in her wool socks.

The door slammed behind her. Complete quiet. She glanced back. The wall of windows made the downstairs a terrarium at night, a spotless sealed world. Amy paced within, her mouth moving constantly, never once looking out, trapped in her inhospitable home.

The night air wrapped around Blue, crisp, the stars sharp, the woods silent but for the rustle of dead leaves as the breeze moved through them. She would have traded her soul again for the chance to swear. Something long and satisfying, something that would have made even Teena whistle in appreciation. Writing it out wasn't the same.

Her boots were on the other side of the door Amy had slammed behind her. Without the boots, she'd lose her bet. Shivering in the cold, she wondered what exactly it meant to give up your soul.

That was stupid. She wouldn't lose. In the morning they'd leave. She'd stop Marcos, ask him for them. He'd help. He owed her that much. Thanks to her, his mom could go on pretending he was perfect. He wasn't the problem; Blue was.

In the meantime, she needed to stay warm. She padded back across the deck, down the stairs and underneath. The ground there was damp and cold, so she pulled a pile of leaves together. Tucked inside, leaning against one of the deck beams, she wrapped her arms around her knees and settled in.

Blue woke with a start at some sound she couldn't classify. The leaves scraped against her neck as she rubbed her eyes. It was still night, the sliver of moon lowering itself behind the trees. What had she heard? An animal? A car?

She wiggled her fingers and toes, trying to work the chill out of them. Now that she was awake, she wouldn't find sleep again. She carried her bag and guitar up onto the deck.

Inside, the lights were still on, but no one was visible. The clock in the kitchen read 2:00. She held her ear to the glass. Nothing.

She tried the doorknob. It turned. Quietly, slowly, she crept across the floor to the stairs. Still no sound beyond the ticking of the clock. This would be easier than she thought. If anyone woke, she'd just run—first for her boots, then out of the house. If Amy hadn't called the cops before, she wasn't going to do it now.

She continued up the stairs, thankful that the stairs didn't creak. Marcos's light was still on. He'd moved onto his bed, one arm dangling off the side.

Blue grabbed her boots and scurried back down the stairs. At the bottom she paused. Something held her there, something she couldn't quite label. A noise just out of range, reminding her of the crunch of gristle between teeth. A hint in the air of something hot, bitter.

She padded down the hall beneath the stairs, the way Amy had gone earlier that night. The same sound again, so soft she thought it might be a mistake, some trick of her ears or the night. Deep down, she knew she should stop. Whatever was going on in that house had nothing to do with her.

Curiosity wouldn't let her leave without knowing. Down the dark hall she went, stopping by a door left ajar. The smell flowed out of the room. She tensed herself to run and peeked around the corner.

It was an office. A computer sat on top of a desk, its lit screen displaying an account whose numbers were all red. Beside it waited stacks of unopened mail, a utility bill on top.

Amy was seated at the desk, one hand on the mail. Her other

hand traced aimless circles in the air. Beside her stood a man. Dark brown hair, blue cotton dress shirt. He leaned over her, one hand on the back of the chair. The sound came from him. He was chewing, his teeth making slight clicking sounds as his jaw moved.

Blue shifted to see what he was chewing. Something pale, gossamer strands that stretched from his chin to Amy's head like fairy chewing gum. Stretched farther as he straightened up, turned his head toward Blue. Amy's head turned, too, her mouth slack. Startled, Blue watched the motion of Amy's hand, identical to the scrabbling of a dying barn cat after Gus Thompson's pit bull had caught it by the neck and shaken it like a toy. Not aimless—futile. Little more than synaptic desperation, her wide open eyes full of . . . shock.

Suffering.

The man grinned, then resumed chewing, the threads stretching farther, thinning, the light fading in them. The sound coming from between his teeth—gristle being ground with pleasure—made Blue's stomach turn. The man's grin grew wider as Blue stepped back, her hand on the door. Amy's mouth moved, too, almost as if mimicking his; a pale bubble swelled between her lips

The man tugged his head back. With a slippery snap, the threads broke free of Amy's head. His jaw moved four more times, the final strands disappearing into his mouth. He raised one hand and touched a finger to the bubble between Amy's lips, watching Blue as if a funny secret rested between them. His finger crooked, the bubble broke, and a wail—pitched so high that Blue felt more than heard it—assailed the room.

Blue ran. Her boots bounced back and forth against her thigh, and she slid to her knees halfway across the main room. She scrabbled back up, kept going, through the door, across the deck, grabbing her things as she went. She crossed the driveway in a bound and headed into the woods, stumbling over fallen logs as boughs whipped her cheeks.

She ran for a long time. All she could hear were the leaves beneath her feet, and her own breath hurricane-loud. Finally, one foot caught in a shrubby tangle and she fell flat out, the guitar giving a loud twang.

She held her breath. No sound came from behind her. Of course, what she'd left behind could follow her without noise. She was sure of it. She closed her eyes tightly, as if that could erase what she'd seen. Not just what she'd seen, but the soft chewing crunch that echoed in her ears.

Eventually the cold seeped through her fear. First thing was to stay warm. She put her boots on and felt the ground beneath her. Dry leaves blanketed the ground; she collected them, crawling in a circle and reaching as far as she could to bring them close. Again and again, until she had enough and could burrow deep within.

SHE DIDN'T SLEEP. AT ALL. BY THE TIME LIGHT BEGAN
to color the sky, she wished she'd never made her deal, had never
even thought twice about Cass. Sometimes she hated Cass more
than anyone else she knew. Hated her for being selfish, for leaving, for not thinking about what it would be like for Blue to be left
behind. Or worse, for thinking of it and not caring. Once she started
thinking about that, she started thinking about everyone else she
hated. Teena, for example, for turning on her.

Only, if she was honest, had it really been that way? Hadn't
she been pushing off, bit by bit, like a diver at the end of the board,
wiggling her toes a little, feeling the bounce? Getting ready to go.
Listening to Teena talking about them moving to Portland together,
knowing it wasn't what she wanted. Not saying it, though. Waiting,
holding on to the *whatever* Teena punctuated every thought with, to
Sundays watching Patriots games she didn't care about, to belonging somewhere. What if Teena had been holding on, too, both of
them afraid to let go?

She examined her hands in the pale sunlight. Both were
scraped up pretty well from catching her as she'd fallen. A smart
person would have packed Band-Aids, maybe even a whole first-aid
kit. Then again, a smart person wouldn't have been caught in the
dark of the crossroads.

A chickadee sang close by, its winter call reminding her of snow, of home. She could have been there, warm, waking up to the beep of the alarm, smelling Lynne's coffee from the kitchen. Not here, with no idea how to find her way out. With that . . . thing . . . from last night lurking somewhere.

A game, that's what the woman in the red dress had called it. Find Cass, win the prize. Only today the game looked a lot more like bullfighting than chess. Even the crackle of leaves as she moved reminded her of the click of teeth.

Her feet hurt as if she'd spent the night kicking concrete blocks with them. She wanted to take off her boots, maybe bury them there, and walk away for good, leaving them the way Cass had left her. Instead, she stood up and stretched toward the rose-colored sky, turning around to examine her surroundings.

The leaves told the story of her dash through the dark. No sense in heading back along that trail. Away from her, the land sloped down. They'd driven up to get to Amy's house last night, so down was clearly the right direction. Who cared what the boots might say—the one thing she wanted was miles between her and whatever might be inside Amy's house.

She hadn't walked more than ten minutes when she hit a steep downhill. Another five and she was on a road. She walked against the traffic, prepared to jump into the woods if a black SUV appeared. Or a police car, or . . . What kind of car would a soul-eating monster drive? Did he even need one? No cars passed, though, and she continued along the shoulder.

The man in the blue shirt had eaten Amy's soul. When Blue had waited at the crossroads, she'd imagined losing her soul as dying. Amy hadn't been dying, though—she'd been suffering.

If your soul was the truest part of you, what did you become once it was gone? A body, she suspected, able to continue on in the world—to eat, to sleep, to breathe. The missing piece would be different for each person. Music, or laughter, or kindness—it could be anything.

If Amy had made a deal, what would she have lost with her soul? What could possibly be worth that?

Saving your sister from the same fate.

She looked down the road, trying not to think about Cass. What made Jed real? Or Jill—what was the essential piece of Jill? What did they risk losing? The man she'd seen with Amy was also the man offering them a contract. She recognized his smell: hot and bad, like something toxic cooked on a Bunsen burner.

The bedtime story Mama used to tell her about the devil at the crossroads had felt nothing like this. "Robert Johnson and his guitar were just too big a temptation," Mama would say. "The devil saw right through him, saw his potential, saw the way he burned to play that guitar, looked right into his very heart and saw it was made of the truest stuff there is, and right then and there, the devil made a choice."

But Robert Johnson had just died young, not lived to have his guitar-playing torn out of him. Blue's decision to make a deal had been all about the gesture, about getting Cass back. It was like a fairy tale; and in fairy tales the suffering never felt quite real. Now, having seen what waited for her, she wasn't sure she would have chosen the same way.

She caught a ride with a little bird of a woman driving a dented green sedan. The woman was headed to work in a town west of Rochester, and she dropped Blue in front of a drugstore there. Blue mouthed a quick thanks and set out, her gear in tow.

In the drugstore, she grabbed a box of crackers and a couple of cheese sticks, along with some hydrogen peroxide and Band-Aids. She paid for them out of the fifty dollars she kept in her jeans. She needed to replenish her stash for a bus ticket. She'd do it in the bathroom, where no one would be watching.

Inside, she worked on her hands first. Hands taken care of, she moved on to pulling her greasy hair back tight with an elastic and brushing her teeth. Somewhat cleaner than she had been before, she opened the pocket of her backpack where she kept her wallet. The wallet was there.

The money was not.

All the money she'd taken out of her account, minus the bit she'd carried in her pocket, was gone. She pulled everything out of her bag, first that pocket and then all of them, but she knew she wouldn't find it.

She'd been so stupid. She'd known when she got back to Marcos's room and found her bag open that she hadn't left it that way, but she'd looked at his house and everything he had and had assumed he wouldn't touch her stuff. Rich kids didn't steal, right? Stupid, stupid. Now she had . . . She took the cash out of her pocket. Thirty-seven dollars and fifty-six cents. Enough for a bus ticket to somewhere nearby. Not enough for a room.

Blue crouched down and rested her head in her hands as the world spun around her. She could hitch, sure, but where would she sleep? What would she eat, once the money ran out? The cheese and crackers wouldn't last long.

A knock at the door made her draw a deep breath, wipe her eyes dry. She shoved everything back into her pack and left.

Outside, the sun shone and the wind tugged at her hair. She walked around the back of the building and leaned against the wall.

What was she going to do? She could go to a police station and . . . what? Tell them some rich kid somewhere in Rochester had stolen her money? She didn't even know Marcos's last name.

Lynne? Lynne would come if Blue contacted her. One e-mail and even now, even after she had walked away, Lynne would come for her. Then she'd demand an explanation, and Blue would have to tell her a story she'd never believe. Lynne would think she was crazy. Maybe she was. Maybe she belonged in a psych ward.

She found some comfort in the thought, in the idea that the man in the blue shirt and the woman in the red dress were accidents of her mind and could be sent away by talking, by the right meds. She'd all but made up her mind to contact Lynne when she remembered the girl in the basement of Bet's aunt's house and the smoke rising from the rags at her feet.

If someone knew Blue's name, she couldn't stay with them for more than three days. Everyone in Eliotville knew her name. What would happen to them if she returned?

She slapped the wall, just hard enough to redden her palm a little. Until she found Cass, she had no home. The only way to keep everyone safe was to keep moving. Everything else she had to work out for herself.

She returned to the front of the building and, for the first time, studied the town around her. It reminded her a bit of Portland—not too big, not too small, not too crowded on a sunny Tuesday in November. She caught a squirrel peering at her from a trash can as she looked up and down the street. The woman who'd given her a ride had said the bus station was a few blocks away. Blue started walking in the direction she'd pointed, hoping a plan would come to her along the way.

One block over she found a park. Not much, just a stretch of grass with a few leafless trees and three benches around an empty fountain. She crossed the street and sat down, careful to tuck her pack under her seat, one shoulder strap looped around her ankle.

The guitar case rested against her shins. *No.* She rejected the idea as quickly as it entered her head. The guitar was worth more than anything else she owned, here or at home, but she'd never sell it. Even before the woman in the red dress had conjured Mama up while playing it, she'd never ever have given it up.

The pigeons shied away as a group, breaking into flight. She looked up to see an old woman approaching. She was creaky, old, and dark-skinned, a dark green beret set atop her thin white hair, a neatly pressed plaid skirt covering tights-encased legs. Blue expected her to choose her own bench, but she made her slow way right up to Blue and sat down so close that she had to tuck her feet behind the guitar case.

"My, that's a little nippy," she said, wiggling side to side. "Careful you don't get frozen in place here."

Her slackened skin pleated around a pair of deep brown eyes that looked unfamiliar; but the smell—the heat, the sweetness and rot mixed together that blew from the woman's skin . . . Blue yanked her notebook from her back pocket.

I'm deciding what to do next. Not staying.

She went back and underlined <u>staying</u> before holding the page up.

The old woman laughed. "Now, now, don't you get yourself worked up, my dear. I'm just enjoying the sun."

Liar!

The anger made her hand shake as she wrote.

You lied about everything. Did you have to take my money? It's not a game, it's just mean.

And then she did freeze, her hand stilling on the page. The snick of teeth chewing, the bubble from Amy's mouth, her hand pawing, pawing. Whatever shape it took, the thing beside her was a monster.

The woman leaned closer, touched Blue's hand and moved it so she could read the words. She tutted. "You can't blame me for everything that happens. I didn't take any money from you."

Blue swallowed.

Amy. You did that, right in front of me.

She paused, afraid to continue. She had to know, though.

Is that what you're going to do to me?

The old woman turned her attention to the returning pigeons. They shuffled forward cautiously, cocking their heads to see whether seeds were forthcoming. "Like I said, you can't blame me for everything you see wrong in the world."

How many of you are there? Mama said—the tightness in her chest came, the one that reminded her that from now on she'd always be a girl without a mother—*you wait for the devil at the crossroads with your instrument + you make a deal. The thing you most want in exchange for your soul. She never said the world was full of devils and that they ate your soul.*

"Child, you've made a deal. That's the only thing you need to think about: your deal. I gave you what you need to find your heart's desire, and I gave you time to do what needs doing. The rest is up to you."

The cold from the bench had risen inside her, inch by chilling inch, until her teeth chattered and her hands shook.

The old woman sighed. The smell of a lit match blew forth from her mouth. She looked down at the watch on her wrist, a tiny silver thing on a band that creased her fragile skin. "It's time for me to be going. Stay focused on our deal, Bluebird. It's the only thing that matters."

She put a hand down to push herself up from the bench, then stopped. Instead, she took Blue's cheeks between her palms and leaned closer, until her papery lips touched Blue's forehead. A shock, warmth rushing in, and something more, something like what had happened at the crossroads; only then it had been taking, and this, the pressure against her head, was gentle giving.

She let go. "That guitar, Bluebird, keep her close. She carries more answers than you can ever imagine." She stood up and walked slowly toward the fountain, raising one leg and then the other to step inside before fading away completely.

Blue opened her mouth, certain her voice had come back. No sound came out, though. She'd felt something going into her. What else could it be but her voice? Unless it was another trick, and now she'd have seizures, or smallpox, or something else terrible. Or maybe it was just a kiss?

Unlikely.

SHE STAYED ON THE BENCH. NO LONGER COLD, SHE OPENED
the case and took out the guitar. At that moment, she would have
taken answers to just about anything, but the guitar said nothing.
Blue gave a hesitant strum. The cold strings responded off-key. She
turned the first peg, listened closely.

The pigeons watched as she focused. Step by step, closing her
eyes and tilting her head, until everything sounded the way it should.
She smiled and opened her eyes. A little boy stood in front of her,
his lower lip jutting out. A few steps back waited a woman who had
to be his mother—same big brown eyes, same full lower lip.

"Go ahead and ask the nice lady," the woman said.

The boy took a step closer. So little; he had to be three, maybe
four. "You gonna play my song." He reached toward the guitar, his
tiny fat fingers curling as if to stroke a cat.

Blue shook her head. She hadn't meant to play anything, just
to hold the guitar while thinking about what she might do next. She
didn't even know any kids' songs.

"You play song for me," the little boy persisted. She looked at
him, and he reached again toward the strings.

She shrugged, ready to pack up, only then she heard something. Music, lacy, like a dulcimer heard from several rooms away

in an old farmhouse. Head up, she stared across the park, searching for someone else playing. No one was there, though, aside from pigeons and the boy and his mother.

The boy. She leaned toward him. The music was somehow inside him, as if he'd swallowed a music box. Only way better than a music box, more like he'd swallowed a real musician and her instrument. It was beautiful.

Okay, so the boy had music inside him. Was it any weirder than the woman in the red dress, or losing her voice, or any of the bad things that had happened? Either the world was full of crazy things, or she was the only crazy one. Schizophrenic—that could be it. She was seeing and hearing things that weren't there.

Unlike everything else, though, the boy's music didn't make her afraid. It made her want to play. She strummed once or twice, then launched into a song Mama used to do for her and Cass, an old blues tune that reminded her of the clink of radiators in the winter, of cold hands warming around mugs of peppermint tea after they came in from playing in the snow.

The little boy shimmied along with the song, clapping his hands off beat, pumping his knees up and down. The pigeons, which had flown off at the first chord, came back in, clucking and cooing. Blue lifted her head to the sun, her foot tapping along. It felt good. More than good—it felt exactly right, as if the world had corrected its orbit.

At the end, the boy's mother handed him something while whispering in his ear. He marched forward and dropped a couple of dollars into the case.

"Carter," the mother said in a stage whisper. "Say thanks."

He didn't, rushing back to wrap his arms around his mother's leg instead. The woman smiled. "Thank you," she said.

Blue flashed her a peace sign, and the pair walked away.

Just like that, she had two dollars more than she'd had ten minutes ago. Maybe the guitar had more answers than she'd assumed.

Blue played right on through the early afternoon. Not constantly—when no one was around, she let the guitar rest in her lap and sucked on her sore fingertips. Real players built up calluses on their fingers. Hers were too soft, and the steel strings wore them raw. As soon as people walked by, though, she was all smiles, the pain her secret.

By the time she knew she couldn't play another song, she'd made forty-eight dollars. There had been other mothers and kids stopping by, a whole little group at one point. At lunchtime a couple of men in suits had listened for a song. They'd each tossed a ten in before leaving together. She'd heard them as they walked away, something about a college band and where had the time gone.

The money didn't come close to making up for what Marcos had stolen, but it gave her hope. The guitar was the answer, just the way the woman in the red dress had said. All she had to do was play. She couldn't believe she hadn't thought of it before. Tish had survived her travel along the Gully by busking. But Tish was a genius, and Blue was just . . . Blue.

That afternoon, Blue started walking, unsure what she should do. She had enough money now for food, and either a bus ticket or a place to stay. Not all three. She'd stayed out in the woods at home with just a sleeping bag plenty of times. That was in a place she knew well, though. And with a sleeping bag—that was the real difference. The night before, she'd managed okay because she'd had leaves for insulation. The thought of spending the night in a doorway with no sleeping bag or leaves made her stomach ache.

Eventually Blue came across a two-story brick building with

HEFFLELAND MEMORIAL LIBRARY printed in black on the white sign on the lawn. Libraries, every one she'd ever known, were warm and welcoming, and full of information. The perfect place to sit and figure things out.

Inside, past an entryway hung with flyers for toddler music classes and dog-obedience training, was a large room. Blue walked quickly past the circulation desk, where a gray-haired woman sat, a pot of orange mums next to her.

The librarian glanced at Blue, smiled, and returned to her work taping a cover to a book. Blue shuffled by, trying not to hit anything with the guitar case. She made her way to a terminal in the center of the room and sat down with her pack between her feet and the guitar to her side. From somewhere farther back among the bookcases came a cough, but no other signs of people existed.

She had a seat, she was warm, she had Internet access. Now what? Should she look up cheap bus fares? Ways to travel without money? How to get the devil to leave your soul alone?

That last seemed the most important, but she doubted that what she needed to know she would find online. She started searching for motels instead. Nothing she found was under ninety bucks a night. Maybe a phone book? She glanced back at the librarian. The woman didn't look up. New problem. Even if she could check out the library phone book, she couldn't check out a voice to use with it.

But the librarian might call for her. Blue looked around, saw no one else, decided it was safe to leave her bag for a minute. She wrote her question out before going up to the desk, taking pains with her penmanship.

The librarian finished taping a label on the spine of a book. Blue handed her the notebook, waited while the librarian read her note.

"Laryngitis is the worst. You're smart to rest your voice instead of trying to whisper." She reached under the desk, offered Blue a phone book. "You can take it back to the table if you want. Just bring it back, okay?"

Blue smiled in response. At the table, she tried motels, found only one that she hadn't seen online. A name alone, nothing about cost or location. No website. She searched the name anyway, came up with nothing.

On to Plan B. She went back to the librarian, her new question printed out. The librarian pushed her glasses back on her head and studied Blue. "I don't know if that's really a place that you'd want to stay," she said at last. "I could recommend some nicer ones."

Blue pointed at her question, mouthed the word *please*. The woman lowered her glasses and dialed the phone. Blue watched, breath held.

"Hello, I'm calling from the Heffleland Library. I'm wondering if you could tell me what your nightly rates are. Yes, and do you have rooms available for tonight?"

The woman wrote as she listened, upside down, so Blue could read it. Sixty-five dollars. She had just over eighty dollars. Enough for the room tonight. Tomorrow, she could make some more money in the park. Enough to get out of town and then . . . Well, the guitar was the answer, right? She'd just keep playing in each town she stopped in.

Get directions for me? ☺

The librarian studied her so carefully that Blue felt that the parts of her face were being catalogued, labeled, and stored away. Close up, she could see the pale powder caught in the woman's soft wrinkle lines, the brown pencil she'd used on her eyebrows. The woman smelled of chicken soup, and Blue's stomach growled.

"I've been reading a lot about the Great Depression recently.

Do you know much about it?" The woman paused. Blue shook her head. Who read about the Great Depression on their own? Was this librarian one of those women who were always taking classes? If Blue had free time, she couldn't imagine spending it in history classes. Then again, she wasn't totally sure what she would want to do. Unbidden, the memory of playing in the park came, of how it felt to have people listening to her music.

"Well, it was a time of hoboes. Drifters. Men without work, young folks without many prospects. A hard, hard time. One cool thing—these drifters, some of them would leave messages in the places they'd travel. A lot of different symbols, a kind of secret language. They warned each other of folks who were intolerant; they pointed out places to find food. One mark, a cat, was the sign of a kindhearted woman. Someone on the road saw that, they'd know they might get a meal or a safe place to sleep for the night."

Blue shifted, wondering where all this was going. All she could think of was the motel room, of a shower and a bed.

"It's a personal interest for me. My father was one of those drifters, looking for work, for hope. There's a story he always told when I was little. One rainy night he was very sick, feeling close to dead. The way he told it, the rain nearly washed the life right out of him. He'd been chased away from a railroad yard, and the nearby town had a reputation for being hard on travelers, and he thought he'd just lie down in a ditch somewhere and meet his maker.

"He sat down next to a mailbox. Glanced up, just because, and saw a little stick cat drawn on the underside. So he dragged himself to his feet and walked up to the house, figuring the worst that would happen is that he'd be shot, and he already expected to die. He didn't, though, because the woman who lived there took him in, and she kept him a whole week, in a warm guest room bed, with more food than he'd had for months. Patched him up, and once he was well enough to move on, she told him that she expected he'd do what he could for others along the road."

Blue looked up, suddenly understanding.

"My father took that debt seriously. I do as well. This world can be the kind of place where a man can die in a ditch without anyone stopping to help, or it can be the kind of place where we all look after each other. I think you might be a person in need of help. If that's the case, well, I have a room you could use overnight."

Blue hesitated. Last night had been more than enough to persuade her never to stay with strangers again. But if she saved her money by staying, then she could buy a bus ticket in the morning and arrive in her next town during the day. Enough time to check things out, maybe even find another park to play in.

The librarian might be like Amy, or she might be the way she felt—warm, gentle, kind. Lou had said to trust herself. This woman, with her salty chicken-soup smell, and the soft creases of her face, and her story, didn't scare Blue.

K, thanks! ☺

THE LIBRARIAN HAD TO WORK UNTIL SIX. BLUE STAYED,
reluctant to leave either her stuff or the library. First, what if she
left her bag behind the desk and the woman stole from it? Hard to
imagine, but anything was possible. And second, what if she took
her stuff with her and the librarian closed up the library and left?
Mama had left. Cass had left. Even Tish had gone. Blue'd come to
assume that within her dwelt something unlovable and easy to leave
behind. She had no reason to believe this stranger wouldn't choose
to leave her, too.

Instead, Blue worked. When she was little, she'd imagined that
the air in libraries was filled with whispers, with books telling their
stories to one another. The air here held nothing more than the
creak and snap of the baseboard heating and the growls of traffic
outside, but there was magic in the order and peace, nonetheless.
Shelving books made her a part of it.

A few kids her age came in after school let out. She wondered
how she looked to them. Like any other new girl, chipped green
polish on bitten nails, curly frizz escaping from the tight elastic
holding back her brown hair. Her jeans had dirt on the knees, and
she kept pulling leaves out of her barn coat's pockets as well as her
hair.

Okay, maybe she wasn't like any other new girl. Maybe just like a new girl who had arrived straight from the woods.

Cass had cared so much about how she looked. Every morning she'd blow-dry her hair into perfect straightness, the edges in a silky taper around her face. She kept her nails perfect, too. Not gaudy—just single smooth colors, multiple coats brushed on until they shone, slick and even and wet-looking. She ordered expensive makeup online, using Lynne's credit card, then paid her back with waitressing tips. You'd never know that underneath it she was as blotchy as any other girl.

At least that was how she *had* been. Was she still the same? Two years ago, Blue had still had braces and had liked to wear snug pink sweatshirts with hoods and zippers. What would Cass look like at nineteen, and would she recognize who Blue had become? Would she look at the faded streaks in Blue's hair where she'd dyed it with red Kool-Aid, alone on a Saturday night, looking for anything to distract her from the quiet? Would she run her fingers through the tangles and say, "I have a better idea"?

"All set?" The librarian had put on a long black coat and a watercolor-print scarf, winding it twice around her neck. Something about the action made Blue shiver. Maybe it was the slenderness of her neck and the casual way the girl in the basement had studied the sparks dropping onto the rags as the others slept above them. But Blue wasn't staying long. She hadn't even given away her real name, so she should have three weeks, not three days. The librarian was safe from her. As long as she didn't stay.

The librarian lived in a little brick house. They entered it through a side door that led into the kitchen. Books lined the inside, on shelves, on counters, in piles on the floor. The woman didn't apologize for the clutter. She just took off her scarf and coat, slinging them over the back of a scarred wooden chair at the table, and stooped to pick up a bowl from the floor.

"I'm still used to feeding two cats," she said as she took a can of cat food from the cupboard. A moment later a black-and-white cat trotted around the corner.

"This is Esmeralda. The other was Chanticleer. There's a picture of him on the mantel in the other room." There was the snap of a can being opened, and the cat at her feet began to purr.

The woman showed Blue a place to leave her boots, by the door. The relief came almost as soon as they were off. She needed another pair of shoes for when she wasn't moving. The whole boot thing wasn't really working quite the way she'd imagined.

The librarian led her back through the sitting room, all the way through to a staircase just past it. Upstairs were two rooms: one clearly a bedroom, while the other was packed full of more books, with a little daybed stuck in the corner by the window.

"You can leave your things here. Go ahead and slide the books around if you need space. I'd pull the shade if I were you. I leave it open during the day, so Esme can lie in the sun, but the people across the way can see right in. I have towels downstairs, if you'd like to use the shower?"

Blue left her guitar on the bed and carried her pack back down the stairs with her. The bathroom was tiny—just room for a toilet, sink, and shower—and the tile was cold under her feet. The water was perfect, though, hot almost to the point of pain; and she stayed in it a long time.

They had a quiet dinner. The librarian had changed into sweat-pants and a ragged-hemmed sweater, and she served them soup in mismatched bowls. Blue didn't care. The food was hot and filling, some kind of soup with beans and corn, and corn bread alongside. She ate until her stomach hurt.

"I'll send some bread with you when you go," the librarian said as she cleared the table.

Blue had assumed that the woman had wanted company. After all—cat, house full of books . . . She had to want people around. By the end of dinner, she wasn't so sure. The woman seemed happy with silence, and her eyes kept straying to a book that lay open on the corner of the table. She hadn't even asked Blue's name, nor offered her own. It was Sharon—Blue had heard her say it on the phone—but she thought of the woman only as the librarian.

Blue'd been so busy wondering if she would be safe that it hadn't occurred to her what the librarian had risked in bringing her home. She knew who she was: just Blue, seventeen, not spectacular at grades or causing trouble, good at swimming and playing guitar. But this woman had only the outside to go on.

Now, standing by her in the kitchen, Blue knew a secret about the librarian. Music came from within the woman, a soft, sleepy fiddle tune designed to be danced to in a dimly lit room.

Another thing she couldn't tell anyone. She went upstairs to her room and lay on the bed thinking about how music played from souls like wind chimes on a breezy day. She wondered what her own might sound like. That was what the woman in the red dress had given her—the ability to hear. She fell into dreams of music rolling in great sweeping waves across the land, along the highways, flooding the cities and washing all unhappiness away.

THE LIBRARIAN HAD TO LEAVE FOR WORK AT 9:30 THE
next morning. "I have to ask you to leave, too," she said, apologetically. "It's not as though I have much to take, but . . ."

Blue had stolen twice in her life. Once innocently—a pencil eraser shaped like an elephant that she slipped into her pocket when she was five. Mama had discovered it when she did the laundry a few days later, and Blue had struggled to remember how it had found its way there. Mama hadn't made a fuss, just stopped in at the store the next day and paid for it as though she'd come to buy it. "Keep things out of your pocket, kiddo," was all she'd said to Blue.

The other time had been on purpose. It was a month after Mama died, and Blue had suddenly wanted a candy bar, more than anything. It wasn't even the candy so much as the feeling, the memory of her and Cass and Mama and Tish on Friday nights before the cancer had come, sneaking cheap candy into the movie theater, the taste of it somehow sweeter, more exotic, than anything they could have bought at concessions.

She'd wanted a candy bar, and she could have asked Lynne for money to buy one, and Lynne would have given it to her, along with a lecture about healthy snacks. She didn't want Lynne's money or her lectures. She just wanted. She'd sneaked the chocolate into her pocket at the grocery and left with one eye on Bill Eagleton talking with the cashier, as if she were daring him to say something. He didn't. No one stopped her. She went around back and ate the candy with great gulping bites. It tasted of sugar and sadness, of nothingness, and she spat the last bite out and walked home alone.

I don't steal things, she wanted to say. *I'd never take your stuff.* She hated that feeling, the same she used to get when she and Teena went into tourist shops on the coast and the shopkeepers had watched their every move.

Instead, she nodded.

No prob. I have to move on anyway. Thx so much for the food + bed.

Packing up, she lingered a moment over her keepsake bag. It contained nothing of value to anyone else: a lock of chestnut hair, harvested before chemotherapy had taken the rest; a tortoiseshell guitar pick; a white cotton training bra; a stone curved in the shape of a heart; two pictures; letters tied with brown yarn. She laid the pictures out, touched the images, the faces greasy with wear.

She lifted one and pressed her lips first to Mama's face, then to Cass's. Mama, wearing a crown Blue'd made her for her birthday. Cass, giving her best Mad Hatter impression in a giant purple hat.

It wasn't just sadness that hurt when she looked at the pictures, it was regret. Sorry wasn't a concept; sorry was a feeling that ate its way down deep inside you and grew until you would do anything to dig it out.

She went downstairs, carrying her things. The librarian looked at the guitar case.

"I assume you have a guitar in there?"

Blue nodded.

"Do you play?"

She nodded again. A little rush hit her, one that said *People give me money to play for them.*

"Would you play for me?" The librarian waved toward the case. "I've never been musical, but I love to listen. My grandfather used to play a fiddle, and my father would try, though he was never very good. I'd love to hear you."

Payment of a kind, for the room and food. Blue nodded. She played two songs. A blues song that Mama played a lot, and one of Dry Gully's standards. Tish had written it, not Mama. Mama's songs were sunshine and woodstoves. Tish's—Blue understood now that Tish's were all about the woman in the red dress, the smell of flame and decay and the heat of her lips on a cold night.

"I feel like I know that one," the librarian said when Blue finished. "Is it something on the radio?"

Blue shook her head.

It was my mother's band, she started to write, then stopped.

She was leaving today, and it had only been two days, but what if she didn't leave? The librarian might figure things out if she knew Dry Gully. Would it still count—would she still be at risk if Blue herself hadn't said her name?

My music teacher taught me. I like the sound.

"Me too." The librarian pursed her lips. "Do you have a sleeping bag in your backpack? It doesn't look big enough to me."

She shook her head.

"Well, that concerns me. Come on." She led Blue back through the rooms toward the stairs, turning aside to open a door leading down into the basement. Blue followed. As the stairs creaked beneath their feet, the image of the girl sitting on the freezer came to her, and she could almost hear the snap of the electric lines in her hands.

This basement looked nothing like the other, though. There were neat rows of fluorescent lights overhead, and neat rows of metal shelves beneath, with plastic boxes bearing labels like DOCUMENTS or RAGS. The librarian went straight to the farthest corner, opened a container, and stepped back, a full purple stuff sack in her hands.

"It's not the lightest or the warmest bag ever made, but it's better than nothing. I have some cord upstairs. We could tie it on your backpack."

They tried. It didn't work, not well. Blue's bag was too small, the seams already stretched to tearing.

"Well. Let's try something else." The woman vanished back downstairs, alone this time. When she returned, she was carrying a frame pack, an old one whose metal frame peeked out from beneath its canvas body.

"This was my dad's." Her eyes shone behind her glasses. "Even after all his travels, he still kept rambling after he married my mother. She loved him anyway, but . . . Sometimes love asks for sacrifices. More than lots of people are willing to make. Anyway, it's silly for me to keep it. I don't hike, and if I did, I'd get something lighter. You take it. You'll get more use out of it."

Blue raised her notebook, but the librarian shook her head. "I insist." So Blue moved the contents of her backpack to the larger one, and the librarian tied the sleeping bag onto the frame. Her old backpack she folded up and stashed in with her clothes.

A scrawled "Thank you" felt too small a thing. Yesterday morning Blue had been crying in the drugstore bathroom, not sure she'd even make it out of town. Now, warm, clean, full, with a sleeping bag and some hope tucked away in the frame pack, she knew she'd make it. She owed the librarian something more.

That thing you talked about, the signs people would draw? I'd write Kind-Hearted Woman on your mailbox. I think you paid your dad's debt.

The librarian looked at her. Something lit her face, like the rosy glow people got around a campfire, beautiful. Blue could hear her as well: the pluck of a fiddle string, a minor key, melancholy and lovely and lonely and hers.

"You take care of yourself," the librarian said. "Travel safe, and stop in if you ever come this way again."

SHE TRIED PLAYING IN THE PARK AGAIN. THERE WERE
fewer people than yesterday, though, and the breeze was stiffer,
making it harder to keep her fingers working. After she'd run
through most of the songs she knew, she'd only added another five
dollars to her collection.

She was examining the Band-Aids on her palms when a prickle
on the back of her neck made her look up. A boy stood at the edge
of the lawn for a minute or so, then headed over.

"Can you play in fingerless gloves? You're gonna freeze."

She shrugged. Her hands were mottled pink and white, depending on how cold any one spot was.

"Don't you talk?"

She pointed at her throat, made a sad face before reaching for
her notebook. It nearly slipped from her grasp. He was right: she
needed some way to keep her hands warm.

"Your throat is sad?" He'd come a few steps closer. Aside from
a scattering of pimples, his cheeks were smooth, his voice a little
high. He had to be younger than she, maybe even in junior high
school.

Bad laryngitis. Can't talk.

"Sucks for you. You sing, too?"

Not like the rest of my family, she wanted to say. What difference did it make, though? It was gone.

Yeah.

He nodded, as if she were confirming things he knew. "Bet it's all pretty stuff, right? You have that look. Longish hair, big eyes, you know. Pretty."

Her cheeks went warm despite the cold. He didn't talk like a junior high kid. Anyway, Cass was the pretty one. Scratch that, the beautiful one. Blue'd try things on impulse and feel funny in the aftermath. She'd put on dark red lipstick, then wipe it all off half an hour later, throw a dress on, change five minutes before she had to leave for school.

The boy kept watching her.

Pretty music? Kind of, I guess.

He looked her over a little more carefully. "You'd probably get more if you sang, but you might also get more guys being assholes, too. You know?"

She gave him a dirty look.

He held up his hands. "Not creeping on you. Promise. It's easier, though, when you're not all alone."

Two steps closer. He looked young—his face, at least—and he was short, but his eyes looked old, like he knew all about life and how things went. Not scary, just more than she expected.

The ache in her feet had been growing, and she leaned forward and rubbed under the ankle of her boots. She needed to move on, in some direction, somehow.

"Your boots giving you trouble?" His eyes were on them now, avid, hungry. She looked at the ragged pair of sneakers on his feet. No way. She was keeping her boots on while he was around.

They're fine.

"'Cause I know a place where you might find some shoes. Maybe some gloves you can play in, too. It's not far."

Lou had said to trust her gut. Her gut had said Jed was cool, and he had been. She'd been right about the librarian . . . and really wrong about Marcos.

Only, had she been wrong about *Marcos*, or about how kids like him should act? She'd looked at his house and everything he had, and she'd assumed that he wouldn't steal because he didn't need to. Couldn't the same have been said about her, the day she stole the candy bar?

She needed gloves, and she needed shoes that didn't hurt when she wasn't traveling.

How far is not far?

"Come on, I'll show you."

His name was Steve. He told her that, along with a general rundown of the town and the places to go and the places to avoid while they walked to the Exchange. That's what he called it, the Exchange, as if of course she'd know what it meant.

When she asked him how old he was, he gave her a funny look. "How old do you think?"

14.

"No way," he said, a little pained. "I'm seventeen."

She raised an eyebrow. He stared at her. "I am. Really. How old are you?"

17.

They rounded a corner, and he cut across a church lawn and down a set of stairs to a door beneath the building. A laminated sign was tacked to the outside—DORA'S EXCHANGE—with hours penciled below. "Come on," he said, holding the door for her.

Inside, cardboard boxes were stacked along the walls. Each was labeled with index cards—MEN'S HATS, WOMEN'S HATS, every category of clothing imaginable. An older woman sat at a card table in the back, knitting with bright purple yarn. She nodded toward them. "Go ahead, take a look."

They weren't the only ones in the room. A man with unwashed hair, his fingers flicking back and forth, mumbled to himself as he gazed into a box labeled LARGE SWEATERS. A man and a woman, clean and neat, whispered back and forth while matching children's mittens in another box. They glanced at Blue and Steve, the woman blushing fiercely. She straightened up, as if to leave, but the man hissed something at her that made her stop.

Steve pulled Blue by her sleeve over to a box of women's gloves and mittens. She thought about the wad of bills in her pocket.

$$?

"Free. It's all free. You're lucky they're open today. And that I found you," he added with a grin.

She peered into the box. It felt . . . wrong. She wasn't like that man, the one who'd be standing on a street somewhere talking to himself later, full of twitches and tics. She had a home. She just wasn't there right now.

Then again, that couple, the man now speaking to the woman at the desk in a low voice about coats, they didn't look like they belonged here, either. And she couldn't go home, not until she'd found Cass. Maybe that made it okay to take some gloves.

Steve didn't struggle with the idea at all. He'd already burrowed into the box, coming up with a pair of black knit gloves. "They have all the fingers, but you could cut the tops off. It'll take a while for them to unravel. Try."

Like shopping with Teena, almost. Could you be homesick for

a person more than a place, even if that person wasn't your friend anymore, never would be again?

She slid her hands in. A faint smell of cigarette smoke clung to them, and the outsides were pilled, and she almost said no. Then she thought about the cost of a pair of new gloves and shrugged.

In one corner were boxes of shoes. Mostly old people's—somber men's loafers, low-heeled women's dress shoes. No sneakers. No snow boots, aside from children's. She tried on a pair of brown leather men's shoes. The tread was worn, and one of the laces had broken, and they were a bit large, but her feet fell silent within them.

They stopped at the table once they were done and let the woman examine what they'd taken—the shoes, the gloves, a green wool crewneck sweater a size too big for Steve. "You know all about the kitchen, right? You come by at five, there'll be hot food Monday through Thursday. Someone's there to help folks find a place, too. The two of you, might be a good idea for you to come and see her."

"We gotta go. Thanks anyway." Steve picked up his sweater and nudged Blue toward the door.

Outside, Blue raised her hands questioningly. Steve shook his head. "Social worker. You don't want to get mixed up with them. I don't, at least. Shelters aren't for me."

What about your family?

He started walking. She hurried to catch up. Walking meant not talking, at least for her. Maybe that was his point.

She thumped on the guitar case, hard. He turned around. "What?"

Scribbling, almost breaking the tip.

That's it? You just walk off?

Why even ask? She'd put her boots back on, and her feet insisted she shouldn't stop, should keep going right on by him and on down the road.

"It's past noon. I need to look for lunch." So he didn't want to talk about his parents. It wasn't like Blue was telling him about herself, either.

Past noon. Lunchtime. In her pocket was a little more than eighty dollars and change. Her money—for food, for shelter, for a bus ticket.

Money she would have spent last night had it not been for the librarian and helping people who needed it. People who didn't come right out and ask for help, ones who waited with sad eyes while the money in your pocket felt heavier and heavier.

I need lunch too. Know a cheap place? ☺

Forty-five minutes later, they sat in the park again, this time licking cream cheese off their fingers. Two bagels, one soda, two straws. Her boots off, tied to her pack, her feet stretched out in front of her in the unfamiliar shoes.

Once finished, she looked over the gloves. A pair of scissors. Add that to the list of things to leave home with.

"Give 'em to me." Steve held out his hand. A jackknife appeared in his palm, fished out of his jacket pocket. Not a fancy one, no screwdrivers and tiny saws. A single blade in a silver case, *PC* monogrammed on the side. She pointed at the letters.

Who's that?

He scowled. "No one. My cousin." He sawed at the gloves until the fingers lay in his hand like shriveled black sausages. "Try now."

She put them on. The edges were ragged, the lengths uneven and thready, but her fingers were free. She opened the guitar case and pulled out the guitar.

Steve sat back, his arm along the back of the bench, while she played a quick tune. When she finished, she propped the guitar between her knees and took out the notebook.

You sing?

"No way. I mean, I can't even keep a tune. People would pay me to stop singing."

She grinned until it hurt. Laughing required noise she couldn't make. Laughing noiselessly was just creepy.

Have you tried making $ that way? ☺

She felt she could tell him things. She didn't know him, he didn't know her. Talking to him was like telling stories to an empty box. She wasn't even breaking the rules of the woman in the red dress, because he didn't know her name.

"No." He suddenly looked sad again, a hallway full of doors that all opened onto women crying, children with red eyes and blotchy faces. A whole house of grief, like Lynne's after Mama had died.

Sorry about before. Thought it was OK to ask . . .

"It's nothing. They just . . . didn't get me. I'm almost eighteen, anyway. I can look after myself." He took his hand away from the bench back. "You really do play well. Not the sort of stuff I expected."

She'd played him another Dry Gully song, "I Thought You Looked the Other Way." It didn't sound right, though, no matter how she tried. In her head, she could always hear Tish's fiddle. Without it, without their voices, the guitar sounded a little lost, a little tired.

Steve continued. "That bit at the end, whoa. That was something else. Not really my thing, but cool anyway."

What's your thing?

"Country," he said without hesitation. "All the way. New stuff, not that old-timey kind."

She made a face. She couldn't help herself. The old stuff, the stuff Mama had had on vinyl—sad, hard lives with just a taste of sweet thrown in—she liked it well enough. More, because it reminded her of curling up in Mama's lap to listen, Mama singing along softly, her breath ruffling Blue's hair. Or the real old stuff, banjos and fiddles with the smell of dirt floors mixed right in—she could appreciate it. Just not the new.

"Better than most of what's on the radio," Steve said. "When I'm older, you know, when I have a job and money and stuff, I'm gonna go out line dancing every weekend."

You ever been?

She untied her hiking boots from her pack and slipped the men's shoes off her feet.

"Nah. Didn't have anyone to go with." He kicked at a pebble on the ground.

No gf?

She regretted asking immediately. If he hated questions about his parents, he might about everything else, too.

He didn't run off, though, just ducked his head down a little. After a minute, he raised it and looked straight at her. "No boyfriend."

She blinked, slow, like a lizard caught out cold. Of course. He hadn't been hitting on her before. He'd just been lonely.

Steve waited, watching, still. What did he want her to say? She'd grown up climbing into bed with Mama and Tish in the morning while they were still half asleep. Maybe Steve had come from somewhere like Eliotville, though, where lesbian musicians were an oddity, and gay kids still suffered at the hands of their peers.

She slipped one boot on, the ache coming quick as the leather hit her foot.

You'll meet someone. Any idea what bus tickets cost?

"Where you trying to get to?" He looked relieved.

Good question. Magic boots weren't enough. She needed a magic map labeled "The Gully." Where would Tish have headed coming east, where would Cass have chosen headed west?

Chicago.

"Chicago?" Steve stuck his hands in his pockets, gave a dead-on impression of a middle-aged man.

Yeah. I think so.

She finished tying her boots, tied the shoes onto the pack in their place.

"It's cheaper to hitch. If, you know, you're trying to save money."

It makes me nervous.

"We could go together."

Could they? As long as the woman in red didn't change the rules, they had time.

Sure, for a bit.

Hurt showed in his face like mud swirling up in a stream. It would have been better if he swore at her. Cass swore. Teena swore, took it to a new art form. Blue did her best to keep up. The thing about swearing was that it made everything okay faster. You said the words, and they were like rocks, then spears, then swords; then at some point they reached an atomic level and the fight was over.

This, though—this silent defenselessness—it was like hurting puppies.

It's that I've got this thing. It's not safe to be near me. Not safe, like something bad might happen to you. ☹

Skepticism joined the hurt. "Are you on the run from the Mob or something?"

Worse. You're safe for a few days, as long as I don't tell you my real name.

"You haven't told me any name yet."

She couldn't help the burst of silent laughter. He was right, she hadn't given a name, and he hadn't asked.

Call me Ishmael.

He laughed, too. "Right. A girl named Ishmael? That's totally believable."

Ok. Try Bess instead.

"So what happens if I find out your real name, *Bess*."

It felt so good to say even a little bit, that she kept going.

Not sure, but I think you might die . . . I made this deal, with—could she really say it?—the devil. To find my sister. She ran away 2 yrs ago + the devil said we'd play a game. These boots are supposed to tell me if I'm going in the right direction + I have to keep moving + she said I can't tell people who I am or stay with them for more than 3 days or 3 wks.

She wrote in a rush, not looking up from the paper once. Steve read over her shoulder, and when she finally stopped, the look on his face had changed again. Sort of sad, sort of uncomfortable.

Because she was crazy. That's what he was thinking. To him, it had to make sense. In health class once, the teacher had talked about homelessness and said mental illness was one of the risk factors. She'd never imagined that one day she'd be in a strange town trying to convince a runaway boy that her story about the devil wasn't a sign of mental instability.

I know it sounds crazy. It's true, though. If I were crazy, wouldn't I make less sense?

"I guess. It's just . . . Did you say 'she'? The devil was a woman?"

She nodded.

"So, if you're crazy, I'm not in danger. And if you're not, we should be able to get as far as Chicago without her, like, I don't know, eating my brains or something."

She's a devil, not a zombie. ☺

Steve laughed. She wanted to join him, craved the way laughter could rise up from her belly, force its way out of her mouth, make her lips stretch and her eyes water. Instead, she just smiled.

THE MINIVAN SMELLED OF PERFUME. SYNTHETIC, OVER-
bearing, nothing like the jasmine Teena had sometimes used, "just
'cause I'm a little flower." This was hard-core old-lady perfume,
mixed with peanut butter and jelly.

They'd waited on a road running north, one the gas station
guy had told Steve connected with Interstate 90. "That's what
you're looking for if you're going to Chicago. Take you right on up.
Shouldn't be more than a ten-hour drive, provided you don't hit no
weather."

They hadn't been there more than ten minutes when a silver
sedan cruised by. Older, nondescript, a man with a crew cut driving,
one hand on the wheel, eyes on Blue. A motion with his free hand, a
summons to the window. A ride, she guessed, though it could have
been anything. She'd seen the car before, not just one like it but that
very one, she was sure. The man, too . . . where?

A honk from a following truck made the man speed past, but a
chill lingered in Blue. When a minivan finally pulled over, twenty
minutes later, Blue grabbed Steve's hand and squeezed.

"It's got a fish sticker. Thank you, Father," Steve whispered.
She didn't have a clue what he meant until he started talking to the
middle-aged woman on the passenger side.

"Praise the Lord," he said. "My sister and I have been praying for a ride. We have an engagement, you see. People waiting for her guitar to guide them."

He gestured toward the case, and she hoisted it a little higher. Sometimes not being able to speak came in handy.

The woman wagged her finger at them. "Now, Fred suggested that we shouldn't stop for you, but me, I trust that the spirit comes in all forms. Doesn't it, Fred?"

The man in the driver's seat grimaced.

"Dears," the woman continued, "you look a little young to be traveling this way."

"Bess, my sister, she's nineteen. I'm along with her because she's mute."

"Oh my." Shock rounded the woman's eyes and mouth into perfect circles. "You know sign language, dear?"

Blue gave Steve a stricken glance. "I'm afraid my sister isn't . . . Well, she was blessed with a sense of music but not a lot more. Her doctor, he calls her a savant."

Where the hell had he gotten that from? She'd assumed everything to know about Steve could be read in his face, but that view was rapidly changing. Seamless lies, smooth and easy as melted chocolate.

"Now that is a pity."

"Ma'am, we were supposed to have a ride, but the man who was to give it, he . . . He wasn't appropriate."

The woman tutted some. The man coughed. "We need to go if you want to get to your sister's. We're already looking at midnight."

"Just a minute. Where are you children trying to go?"

"Chicago, ma'am, but we're grateful for any ride."

"Oooh!" The woman clapped her soft hands together. "I told

you, Fred, I told you there was a reason to stop for them. We're headed to Chicago, too!"

And with that they were in the backseat of the minivan, Chicago-bound. Blue nestled into her seat, traded her boots for shoes, and tuned out the Christian pop on the radio.

By the time Chicago grew near, Steve had cemented their credibility with the woman via evangelical wordplay. Blue had spent plenty of time on the road with Mama and Cass and Tish, but their games had consisted of collecting license plates and making truckers honk. She couldn't have quoted anything from the Bible, aside from *In the beginning*. Steve, on the other hand, tossed off Bible verses effortlessly. It paid off when the woman insisted that they come to spend the night at her sister's house.

As she listened to Steve in the dark, Blue felt she knew his voice, only it wasn't a boy she heard. From time to time, under the flicker of the highway lights, she heard not the scratching notes of adolescence, but the betrayal of a soft clear girl's voice.

Click. Click. Click. The sounds of the turn signal, the beat of the Christian pop. She touched Steve's hand, ran her fingers over the almost hairless skin, the heat of the damp palm. He looked at her. *I was blind, but now I see* . . . Did that come from the Bible, too?

THE WOMAN'S SISTER WAS AN OLDER, PLAINER VERSION
of her. Her house reeked of cinnamon potpourri. Her walls were
covered with framed examples of embroidery—Bible verses, puppies, fir trees.

She stared at them, Steve and Blue, as Cynthia spun their story,
embellishing it with bits of her own creation. Blue had become a
musical prodigy with the IQ of a toddler, Steve her devoted brother,
protecting her from the forces of darkness. "You can see it in their
faces, Ruth. Lambs, both of them."

The only thing Blue could see in Steve's face was something
she wasn't sure either woman would appreciate.

"Well, I don't know. . . ," the woman started at last.

"Ruthie, look at them. You've got the space over the garage."

"Oh, Cyn, the heat's not even on out there. And I've been stor-
ing all my old stuff . . ." She touched the cross she wore on a gold
chain. Blue wondered idly what would happen if she touched it.
Anything? Would she burst into flames? Would it?

"Oh, okay. Fred, you'll show them up? You'll have to use the
bathroom in here. And it'll be cold—the space heater should help
some. Cynthia says you're good people. I hope you prove her right."

The space above the garage was cold, but it was also a room, with lacy curtains on the windows and wooden floors. Large sheets of canvas had been tossed over the floor and what appeared to be stacks of boxes in one corner. After stopping downstairs for the bathroom, Blue found Fred manning an electric pump, inflating an air mattress, while Steve watched.

"Check with Ruth. She must have sleeping bags somewhere. If not, she'll have blankets. Those women like to be prepared. No sense in Armageddon leaving everyone cold."

"Yes, sir."

"Pillows, too. No reason to suffer."

"Thank you, sir, for setting up the mattress. I don't want to keep you from your own bed."

"I want to see that the heater's working properly. Those things can be dangerous." Fred plugged the mattress, grunted a little as he stood up, pump in hand.

Steve left in search of pillows and blankets.

Once he'd gone, Fred held out something, a small laminated rectangle. "I took the liberty of looking in your bag while your *brother* was asking for the pump downstairs. I know who you are, Blue Riley, and where you're supposed to be living. I know your mind is plenty sharp. I can see it in your eyes. The only reason the women don't is because it makes them feel good about themselves. I'm giving this back to you, but remember. Either of you take a single thing, do any harm, well, things will go bad for you."

No.

What time was it? When they'd entered the car, it had been daylight. By the time they went to bed it would be after midnight. Two days gone. She'd have to leave as soon as she'd gotten some sleep. No harm to him, and some good for her.

"I have pillows enough for an army." Steve burst in, arms full. "Bess and I are much, much obliged to your family, sir."

Fred glanced at Steve, gave a quick nod. "You two be good up here. I expect they'll have breakfast for you in the morning."

Once he left, Blue let out a long shuddering breath. Steve looked at her curiously as he dropped the bedding on the mattress. "Something wrong?"

She shook her head. No reason to tell him about the license. They'd leave the next morning without letting on that they weren't what Steve had said. No trouble at all.

STEVE WENT TO BED IN HIS CLOTHES—JEANS, T-SHIRT,
oversized flannel. In the glow from the streetlamp outside, she
studied the plush roundness of his chin, the sheen of his eyes as
he looked at her, then away. Easy enough to leave things the way
they were, easier, even, without a voice. The perfect excuse to say
nothing.

Except . . . Except what? The urge that led her to touch his
cheek, to run one fingertip over the smoothness there, there
weren't words for that. Language was so clumsy at times like these,
as she traced the comet's tail of wet heat trailing from his eyes.
She found his hand, touched it to the tears and shook her head.

He shivered a little. "What . . ." Maybe he didn't have words,
either. Maybe some spaces couldn't be filled by language. Born
into the wrong family—she'd known other kids that way. Beck's
little brother, his head full of numbers while Beck and his dad
debated the finer points of deer season over dinner. Susie Boucher,
raised in a house of china figurines and pressed tablecloths, her
blunt-cut hair held back with a green rubber band filched off a
bunch of kale, standing in the rain for hours in waders and a straw
hat, fishing.

But what did it mean to be born into the wrong family *and* the wrong body? What could she possibly say about that?

He drew a breath. "Sometimes I want to go home more than anything, you know? I want them to come looking for me, to say they're sorry, that they want me back. Some nights, when I can't sleep, if it's cold and I haven't found a good place to crash, that's all I can think about."

She kept still, afraid even movement would stop his mouth.

"It's like I asked too much. Like, if I'd said I was a boy, then, maybe. But a gay boy? It . . . My mom couldn't even talk to me. I saw this show on TV, about kids like me, and how their families had helped them, and I thought maybe mine would come around. I tried, I tried so hard. They said it was against God. Can you imagine, being told even God would turn his back on you? I didn't know what else to do. I just left."

No one gets to tell you who you are. That lesson had come from Tish, not Mama, in a fight she never should have heard. "If I wanted someone to tell me who and what I should be, I would have stayed home. I'm a goddamn rainbow, Clary, and I get to show all my colors, even the shit ones," she'd said.

Mama had laughed. So had Tish, after a minute. Laughter, quick and sweet and sad. Then, "Tish, I love your colors, but I can't keep along this road forever. There's an end somewhere."

There had been an end, just a few months later. End of Dry Gully. End of Tish's husky voice complaining at the light in the morning, the way she ran her fingers through Blue's hair, back and forth three times. End of the way life was supposed to be.

Blue had never been alone, though. Never had any doubt that people loved her, even when she hated them. She followed the curve of Steve's arm to where his hand was tightened into a ball. Slowly unworked the fingers and slipped her hand into his.

The next morning everyone gathered at the bar in the kitchen. Ruth fried bacon on a giant skillet, while Cynthia twittered about them. Steve offered to help more than once. Each time the women turned him away, patting his back and thanking him.

As Blue sat, a knot of anger grew inside. She couldn't put her finger on what it fed on. Maybe it was from watching their smug, well-fed faces, watching Steve call Fred *sir*, talking politely with the women. So sweet, even though his own nice, religious parents drove him away. Weren't these people the same?

Too easy, said a little voice in her head. *Fuck you*, said a louder one. She swallowed both with an unchewed wad of bacon, none of it passing easily.

"We were talking, earlier, before you came down, about a little plan Ruthie and I hatched." Cynthia gave her a rosy smile. "Ruthie has a little prayer group, some adults, some young people like you, and we'd love for you to play for them. In exchange, you could stay here for the day, and then we could drive you to meet up with your church in the evening. Steve said it wouldn't be any problem at all."

Blue glared at Steve. He gave her a pleading look. "She can't really decide for herself," he said. "I make all the decisions for us. It's really nice of you to ask her, though. The answer is that we'd love to."

Blue pushed away from the table and left. Out the door, up the stairs to the garage, opening the top of her pack, pulling out the keepsake bag, touching each item in turn as the urge to ball up her fists and hit something faded. She put everything back.

It didn't take Steve long to come looking for her. "What's the problem? I got us lunch and dinner and a warm place for the day. All we have to do is go to play some music."

She grabbed her notebook, writing in heavy lines.

We? Me, you mean! I have to PLAY!!! You assumed I'd want to. Guess what? I don't play church music.

"You don't have to. No one's going to know what you play, not if you're not singing the words. Play something pretty, it'll be fine."

Something pretty? For a moment, she felt the way Tish had always looked: dark eyes, tattoo on her neck, lipstick the color of drying blood. Tish didn't play pretty. She played real.

Tish played the fiddle, though. Blue played Mama's guitar, with fingers that were sore because she hadn't played enough to harden them, without anything to boost the sound, with a limited repertoire. Maybe she was doomed to sound pretty.

They're fakes.

Steve flinched. "They're nice. They're good people."

Fred knows we're lying.

She wanted to leave it at that. Steve looked as though he might cry, though.

He knows. He even knows my real name. If I stay past midnight, she'll hurt them.

A soccer game of emotions bounced around Steve's face, disbelief, and anger, and fear, and . . . want. He wanted something, and she was keeping him from it.

"You're just saying that. You don't want to stay and you're making things up. Maybe you even made up the whole story you told. Or maybe you're nuts."

Maybe I should just leave then.

She almost went back and underlined it a second time. All she had to do was pick up her bag and her guitar and walk out the door.

At the moment, she felt she could hike all the way across the country, one step after another, faster and faster, Steve and everyone else left far behind.

"No, you can't. Please. If you go, they won't believe me. I need you to stay. I don't have any money, and I don't have a place to go, and I need your help." His face had gone blotchy, red spots around his eyes, on his cheeks, his eyelashes clumping from unshed tears.

He needed her. She needed to keep moving, but he needed her, needed this one thing she could do for him. All she had to do was play. Steve would understand about leaving before midnight. It would work.

She reluctantly nodded.

She meant for it to work, but as the day wore on, she meant it less and less. She didn't feel like a person to them—just an open square on their Good Christian Bingo card.

Teena's gram had gone to church every Sunday. When Mama had died, she'd taken Blue's hand between her two warm withered ones and squeezed. "There's no fairness to who comes and who goes," she'd said, eyes tight on her. "Never is. Only thing to know is that you had a mama who loved you, and that she's far away from suffering now. Only thing left to pain her is how her babies are, and we'll show her that you're surrounded by love."

She was the kind of church folk that Blue could understand. She would have had beautiful music inside her, Blue was sure of it. These women, theirs sounded as if it came through speakers that had been wrapped in blankets. She could hear dead air where the notes should have been, spaces that lengthened as they complained about someone's daughter on welfare, about having to pick up the tab for her and the child she'd had without a husband, about her laziness in not getting a job with a local maid service. If they'd met Blue and Steve as runaways, if Steve hadn't sounded one step away from being a minister himself, would they have ever taken them home?

She didn't think so.

The cold bit into Blue the way only a damp sullen chill can. She zipped her coat up to her chin, pulled on the fingerless gloves. When the breeze blew hard against her, she longed for the missing fingers.

It felt good to use her boots. A tidal feel, as if she were water and they were the moon. She kicked at pebbles as she moved, hitting them back and forth across the empty street. The neighborhood was silent. No kids playing outside. No cars driving by. Not even curtains parting so old ladies could give her the evil eye.

She kept going. The street ended in a T, and she turned right, following the curb. Back home, roads meandered. They wiggled like the contents of the night crawler cups sold in every package store in rural Maine. Not so here. Straight lines, neat as graph paper.

Another right, same old sights. Right, left, right, Blue's feet thudding on the pavement, legs relaxing, getting into the groove. Maybe Cass was here, in one of the houses, sitting at a table, reaching for a phone.

The smell drew her attention first. Burnt oranges, heat . . . She looked up.

The woman stood beside the curb. Tan coat belted at the waist, blond hair blow-dried and hair-sprayed into that middle-aged do, the one worn by teachers and tellers and secretaries everywhere.

The woman raised a hand as Blue neared. "Lovely day for a walk, isn't it?"

Blue shrugged. No paper. No pen. No way to talk.

The woman took a few steps toward her, near enough to show the pencil marks on her carefully made-up face. "It's the kind of day perfect for moving on, don't you think?"

A snapping sound accompanied her words, the click of a static charge. In the sunlight nothing glowed, but Blue could feel the heat of the sparks.

She tapped at her wrist, pointed up at the sun, shook her head.

The woman smiled, a you-should-have-done-better-on-your-exam smile. "Two days, Bluebird. You let him know your name. The clock rolls over at midnight. You'll only have yourself to blame if you don't leave on time. And what about the other one? Just because he doesn't have your name yet doesn't mean you're not a danger to him."

Blue shook her head. Frustrated, she stomped her foot and grabbed at her throat. *I want it back*, she thought furiously.

"Want? Who doesn't want something, Bluebird?" So the woman could hear her thoughts. She shook her head. "'Want' is not 'deserve.' 'Want' isn't even 'need.' I think it's time for you to be figuring out how to move on."

19

THE GROUP THAT GATHERED THAT EVENING WAS MOSTLY women like Ruth and Cynthia, with careful hair, rosy faces, soft hands and wedding rings, and little gold crosses hanging over snug sweaters. Everyone squeezed closer, talking loudly around her.

"This is her, one of God's little angels. And this"—Ruth put an arm around Steve—"this is her brother, who has devoted himself to caring for her. Just as sweet as sugar itself."

Steve smiled, even blushed a little. Blue knew his problem now: he wanted them all to like him the way his parents didn't. To see him for who he knew himself to be. She hated him for it. He was using her to make himself seem special. So was Ruth.

They wanted special, she'd give it to them. She knew exactly which song to play. She wasn't anyone's golden pass to goodness.

But first, she had to sit through a meeting that droned on for an hour or so. She retreated deeper into the angry space in her head. If there were color to it, it would be red, like the crossroads woman's dress, like the blood that had scabbed on her scratched-up hands. Like the pulse beating in her neck.

Finally, Steve put his hand on her shoulder, and everyone clapped, and she stood up, a little bewildered, which made them clap more. "So special," she heard one woman whisper. She gripped the handle to the guitar case so tightly she believed she could have counted every stitch on the edge.

They'd made room for her on the bench in front of the little upright piano. She laid the guitar case beside her, opened it, running one hand over a hymnal as she did. Nothing. No flame, no voice of God, nothing at all. She suspected it would be the same even if she stroked a Bible.

She tuned quickly, took a breath, and played a warm-up tune. Just pretty, the sharp plucks of a music box, slowing toward the end as if the box were winding down.

Everyone clapped politely. They knew it wasn't a song, wasn't even enough to be a fancy instrumental. She touched her fingers to her lips, blowing on them just a little. Took a pick out of the case. Smiled as sweetly as she knew how.

The song felt like fever through her hands. That eager to come, that caught between dream and reality. Mama was in the chords, and the smile she always gave Tish as they hit the chorus together. Tish was there as well, a pair of raven wings spreading out from her shoulders as the missing fiddle sounded in Blue's ears. More than anything, she could feel the empty space in her throat, the place where the words wanted to come from, the story they could tell, the change from purr to growl and back again as the song progressed.

Belief. That's what it took to play for a crowd. That's what Mama had had. And for the first time, ever, Blue felt it within herself.

She enjoyed the applause at the end. It wasn't the music they applauded, she knew, it was the idea they had of her. She'd succeeded because she'd gotten them to applaud a lie.

Steve looked happy enough to burst when he led her out of the room. She pushed quickly away, losing him among the people coming into the kitchen for coffee.

She made it to the bathroom, locked the door, and studied herself in the mirror until the noise from outside had subsided. She came back out, turning away from the loud buzz in the kitchen. There was nowhere really to go but down the hall and into Ruthie's study. She pushed the door open, stepped in, froze.

"You do have a way of turning up," the man in the blue shirt said. He grinned as he spoke, revealing smooth, straight white teeth. He was alone, but he chewed a few times, as if she'd caught him at a snack.

Run, Blue's mind said, but her feet stayed put. Each breath rose and fell as if being sucked through mud: thick, sluggish.

He looked at her, head cocked. "I don't think you're ready to sell yet. Soon, though. That performance moved you along nicely." He sniffed the air. "Like waiting for a roast to be done. Don't worry, I'll find you when it's time. Buyer's market, after all." Bigger grin, more teeth. His breath smelled of cold wet rain, of sorrow by a graveside. "Fire sale! Bargain basement prices! Buy one, get two free! You know the drill, don't you?"

Blue's feet woke. One step backward, two, the doorframe behind her, his grin growing even wider. With a sudden movement, he raised his hand and snapped his fingers.

She ran. Down the hall, back the way she'd come, past the kitchen, and smack into Steve. "There you are," he said, a touch of panic in his eyes. "I didn't know where you'd gone."

She grabbed his sleeve, dragged him into the garage. He stared back into the house. She looked, too, at the empty hall, nothing alarming at all behind her.

Inside her, something tipped, something heavy and hard, concrete pouring down, coating everything. She was crazy. Maybe the crossroads were a dream. Maybe the only danger she faced was her own mind.

❖ ❖ ❖

Steve, backed up by Cynthia and Ruth, insisted they should stay the night. Blue didn't want to fight, didn't even know what she'd argue, so she just lay down on the air mattress and waited, pretending to sleep. She had to leave. Maybe none of this was real, but she couldn't take the chance of something bad happening. Once things got quiet, she'd grab her bag and start walking.

In the meantime, she tried to piece things together. She'd assumed the woman in the red dress and the man in the blue shirt were the same. But every time she'd seen the woman, her appearance had changed, while the man's did not. Could there be two of them, some sort of evil yin and yang? The woman sucked people in and the man destroyed them?

It didn't fit, not with Mama's stories, not with what Blue had read. She imagined the man and the woman sharing an office, the woman rising from a desk with wilting roses in a vase, brushing the fallen petals away. Smiling, taking Blue's coat, running her hand against Blue's neck as she did, making chills and heat rush together where she touched.

"He'll see you in a minute," the woman said, in that voice like smoke. Blue nodded. "He'll see you in a minute," the woman said again, only this time she sounded different, like Mama. "You don't need this, Blue. You don't need to wait. He'll only be a minute and you need to go—"

Blue jumped. The room was lit by the streetlights outside. Steve was curled up in his sleeping bag, fast asleep. She ran a hand through her hair, confused, then saw the glow of Steve's watch.

11:55.

Fuck.

She jumped up. Somehow, she'd fallen asleep. *Stupid, stupid.*

She grabbed her sleeping bag, wadded it, and strapped it to her pack, the edges trailing behind. Everything else was already in the bag. She slipped her feet into her boots, laced them tight, hoisted the pack to her shoulders, and grabbed the guitar. She tripped over Steve's foot as she went, and he let out a surprised cry.

"Hey!" he called as she rushed down the stairs. She didn't stop.

THE COLD WAS INTENSE AFTER THE WARMTH OF THE sleeping bag. It cut through the lingering touch of sleep within seconds. *Move*, her boots said, and she agreed.

She heard nothing but the sound of her own steps at first, the occasional crunch of ice beneath them. Then, from behind, came the racing slap of other feet. She didn't bother turning. By the time Steve caught her, he was winded, puffing two breaths for her one.

"Why'd you take off?" He had his bag, too, clothes hanging from the pockets. She just stared at him, not slowing.

"I don't believe you. You were in the middle of a church group and nothing happened. If you really were, you know, touched by the devil"—he spit out the word, as if it might call down a volley of brimstone—"if you were, then you shouldn't have been able to . . ."

Play for the nice people? Why not ask the man in the blue shirt about it? She felt a lurch inside her like a twisting fish at the thought of his chewing. Who had been his victim there?

"They would have given us a ride in the morning. Do you even know where you're going?"

No idea, but her feet liked what she was doing, so she'd keep doing it. Steve struggled to keep up, taking two steps to each of her determined strides.

"You don't even have any proof that that woman is dangerous. She could have just been—"

She spun on him. One finger deep in her mouth, pointing to where her voice should have been, as she dared him to argue. He froze. She shrieked, or made the motions, her lips stretched tight, while the night continued on undisturbed.

"How do I even know you lost your voice that way? Maybe you never had one."

Out came the notebook from her pocket.

Right. Just like maybe you keep all your clothes on when you sleep because you're cold, not because you don't want anyone to see what's underneath.

He flinched. Even in the dark she could see it, as sure as if she'd swung at him. His voice was steady, though. "That's my business, not yours. I'm who you see." Now a quaver, close to tears. "I'm a boy. People who really care about me see that."

She started walking again. It was like cutting into a potato, that satisfying slide through the crispness, just enough resistance to make it feel real. She'd cut into Steve, and he deserved it, for ignoring what she said, for siding with the others.

Only he didn't. Not really.

Not at all. He was flying in circles, looking for a safe spot to land. She was flying long-distance, over water, over land, heading someplace she didn't know, could only feel in her bones. Just because they weren't doing the same thing didn't mean she had any right to hurt him, even when it felt good.

She looked back.

He was standing in the middle of the road, a shirtsleeve hanging from his pack almost to the ground. His eyes glittered, thin lines shining on his cheeks. She walked back.

Right. Not my business. My mom used to be in a band with another woman, Tish. Tish always said that anyone worth more than a drink—

She paused, embarrassed to write the words.

—and a grope would always be able to see the little grain of truth in the heart of the pearl.

It looked weird to her written out, rather than said in Tish's casual way. She didn't follow it with the rest, that most of the world was only interested in the shine of the pearl, not what made it.

Steve gave a little shrug. "That's kind of weird. And, um, not the kind of thing an adult should say to a kid."

That angry streak rubbed back up to the surface, irritating everything along the way. She pushed it back.

She wasn't saying it to me. Just saying it, ya know? You coming?

Tish also used to say that people needed to understand that anyone else's life wasn't theirs—not theirs to judge, or applaud, or anything. Once you started thinking you had that right, then you started thinking you had other rights, too, rights having to do with control and decisions and all sorts of wrongness.

After a minute, Steve caught up with her. She slowed a little, and he walked more comfortably. Without stopping, she grabbed the sleeve dangling down and shoved the end back into his bag.

After what felt like hours, they left the neighborhood behind and hit a grid of roads. There was traffic as well, not tons, but cars passing, the occasional truck. Steve thought they should try to hitch. Blue still didn't know where to go. Her boots said *Move*, but they didn't come with a compass, at least not one she'd found.

As long as they kept moving and kept away from the wake of

passing vehicles, she stayed warm enough. Stop even for a minute or two, and the cold worked its way in, icy tendrils along her cheeks, down her neck, through her jeans. She wanted to be in a house. Not just any house. She wanted to be at home, in her own bed. The more she thought about it, though, the more she didn't know where that bed would be. Was home a place or a person?

She kept looking up, expecting to find stars. Instead, she saw only the yellow glow of the city. At one point, she imagined it a giant fire, the flames reaching out toward her; only, they chilled rather than heated. Cities drew people, that much she knew. She tired of them quickly, though. Sound and light and busyness, people looking down at their feet or straight ahead, instead of at one another. Mama used to drop coins into cups, smile at strangers; she'd give directions, or at least encouragement when she didn't know how to get somewhere. There had to be lots of people there like Mama and like the librarian, but it never felt that way to Blue in a city.

There was no way to avoid Chicago, though, not with it right in front of them. And, on the plus side, cities made it easier not to stick out. Small towns told everyone's stories—during lunch at school, in the aisles of the grocery. Maybe, in Chicago, Steve could be *Steve*, not whoever people insisted he was.

He tapped her arm. "Bus stop. We could wait and see what comes."

Blue felt in her pockets. The money was there. Plenty for a city bus. They'd be warm in it. They might even be able to sleep. Though she felt wide awake, she knew she'd crash as soon as she started to warm up.

She nodded. They set their packs down on the bench. She immediately regretted stopping. The cold didn't creep; it attacked, racing along her frame like a tidal wave. Hopping from foot to foot did almost nothing, and her feet began to ache as well. She couldn't switch into her shoes, not without chilling herself further, so she walked in small circles.

Steve wrapped his arms around himself and shivered. After a few minutes, Blue joined him, moving in close enough that their breath met between their faces. She put her arms over his shoulders. It felt like a mistake at first, the heat escaping where her arms were no longer pressed against her body. New heat formed, though, between them, in all the places their bodies were close. Now they each had only their backs exposed to the wind.

They stood like that for a while. Eventually they lowered their heads to each other's shoulders, and Blue slipped in and out of a dream state, the lights flickering around her, the world full of a guitar and a banjo, their notes twirling round and round together. A song like she'd never heard before, melancholy and joyful at the same time.

It ended when Steve stepped away from her. "Look," he said.

A silver sedan idled just down the street from them. It rode a little low, as if there was something heavy in the trunk. The man at the wheel had graying hair in a buzz cut. He watched them, one finger tapping time on the steering wheel. When he caught her eye, he nodded.

A different kind of cold raced down her spine. She shook her head, one hand out to grab her guitar. Steve didn't move. "He could give us a ride."

She needed her voice. She needed to ask Steve what kind of guy picked up kids in the middle of the night, what kind of guy kept showing up wherever she was, whenever she needed a ride? It was him, she was sure of it—the same guy who passed them before Cynthia had picked them up.

He had no reason to follow her. He wasn't the woman in the red dress or the man in the blue shirt. He was just some weird old guy, and she didn't want to know what he wanted.

Another car flashed its lights, and both drivers drove on by, the man watching as he went. It looked as if he smiled as he passed, fleshy, feral. Patient.

A BUS CAME SOON AFTER, DRIVEN BY A DARK-SKINNED man singing a blues song in a gravelly voice as he opened the door. He stopped midchorus to ask where they were going.

Blue just handed him a pile of money. He took a long, slow look at her, at the guitar and the backpack, and at Steve. "Now that's a whole lot more than you need to give, young lady. Tell you what." He sorted through the bills and change. "This much'll take the two of you as far as I go, and if you settle in the back, I'll turn the heat up for you."

She could have kissed him. She and Steve bumped their way down the empty bus to the back, where they each took a seat and spread out. Pack between her ankles and one arm around her guitar, Blue loosened her bootlaces, pulled the tongues out, and soaked in the heat that rose around her.

The sky was light when she woke. Steve was snoring softly, his head resting on his bag. The bus wasn't moving. There were no passengers, no driver.

She looked out the window into a yard full of buses. Not the kind she expected, though. Some had missing hoods, some had dried vines twining around the flat tires they rested on. Most of the doors were open. The bus next to theirs had an abandoned bird's nest on the dashboard.

They had gotten on a bus, a real one. She remembered it—the driver, the songs, the heat. The heat! She should have been cold, but she wasn't. She sidled down the aisle, out the door, ready to touch the engine and see if it was warm.

It wasn't. It was possible the engine was warm, somewhere. Just not here. The open hood revealed empty space, dried grass poking up through the snow.

She hurried back in. The sound of her steps woke Steve. He rubbed at his eyes as she whipped out her notepad.

You remember the bus last night?

She shoved the note at him. He read slowly, gave her a bewildered look.

"Of course. Why?"

She pointed out the window.

It's a bus graveyard. Ours doesn't even have an engine!

He couldn't take her word for it, of course. She led him out of the bus, watched his eyes widen as she waved her hand in the empty space.

"But . . . We drove here. The bus driver . . . You saw him, right? Skinny guy, big voice."

Yeah. Sang a lot.

Sang like someone auditioning, pulling out all the stops.

She looked around. Skyscrapers rose before them: the gateway to the city, the sunlight turning their glass to gold. A chain-link fence surrounded the yard. Even the fence was old, the top pushed down here and there, holes cut in places.

We should get moving. It's gonna get cold here. I'm hungry.

"Okay. Do you still have money?" he asked. Then he shook his head. "No, wait. We rode a real live bus last night and we woke up on a dead one. This isn't possible."

Oh, Steve. She would have said it if she could, complete with a big sigh. Somehow she'd become an expert on things that did not make sense.

It just happened. I know it's freaky, but it got us here, right?

She reached in her pocket and counted what she found as he read. Counted it again.

I could have sworn the driver took $5.

Steve watched, the color draining from his face. Stolen money mattered more than magic buses. "Did he take more?"

She shook her head and thumbed through the bills one more time.

Nothing. There's plenty of $ for breakfast.

And lunch, too, and dinner, but after that . . . ? She gave Steve a smile meant to be more cheerful than she felt.

They didn't have to walk far to find a diner. The Bluebird Diner. Its sign, the paint chipped away until it merely implied the original shapes, showed a little bird perched, head cocked, a bit of faded blue left on the wings. Blue felt warm as she went in, as though the place had been made for her. The inside was as weathered as the sign—torn vinyl on the seats, the air greasy in her lungs. She didn't care. She would have eaten a vat of lard, had someone set it down in front of her.

The good sign was that there were plenty of customers. Working-class people in jeans and uniforms and worn shoes. At home, the local diner filled up with loggers and truck drivers and kids coming in after school for french fries and ice cream. On the weekends, there'd be families out to dinner, sometimes even her and Lynne. Real people, just like here.

The cook, visible over the half wall around the kitchen, worked in a clean white T-shirt, a baseball cap backward on his shorn head. He sang show tunes as he flipped eggs, his foot tapping time. The whites of his eyes showed yellow against the dark of his skin, and she had a flash of Mama toward the end, the yellow seeping into her eyes, her hands, everywhere. Sometimes she'd be confused, not sure of the day or time, and sometimes she'd see Blue and light up, saying, "Come sit with me, baby, tell me a story." Blue would sit down, feeling as though she'd been ripped into two jagged pieces. One half of her would long for the chance to escape, to run anywhere her mother wasn't dying; the other half would hold Mama's hand, determined to never let it go.

They ordered pancakes and sausage and eggs and coffee and ate it all, never looking up from their plates. With food in her belly and the sun shining through the window and onto her bare arms, Blue felt her certainty begin to return. She could find Cass. She could find a corner and play her guitar and make some money, enough to have a place to sleep. She could hitch a ride, enough rides to get her where she needed to go; and as long as she kept playing, she'd have money. Maybe Steve would stay with her. After all, he didn't really seem to have anyplace to go, and he didn't know her real name, so they still had time.

Steve swallowed the last of his coffee with a sigh. He'd drunk three cups, each one with five packets of sugar and a couple of hits of cream—more like syrup than coffee.

"What song did you play last night?"

Last night? Last night was the bus, and the singing driver, and

. . . the church group. The man in the blue shirt, his grin—*It's a buyer's market, little girl.*

Don't think about that. Think about what you played. She couldn't help her grin as she pulled out her notebook. Steve smiled back with sunny curiosity.

Tell me to come to church with you, baby.

Tish sang this one, Mama chiming in on harmony.

This is what I'll say, / That house you're wanting me to enter / Ain't any place to stay. / Show me something worth my worship, / A forest, just one tree, / The sweet taste of your neck now, / That's true enough for me. / I ain't got no time for hearing, / That who I am is wrong, / I ain't got no time for hearing, / that we don't belong. / I believe in your sweet touch, / I believe in me, / I believe those fires they're fleeing / They've set their own damn selves.

Steve came around to her side of the booth as she wrote. She paused, trying to remember the next line, and heard a small sound, almost like grinding teeth.

Steve's face—white, then dark red, the color racing in. "You—" he started, one hand punching against his leg. "How could you? You played that? You went to a Bible group and played that?"

She looked around the diner. A few people looked back. It had been funny, playing Tish's song to all those people who thought she was some innocent tool of God. It had been a joke, one Steve should have gotten.

He clearly didn't. "I can't believe you. You were just making fun. Making fun of them. Of *me*."

What was he talking about? She wasn't making fun of him. They'd been playing along. All those Bible verses, all of that . . . It had just been a game, one Steve understood because of his family.

Only . . . Steve looked as if he were going to cry. Didn't *look* like it—was actually crying. "I thought you were cool. I thought we were friends." Before she could stop him, he'd grabbed his pack and left, stepping out the door and into the morning foot traffic.

BLUE DIDN'T RUN AFTER HIM. SHE FINISHED HER COFFEE,
paid the bill, and left the waitress a handful of change as a tip. It was
a joke. He'd been living off her money and her playing, at least for
the last few days; and she'd made a joke that didn't even hurt the
people there, since she was sure none of them had ever even heard
of Dry Gully, let alone knew their songs.

She hadn't hurt anyone by playing the song. All she'd done was
made it bearable for herself. If he didn't get that, who cared? She
didn't.

Only she did. Walking down the street, she felt Steve's absence as
keenly as if she'd lost her guitar. The sidewalks were crowded with
people, the streets with cars, and yet every corner he wasn't on felt
as empty as each morning she'd woken without Cass in the bed
across the room.

Breakfast had shrunk her funds to under sixty bucks. Should
she keep moving, or find a place to play and make some money?
She was willing to bet that the Gully passed through Chicago. Cass
had to have been here, maybe even still was. The clatter of traffic,
the honk of the horn from the fourth phone call—they could have
come from here.

Come on, boots. Tell me where to go. The crowds were thinning as rush hour drew to a close. Time to move.

She made a rookie mistake, walking herself round an entire block and returning to her start point. *The boots should have known,* she thought, and a thrill shot through her at the idea that there wasn't a change because she'd located Cass.

But when she tested out a left turn and walked a block away, there wasn't a change, either. She was pretty sure the pull was stronger now than it had been in Maine, so maybe the problem was that the boots gave only general directions until she got close. Right now she needed to keep moving and remember not to take all left or all right turns.

After ten minutes or so, she paused by an appliance store, waiting for the walk light in the intersection. She glanced over, looking first at her reflection in the glass, then at the image on the TV there. What she saw brought her to a dead stop.

Final contestants chosen for Major Chord, the captioning read. *New band Forgotten Highway features frontman Jed Radley and songbird Jill Brantwell.* Forgotten Highway? What had happened to Mr. Chicken? To Bet and her careful artwork? There, stretched over a fifty-inch screen, were Jed and Jill, smiling, holding hands. "*It's a dream come true.*" She could see Jed's mouth moving. "*It's a great group of musicians showcased this year. Huge talent.*"

The screen flickered and they were gone. The honk of a horn, the change of a light, and she was gone as well.

Eventually she reached Union Station. At first glance, she assumed it looked familiar because of movies. But surely she'd seen the pillars before. She could feel Tish's arms holding her, hear Mama saying something about a delay, laughter, the rough canvas of Tish's army surplus jacket gathered up in her fingers. They must have come to Chicago to play. She knew the building, the color of the sky above her, the way the noise echoed around her. Even the lines of the tall buildings to the side and the dark squares of their windows were familiar.

They had been there, together. Happy. When? She'd been little, if Tish had been carrying her.

"Looking for someone?" A man waited by her elbow, grinning as though he knew her. Reflex sent her sideways, away.

He was about the same height as her. Tanned, but a fake tan, not the kind from a November trip to Florida. He kept his mouth almost completely closed, showing only a hint of teeth.

She nodded. Should she have? Or should she walk away?

"Beautiful day." He stayed put, as if waiting for the same imaginary person. "That's a lot of stuff you're carrying. Where you coming from?"

Stay clear of any man that comes up to you all friendly in a bus station, train stop, that kind of stuff. They come on all sweet, you know they're trouble—that's what Lou had said. Did this count as sweet?

Didn't matter. The answer was in the twist in her stomach. She gripped her guitar more tightly and headed toward the doors.

The man kept pace with her. "Why don't you let me carry that for you? You don't want to wander around alone if your friend doesn't show. I know what it's like—big city, not knowing where to go. I can help you out. I'd be happy to." His hand was on her guitar now, bumping against hers as she tried to walk faster. Not much farther to the door—then what? She imagined herself grabbing at passersby for help. Every encounter she envisioned ended with the police contacting Lynne to come get her.

"Come on, lemme help. The city's tough at first, but with a little help it can be a real nice place." She'd been looking away, trying not to catch his gaze, but he kept moving closer. Her heart began to pound as she ran through everything she could remember from the self-defense class she'd had in gym.

"Let's start with your name." Nudging as he walked, herding her away from the doors.

She'd have to shove, and then . . . run?

"Hey, been looking for you." Now someone else was approaching. A girl, a little shorter than Blue, her dark hair done up in tiny pigtails, some of them blue, some black, a few wrapped with green thread. She had a ring through her nose, another through her lip, and she wore a black leather jacket.

"Fuck off," the man said. He tried to put his arm around Blue's shoulder. She swung out with the guitar case, hitting him in the knee. She winced at the jangle from within.

The girl grinned. "Fuck off yourself. Rat says he already talked this whole thing out with you. Says you should know better."

"Fuck Rat, too. He's got no say over my business, and neither do you." He opened his mouth wider now, and his teeth were jagged, yellow and brown. He stuck his thumb out at Blue. "You're a bitch, too, but for your own good I'll tell you that if you go with her, you'll regret it. Rat's no walk in the park."

"Yeah, like she'd listen to you. Get out of my face before things get serious." The girl didn't look half as tough as she talked, but the guy backed down. He left slowly, watching them as if he could light them on fire with his eyes.

Nothing happened, though, beyond him leaving and the girl lighting up a cigarette. She offered it to Blue. Blue shook her head.

"That, my friend, is a crappy little piece of humanity. Smart you, not going with him."

Blue shrugged. She didn't trust the girl, either, but given the choice between the two, well, she'd made her choice.

"Where you headed?"

Not a yes-or-no question. She could walk off, or she could get out her notebook. Or she could try for a game of charades, but that was a stretch.

Notebook it was.

West.

The girl's eyes narrowed a little. "You deaf? Read lips?"

Blue shook her head.

Try me.

She turned around.

"Doesn't everyone go west?" A whisper carried in a puff of cigarette smoke.

Blue turned back.

Don't care about everyone. Just me.

"Got it." Another drag, another wave of smoke into the crisp air. "Listen, you should come with me. Rat's got room. You could play us a song or two."

Pit of the stomach said no, even though loneliness said yes. She shook her head.

Gotta keep moving. West isn't gonna wait for me.

"Whatever," the girl said, dropping the butt and stubbing it out with her toe. "Don't get caught in the cold, and be careful with that thing." She pointed at the guitar. "Police catch you playing without a permit, you'll get a big-ass ticket."

BLUE STRODE AWAY AS IF SHE KNEW EXACTLY WHERE SHE
was headed. *I'm a girl with a guitar and a giant backpack with a sleeping bag strapped to it in the middle of Chicago, and I was standing outside a train station. Bad, bad idea.* Better to go, anywhere, as long as she looked as if she had a plan. Otherwise, someone else would be along to *help* her.

She kind of needed help, though. If the girl was right, then she couldn't count on playing to make money.

The truth was, she didn't have a clue what she was doing, or where she was going, or even whether she was doing it for good reasons or crazy ones. And at some point—not having a watch or a phone meant that the hours slipped by unnoticed—it was going to get dark, and colder, and she needed be somewhere safe for the night.

Was this what Steve had dealt with every day since he'd left home?

Blue kept walking, on and on, until she reached a park. Not the sort of park she knew from home, the kind she'd played in when she met Steve. This one looked as if it belonged someplace else, Europe maybe, with plantings of shrubs set in geometric patterns across snow-dusted stone, deserted benches along them. Past the far edge ran another road, and beyond that was the lake.

In the middle stood a huge fountain, totally empty, all gray stone and stillness. Green sea horses rose from the waterless pools around it. She was so intent on them that she didn't notice the one filled bench until its contents shifted. A lone figure in a familiar ski jacket sat hunched there, his knees to his chest, his eyes closed.

She ran to Steve, her guitar bouncing against her thigh. He looked up at the slapping of her feet on the stone.

"What are you doing here?" His eyes were red-rimmed. His nose was red, too, and there were salt marks along his cheeks.

Walking.

She wanted to shout at him, pick him up, and hug him. Instead, she handed him the paper.

He shook his head. "Just walking?"

She'd missed something big. She understood that much, but the rest was a mystery. Now that she was through feeling mad about it, she wanted to understand what *it* was.

I don't get why you left. It was just a joke. I was mad at the way people were treating me + I don't believe all that religious stuff + they didn't know what I was playing. Just a private joke, ha ha.

She crouched down closer to him. It was warmer there. Well, not warmer so much as less windy. Remembering the bus stop from the night before, she leaned close, kneeling on her pack. Their bodies made a tent, a cozy world of their own.

"It wasn't just them you were making fun of, 'cause that's what you were doing. Making fun. Me, you were making fun of me."

But how can you believe that stuff, when they don't believe in you?

"It's not whether they believe in me that's important." His face was paler in their shadows, his lips seashell-pink waves. "My parents raised me to believe. I liked church. It's . . . I don't even know how to explain it to you. Everything else is so messy and noisy, and here's a space where we all share the same words, the same things. Even when we're not like each other. Even when I'm not like them."

But—

That was the part that didn't make sense. She'd spent her first year in Eliotville being not like anyone else, and she'd hated it, had studied Teena carefully—hair, clothes, favorite ice cream—and copied what she could. If that hadn't worked, she would have found a cave to stay in.

"Everyone knew. The kids at school, they picked on me. My mom would buy me these dresses, or, like, blouses with little bits of lace on them. I wouldn't have anything else to wear, and I'd feel like, I don't know, like that thing in the labyrinth—" Steve looked at her, and she shook her head, not sure what he was talking about. "That monster, the one that was part bull, part human. The other kids could see that it was all a costume. One time—" He stopped, shook himself free of the memory.

"I know it's gonna sound stupid to you, but I used to read my Bible at night. Not the scary parts, not all that bad stuff, but the parts when Jesus speaks. You know the Sermon on the Mount, that list of people who God loves? I felt like I fit there somewhere. And things got all ugly, and it wasn't just the kids, it was my parents, pushing harder and harder, and there was this one place, you know, this place where I'd read those pages over and over and knew that there was room for me.

"Things got so bad that I, you know, I thought maybe, about this bridge near our house."

She touched his hand, felt as close as if it were his heart.

"I went there, and I didn't want to. I really didn't. I'd seen things online. I knew I wasn't the only kid like me, I was just the only one like me *there*. I wanted everything to stop hurting, I wanted it so bad, but I stood on the bridge and I felt like I wasn't alone, like someone was there, holding my hand. So I told myself I could always make that choice, right? I mean, the world is full of bridges. But right then, knowing about all those bridges, I could go ahead and do whatever I wanted with life, because I'd always have a choice."

And the person holding your hand . . .

She'd been more than stupid. She'd been cruel. Maybe the man in the blue shirt had been on to something when he told her she was almost ready for him.

He nodded. "So you were laughing at me, too. At what I believe."

She'd been wrong. Teena's gram had had two daughters die, and she still talked all that love and belief stuff. People hurt, and they found things that held them together, and for Steve, it was a story of the meek inheriting the earth, and for her, it was the devil who waits at the crossroads, giving and taking all at once.

I'm sorry. I was mad + I wanted to take it out on them. I don't think they were nice people. Not the way you are. I don't feel bad about them, but I do about you.

"It doesn't make a difference if they were nice or not. It's what *you* do, you know? Whether *you* choose to act mean or nice."

I'm sorry. ☹

She could write it again and again. The question was whether he heard it, given the flimsiness of the paper, the word.

He looked at her, his eyes seeing deeper, further than hers did. "We should go find a place to stay, don't you think?"

They walked back out to the road. Traffic hurried past; the only vehicle in the metered spaces was a beat-up van with Illinois plates and a skull-and-crossbones sticker on the crumpled back fender. "Maybe we can find bagels again," Steve was saying as the van's passenger door swung open and the girl from Union Station stepped out.

"Yeah, it's them," she called back over her shoulder. The back doors popped open, and a couple of guys got out. One grabbed Steve, an arm around his shoulder, hand resting on his mouth, like they were goofing around. The other pushed in close on his far side.

Blue grabbed her notebook.

The girl laughed. "See, like I said. Totally can't talk at all."

The driver's door opened now. A skinny guy emerged. Tall, wearing a T-shirt and jeans, a tattoo of Elmer Fudd on one forearm, a shotgun wrapped in barbed wire on the other. He grinned. "You're the shit, Florida." He walked up to Blue. "And you, little girl, should probably hand that guitar over to me."

SHE HAD NOWHERE TO RUN OTHER THAN ACROSS THE
park, across the road, into the lake. It was just her and Steve against
the others, and Steve was already surrounded. She glanced toward
the distant lake—too cold to swim, and certain to destroy the guitar,
even if she could make it there. A hot prickly sweat covered her
body.

She shook her head. The man laughed. "Listen, babe, you can
do your whole little tough girl thing, get it out of your system, but
face it. You're outnumbered. You're not half as tough as you think.
And unlike you, I have no problem breaking that guitar in half just
to spite you if you don't hand it over. Or your boy, either. He looks
even easier to mess up."

The thought of letting go of the guitar case was as unimagin-
able as sticking her hand into a bonfire. She reached for her notebook.

What if I gave you my $ instead?

He raised an eyebrow. They were pale, his eyebrows, and long,
the coarse runners of hair almost invisible against his skin. She
couldn't even think about the rest of his face, just those eyebrows
and the way she hated them.

"How much we talking?"

Almost 60, I think.

He laughed, thin pink lips stretching to show a front tooth sharpened like a snake's fang. "You're funny. Sixty bucks isn't even enough to bother blowing my nose on. Or did you mean sixty cents?" More laughter, the girl joining in.

If 60 bucks is nothing to you, get your own guitar. Why take mine?

"Why? Because I'm in the mood for it. Because that guitar might be the one thing I've wanted all my life—right, Florida?" The girl nodded. "Because I want you to do what I ask, and right now I'm asking you to hand over the fucking guitar. Mal?"

The man holding Steve raised his arm and tightened it against Steve's neck. Steve's face began to turn red, his mouth opening in little fish gasps.

"Hand over the guitar."

The man flexed his arm further, and Steve scrabbled at his wrist with both hands. She looked down, at the handle, then handed it away, as painful as tearing the skin from her palm.

The man took the case as carelessly as if it were a block of wood. "Good girl. Let's get going. Florida, you gonna escort our guest?"

The girl bent at the waist, one hand raised in a flourish, before shoving Blue toward the van. The man tossed the guitar case in the front and took the driver's seat. Steve was bustled into the back with the guys. Blue and the girl ended up on the bench behind the driver.

The girl leaned back, her feet on the seat ahead, and lit a cigarette. She offered it to Blue. Blue shook her head.

"Ya don't talk at all, huh? Like, if I put my butt out on your arm, you wouldn't even squeak?"

Blue didn't respond, other than to stare at her levelly. *Don't show fear, never, ever, ever,* that's what Tish would have said. Even when the thought of the red tip, the pain, the empty space where her scream should have been tied her insides in knots.

"Florida." The girl held out her hand to Blue. Her grasp was surprisingly soft, her nails gnawed to the quick. She didn't look older than high school, but everything about her was worn out. She wore a thick layer of makeup; there was a blood spot in the white of one eye and a puffy swelling around one of the piercings in her left ear.

"That's Rat," she said, shoulder lifted toward the man in front. "Those are just the boys back there."

"Fuck you," said one of them.

Florida laughed. "Really, they're just walking dicks. Ain't much more to them. What's your name?"

Did it make a difference what Blue said? As if she'd picked up on Blue's thoughts, Florida grinned. "Not like you can fuss about what we call you. Gonna call you Interstate, 'cause you look like you've been going a ways."

Interstate. The name actually felt good.

She heard snickering from behind. When she turned to look, one of the guys was making a cupping motion at Steve's chest while the other one laughed.

"What's the racket, boys?" Rat didn't look back, his attention on the road, one hand resting on the steering wheel, one on his thigh.

"This one, he's as much a boy as I'm a pony."

Rat shifted his gaze to the rearview mirror, there and gone in a flash. "Ya don't say. Well, that makes things even nicer, don't it. We got us some specialty items."

The knots inside Blue tightened again. She chose a clean page in her notebook and wrote.

What's the deal? Where are we going?

Florida looked at the page and laughed. "You think you and me are going be all cozy, write notes back and forth like we're in school?"

Blue jerked her head back.

"Do you think she really has a sore throat?" Florida called to Rat.

Rat shot another glance in the mirror. "Nah. Sore throat you can still whisper. If she had a voice, she'd use it."

Florida leaned close to her. "Thought so. Can't even make a peep, right?" She tapped her ash out onto the floor.

It's temporary.

Even as Blue wrote it, she knew she had no reason to trust the woman in the red dress. She could do everything right and still lose. These could be the last months of her life, and she was spending it in cold places, without Cass or any idea where she was. Without her mom, or a home.

Without anything.

THEY PARKED ON A SIDE STREET IN FRONT OF A PAWN-
shop. "Keep an eye on that one," Rat said, tilting his chin toward
Steve. "I got Interstate."

Blue sized Rat up as he waited by the van door for her. Not
huge, but wiry, like the guys working at Teena's uncle's garage. She
half-expected to see a wrench in his back pocket, oil on his fingertips. There was nothing, though—only clean hands that gripped her
guitar case handle too tightly for her to even think about wrestling
it free.

"You give me any trouble, I got no problem with putting my
foot right through this," he said, giving it a little shake.

That was the other part of sizing someone up—deciding
whether they'd actually do the things they threatened. She'd learned
that from Tish, too. A swollen lip, a black eye, her laughing at the
table with Mama. "So I wasn't at my best," she'd said. "Figured it
was all talk, you know? You girls always remember that—you need
to know whether the bastard saying they're going to take a swing
is actually going to swing, or if they just like to hear themselves
talk."

Rat looked like someone who'd have no problem doing anything he said. It was the way he talked, the way he studied her, as

if she were an engine instead of a person. She couldn't risk him destroying the guitar.

She followed meekly along, down a narrow alley that channeled the wind into something fierce. They stopped in front of a NO TRESPASSING sign, hung on the back door of an empty building. Rat opened it.

"After you," he said. Blue stepped through cautiously. Florida bumped into her from behind.

"Come on, move it, don't leave the rest of us to freeze out here."

Inside wasn't much warmer. There was no wind, thanks to the cardboard and duct tape covering the broken windows, but no heat, either.

They kept moving. Florida took the lead, heading to a door with a skull and crossbones spray-painted onto it.

Inside, the walls between several rooms had been broken open with a sledgehammer, leaving jagged holes to step through. A collection of space heaters, their extension cords bundled together and run through a hole in the wall, glowed red. More extension cords powered a few lamps. In one of the rooms she could see mattresses on the floor; through another were cardboard boxes full of what looked like applesauce cups and breakfast cereal.

A pair of ragged couches sat in the corners of the room they'd entered. A flat-screen TV was mounted on one wall. One of the men turned it on to a football game.

"Get me a beer," Rat said to him. "Florida, check our guests out." He stepped aside. Florida took hold of Blue's pack. Blue gripped the straps tight and held on.

Rat threw the guitar case against the wall. It hit with a thud and a jangle. She jumped toward it, but Rat caught a fistful of her hair and yanked her back. "No," he said, flat and cold. "You don't do things without permission. Maybe wherever you come from, you did, but not here. Give Florida your bag and don't make a fuss. Not that you could anyway." He laughed, delighted with his own wit. "Not that you could. You got that?"

Her scalp burned, and her face, and her mind. She wanted to punch him, and she thought about it, but he'd smash Mama's guitar.

She heard the click of a lighter by her head. Rat pulled harder on her hair. "You see this?" He held the flame under her nose, close enough to sting. "I got no problem setting your pretty little guitar on fire and watching it burn. So we could do that, or you could behave. Take your pick."

He was so close that she could hear the music under his skin, jangling piano, sharp and hard and piecemeal.

She loosened her hold on her straps. Florida took the pack off her back, and Rat let go of her hair. The contents didn't look like much as Florida spread them out on the floor. Blue reached out as Florida emptied the keepsake bag, but stopped herself when she caught Rat's look.

"What a load of crap." Florida fingered the guitar pick, the packet of letters. She held up the training bra. "You really that flat?"

Blue kept her hands in her pockets, her face blank. Florida was looking for cracks, for someplace she could reach into and hurt Blue. The cracks were there, but if Blue didn't react, Florida would never find them.

"Nothing good?" Rat tapped Florida's shoulder. "It's okay. Gonna wait and see if the others bring anyone in, but I'd say we got a good haul. Mute and a boygirl. Val always pays extra for freaks. Good for kinky shit."

Florida kicked her shoes off and sat on the unoccupied couch.

"You gotta give me something extra this time, Rat. You wouldn't have them at all if I hadn't found her. Right? Whatcha gonna give me?"

"Your cut, same as always. A place to live where you don't have to peddle your ass, same as always. You got a problem with it, you can get out." He finished off the beer, crushed the can in his fist.

Blue knew better, but she couldn't help herself. She needed to know that the guitar was okay. She took three steps toward it and ran smack into Rat. He grabbed her shoulder, dug his fingers in until it hurt. "I didn't say you could look at that, did I? In fact, I don't think you asked permission. Did she?" He panned the room, eyes wide.

One of the guys on the couch said, "Didn't hear nothing come out of her mouth."

"That's right. You know why? Because she can't fucking talk. She has to write everything down." He snagged the notebook out of her back pocket before she could stop him. "I bet we can look in here and see everything she's said for the last, what, week? Month? Year?"

He flipped it open, read the first page he came to. "Right. You offered me money. Give it over. We'll consider it rent." He wiggled his fingers.

She handed it to him. Everything she had left. She'd already told him how much, couldn't pretend otherwise. It wasn't the money she cared about.

He grabbed her hand and twisted it to examine the ring on her finger. "Not much, is it? Not even worth the effort to pull it off your finger." He let go.

A bauble, that's what Tish had called it the day she gave it to Mama. But Mama had kept it on her finger through everything, right to the very end. Blue resisted the urge to touch the turquoise for fear she'd draw his attention back to it.

She took her notebook from him instead.

I gave you my $. Can I plz have my guitar?

She put the please in even though she didn't think it belonged there. The guitar was hers; Rat had no right to touch it.

He thought otherwise. "Not yours, not anymore. You gave it to me." He stared at her. She pressed her nails against the skin of her thumb in her pocket and stared back.

He didn't like it. She could read it in the tightness around his nose and mouth. "Listen, I got no reason to be nice to you. You're just a load of freight, something I'm holding until the buyer shows up. Like cattle, see, like a dumb old cow waiting in a stock car for her trip to the slaughterhouse.

"But here's the thing. Even those stupid cows got to have manners. That's where cattle prods come in, you know. They don't behave, they get the daylights shocked right out of them. We could do that, right here. See those cords over there?"

She didn't want to look, but she did, drawn irresistibly to the thick bunches of extension cords taped together, running along the floor and through the wall.

"Now, the way we get power is to just tap into it ourselves. Run our own lines. Works just fine, provided you don't mess with things. You mess with things, well, I don't want to think about how that might feel. Probably wouldn't leave too much of a mark. Just on the bottom of your foot, or where your hand touched the line. Probably a nasty smell, all burned and shit."

It's nothing, he's talking crap and he's not going to hurt me. Only, she knew she was wrong.

"Here's the deal, Interstate. I want to know what kind of cow you are—one who understands her place or one who needs a prod. Got it?" He waited for her to nod. "You want to look in that guitar case. I want to know you'll behave. So you do what I want and I'll let you look."

She looked at him, her hands trembling against her thighs.

"You want to see the inside of that case, you give me a kiss."

An involuntary step backward, one she wished she hadn't taken as soon as she saw the flicker of cruelty. "Look at her. You'd think her lips were fricking gold."

"Let me instead. Let her be."

She'd forgotten Steve completely. His voice buoyed her even as she shook her head at him.

"No way. Her guitar. She needs to deal with it. Come on, either a kiss or you say good-bye to that guitar. Your choice."

Kiss.

He crooked his finger at her and made her lean in. His breath smelled of beer, and she almost turned away. Then his lips reached hers, and his hand was on the back of her hair, and his tongue in her mouth. Control became something she'd never had, something she'd never have again, not as long as he was alive. His hand tightened against her head until she stopped trying to pull away.

Then he loosened his grip, moved his head back, and talked, voice low and intimate. "See, real nice there. Manners are all I expect. You give people what they want, they got no cause to give you trouble." He took a step back. She wanted to spit the taste of him out on the floor and brush her teeth until her gums bled.

"You go ahead and take a look."

The guitar. She almost didn't want to touch it now, but she needed to know. She knelt on the floor beside it. Tears burned at the corners of her eyes as she opened the lid.

Nothing broken. She traced the veneer—smooth, hard, intact—and plucked a string. She bit her lip at the reassuring twang.

Then his hand lowered on her shoulder as he pulled her away. "No way. You bought yourself a look. That's all. Guitar's mine."

She hated him. Hated him more than she'd ever hated anyone, more than she'd hated Mama in those flashes of time when she blamed her for dying. More than she'd hated Cass for leaving, Tish for vanishing. So much hate that she felt she would explode into pieces.

Mine.

He didn't even look at the note. "You got to look. You know it's okay. You want it to stay that way, you and your little boy-girlfriend there are gonna go in the other room and stay nice and quiet. You cause any trouble at all, I'm gonna smash the hell out of this guitar, then see how much you light up when I plug you in. Understand?"

Blue could hear her pulse in her ears as she stood up and started toward the other room. Then she stopped. She had one chance, a long shot, but she'd take it. She scribbled five words down in her notebook. Went back and handed it to Rat. This time he looked.

His lips stretched in a satisfied grin. "Nice to meet you, Blue Riley. Still doesn't get you that guitar, but you can take your pack with you to the other room."

She collected her things, thinking all the while. *Burn 'em down. If I don't get my voice or my sister, you owe me that much.*

I'm sorry.

She underlined it twice for good measure.

Steve wouldn't look at the page at first. When he did, he shrugged.

Me, You're here bc of me.

"Yeah, maybe, but who knows where I'd be." He whispered, his voice drowned out by the TV.

Not someplace worse. ☹

He didn't answer. There were times when he looked a thousand years older than Blue did, times that reminded her that she knew nothing about his past and how long he'd been traveling. _Traveling,_ as though he weren't a kid with no money and no family, and, as far as she could tell, no friends.

Except her, and look what she'd done to him.

I'll get us out.

He gave a jaded shrug. "You think I haven't heard those things before, or worse?"

She touched his hand. He didn't pull away, but he didn't seem to notice it, either. She went to her notebook instead.

My mom is dead + my dad was a sperm donor. I have my Aunt Lynne + my sister, if I can find her. That's it.

Steve shook his head. "You don't get it. It may not be a lot, but you have them. I don't."

Yours might come around.

He grimaced. "Even if they did . . . why would I want them? Why would I want people who took me in because it was their duty, not because they loved me?"

Being the girl with no parents had bought her a lot of sympathy over the years. Losing her mother brought an ocean of sad, but it didn't erase all the ways in which Mama had loved her. Even when things sucked, she had that.

If she ever met Steve's parents, she'd be sure to tell them her name, too.

You have me. I ♥ you.

And if he had her, did she have him, too? Was there a future in which they would talk about the time they'd ridden a ghost bus into Chicago, only to be captured by human traffickers?

Crap. She jerked away.

"What?"

You heard my name!

"Yeah. Blue. It's pretty."

He didn't understand.

I told it to Rat because I want her to get him—the woman in the red dress. But now you know.

"So?"

Still he didn't see it.

So she'll get you too, unless—like being swept over a giant waterfall, no way to turn back—*I leave you.*

"Leave?" As if getting up and walking out of the room were an option, Blue simply leaving him behind.

We have to get out of here together, but . . .

She'd done it for nothing. If she and Steve got away from Rat, the woman in the red dress would still come for Steve.

She examined the room around her. A bucket in the corner with a garbage bag laid over it. A gallon jug three quarters filled with water. And, coiled on the floor, a pair of chains with a manacle on one end, and a hook attached to the wall on the other.

They had to get out.

At some point the TV changed from sports to entertainment. "This year's *Major Chord* has a lot of surprises in store." Blue leaned forward to peer through the hole in the wall. The smiling face of the man in the blue shirt was stretched across the screen. "We've brought together talent from the heart of America, places your viewers will recognize as their own neighborhoods." His smile broadened, revealing his teeth. "Remember, anyone can rise to the top. Hard work is all it takes."

If that were true, Blue thought, *Mama and Tish would have been superstars.*

The interviewer, her ribs visible where her dress plunged down from her bony shoulders, gave a plastic smile. "That's good news for all of us excited for the new season. Of course, the band Forgotten Highway is stirring real interest. Who can resist true love? Jed and Jill are just made for each other, aren't they?"

They switched to a shot of Jed emerging from a limo, Jill just behind him. His hair had been streaked and it gave him a surfer look. Different band name, different hair, fake romance—what remained of Mr. Chicken? Was that part of what they were giving up?

No, Blue knew the real answer. She scanned the sidewalk for Bet. It took a minute to find her, but there she was, in a long skirt and a long-sleeved shirt, looking overdressed in the glaring sunshine. She smiled awkwardly as she was pushed to the side.

"So that wraps up our coverage of *Major Chord* for tonight. Tomorrow, we'll be back to recap the opening show, plus take an in-depth look at mystery girl C. R. Smith. We'll also reveal the final judge for this season, and boy, it's a big one! Next up, a taste of country cooking with country music sensation Twylee Mathers."

When Blue moved back, she bumped into her pack. The things Florida had pulled out and shoved back in spilled out over the floor.

Steve fingered the worn training bra, looked at her. She took it away, rubbed it between her fingers.

It was

Blue paused, scratched out the words.

My mom died of cancer. Before she did, I think she tried to do all the things she thought she'd miss out on with us. My big sister Cass needed a bra. I was 9 . . . well, I still don't really need much of one. Anyway, Mama said we'd buy me one too, just in case.

Only it had been much more than that. The three of them had gone to Sears on a Sunday. Mama'd brushed aside the salesclerk and led them through the lingerie as if it were her natural habitat, as if beneath her clothes she wore exotic things, not cotton underwear with worn elastic and a sports bra.

Mama and Cass had tried on padded bras, and leopard-print bras, and, accidentally, a nursing bra that made them all laugh until they cried. After Cass had made her choice, they went to the girls' section. In among the bags of neatly rolled underwear and paired socks, they found three different training bras. "Go on, Bluebird. Pick the one you like the most," Mama said.

She'd picked this one. Plain white cotton, with a narrow strip of trim around the band. She liked the feel of that trim under her fingers, and she liked the smile Mama gave her when she chose it. And now it lived in her bag of treasures, because sometimes a bit of cloth could feel like love.

Steve cleared his throat while she brushed at her eyes. "And these?"

The letters. It made her a little sick to look at them.

They're for my sister. They were from her father to our mother.

"You mean, your sister's father wasn't yours?" Steve stammered a little.

My mom got pregnant on the road. She was a musician. The guy was too, only a big name. They didn't stay together. She decided she didn't want Cass to be alone, so along came Donor 707. I don't know anything abt him, other than he was good at science.

"What do you know about your sister's father?"

More than she wanted to. More than she should have. If only she hadn't gone looking. Sometimes you do stupid things for stupid reasons, like wanting to get someone's attention, only in getting their attention you rip the kite that is your life right off its frame so it collapses on the ground.

Not much.

NOT LONG AFTER, RAT TOOK A CALL. ONCE HE'D FINISHED,
he spoke to the others. "We're gonna have to drop them off for Val.
Florida, go out and get your smokes. The boys can get the van ready
to go. We get this done and I can get home to my old lady."

Blue tapped Steve on the shoulder as everyone but Rat left. This
was it. If they didn't get out now, they never would.

In the dim light, she could see Steve nod, face pale. No way to
write everything out. She had to trust that he'd follow her lead. First
step: she dropped to the floor and, hands gripping her stomach,
began to roll.

Steve grunted as she banged against him. Rat leaned back, trying to see them. "What the hell's going on in there?"

"Nothing," Steve said, just enough fear in his voice. Blue kicked
the plastic bucket, the handle clanging against the wall.

"Doesn't sound like nothing." Rat came to the hole in the wall,
a floor lamp in his hand. "What's she doing?"

"I don't know. She's been having this pain off and on for a couple days." From the corner of her eye she could see them both staring at her. She rolled farther, mouth open in a moan that couldn't
come. Farther in. He had to come farther in.

"She been screwing around? Knocked up?"

"No. I thought it was getting better, but this is even worse."

Another roll, almost all the way to the wall. She arched her back, waited, the chain along the curve of her waist.

Rat walked toward her. "What's going on with you, Blue Riley?" He bent down.

She had one goal, every muscle in her body moving toward it. She took the chain in her hands and rolled to the other side, her arms rising to loop it over his head. He jumped too fast, the chain sliding down his body and tightening near his knees, not his neck. She jerked. He fell.

In her mind, it was smooth and quick, and ended with Rat tied up and her and Steve running away. He fell on top of her, though, one knee driving into the underside of her forearm, one hand on her hair.

"Fucking bitch," he hissed. Before she could move, he sat up on her, hands around her neck. "I don't care if I leave marks." His hands tightened.

She pressed her feet on the floor and pushed up, trying to unseat him. He didn't budge, too much weight for her to move. Her hands rose of their own accord, scrabbling at his arms to no avail. As the pressure built in her head, her vision filled with flashes of light.

Then there was a dull thud, like a down pillow swung hard. Rat's hands loosened and she drew an agonized breath. Another thud, and he rolled off. Blue looked up and saw one of her boots swing past to catch Rat in the ribs. Her boot on Steve's foot.

It hurt to breathe, but she sucked in great lungfuls of air anyway. Another thud sounded, only this time it was mixed with the splintery crack of green wood. Rat gave a gasp, as much pain as air in it.

She looked over. Rat lay curled on the floor. Steve stood next to him, staring down in disgust. Not at Rat. At his own feet in her boots, and at the dark spots that spattered them. "I'm sorry," he whispered.

Rat shifted slightly. The blood on his face distracted her from what she should have seen: his hand curling around the chain beside him. By the time she noticed, it was already too late.

She yelled. Nothing came, of course. Instead, she heard the chain sliding through the air and hitting Steve's legs.

Steve dropped to his knees, surprised. Rat was up, his hand swinging again. This time the chain caught Steve across the cheek. His hand went up to where the blood ran down, the drops falling from his chin.

Rat tightened both hands around a length of chain. "Stupid fucking idiots. You really think the two of you are going somewhere? Not the way you want. I think one of you's headed to Val looking ugly"—he bent down beside Steve, as if to help him—"and one's headed in a box."

He dropped the chain over Steve's head, drew his hands together behind Steve's neck.

Blue jumped. Up, forward, straight into Rat. She grabbed the little fingers on his hands and tried to pull them back. Steve's hands scratched at the floor, his mouth open in a silent gasp. Blue let go of Rat's hands, ripped back the collar of his T-shirt, and sank her teeth into his shoulder.

He dropped the chain and spun. She jumped away, spitting out his blood as she went. *Get up, Steve!* she wanted to yell, but could do nothing more than stomp her foot before Rat came at her again.

She ran into the other room. Her foot snagged in the extension cords and she grabbed the stem of a lamp to catch herself. Then Rat was there, and she was swinging the lamp with both hands. His nose gave under the impact with a crunch. Everything was the color of blood now. She froze, but Steve was suddenly beside her.

"Come on!" he yelled. She obeyed, pausing only to grab what she'd been watching for the whole time. The guitar case in hand, she ran after Steve. Behind them Rat was giving gurgling cries, but they kept going down the hall, through the dark, to the door. Into the night, into the alley, and beyond.

IT WASN'T UNTIL THEY HAD LEFT THE ALLEY FAR BEHIND
that Blue realized how many things she didn't have. A coat. Her
pack. Her boots. No, Steve had her boots, but that left her in socks.
She was shaking, not just from the cold. She looked behind them,
saw no one, stopped. The adrenaline came up as a wave of bile from
her stomach, and she spat it out on the street.

"Keep moving," Steve said. "They'll find us."

She followed him. Her keepsake bag, all her things: she'd left
them back there. Along with what it was like to never have been hit
and to never have hit someone back.

They kept going. The streetlights were on, and above the sky
glowed orange. Every so often, water splashed her face. Snowflakes.
Just a few, but it wouldn't take many when you had no shoes, no
coat.

No notebook. She couldn't even talk. There was nothing to do
but keep moving forward.

Even her ability to do that was fading, fast. Her neck hurt, and
her feet were numb, and she would have done anything to be warm,
only she was sure she would never be warm again.

Looking at Steve didn't help. Scarlet marks ringed his neck, the
outline of the chain links clear on the white skin. Scarlet on his

face, too, and on the collar of his shirt. Blood dripped from his cheek.

"It's okay," he chanted. She bumped against him, and he didn't even look at her, just continued on, walking, repeating. *Shock*, she thought, the word floating through her mind and out again, to be replaced by *Cold*, and *Tired*, and *Are they behind us?*

Dark and noise—cars driving by, people shouting to one another, music coming from somewhere. Music. Lou had said that musicians look after one another. Blue took Steve's hand, headed toward the sound.

The cheerful bounce of ragtime on a piano rang out from somewhere above them. From somewhere behind came the slap of running feet. Blue grabbed Steve's hand and yanked him toward her, pressing them both against a door.

The footsteps died away. Above her the piano continued to play. She tried the doorknob. Locked. A little brass plaque on the wooden frame read NELL BROADHURST CENTER. Blue banged on the door, hard. Nothing. There was a buzzer set to the side. She hit it.

"We're closing up," came a lush voice, the piano in the background.

Please hovered on her lips, could go no further. She began to cry, silently, leaning against the frame. *Please.*

Steve stirred beside her. She looked at him. "Please," he said. "We're hurt and we need help. Please let us in."

Silence. Blue clenched her fist to her mouth, as if her screams might come out, as if the world would hear them if they did. Then, from somewhere inside, came the tap of high heels on the floor, the click of the door opening. A brown-skinned woman in a green dress stood there, her red lips opening, speaking.

"Babies, you better come in. Let me see what's happened to you."

Inside, the world stuttered along like snapshots instead of film. Someone wrapped a blanket around her shoulders and put an ice pack on her neck. Someone else was talking about Steve and stitches, about ERs and sympathetic doctors. Steve talking, too, his voice raspy, whispery, saying "She can't talk," saying "Please no," not saying her name, not to them. Saying something else instead—"Interstate"—and she absorbed it all, the warmth, the quiet, the gentleness.

"I don't want to leave her." Steve, close by.

The woman again. "Baby, you gotta get that cheek taken care of. She'll be safe here. Javier'll look after her."

She looked at Steve. Suddenly a little cloth-bound notebook with a unicorn on the front and a silver pen were pressed into her hands. "You need it more than I do," said the woman, smelling of clove and roses as she held her warm hand against Blue's cheek.

Blue took the notebook.

Will you be OK? Who are they?

"It's okay. They understand," Steve said.

"He doesn't want to leave that cheek open, hon. Scars are butch and all, but he doesn't need them to be handsome, does he?"

Blue nodded. She wanted to say something more—anything, really, anything made with her mouth and her tongue and her throat. Not flat words on a page. She took his hand instead, squeezed it, hard, looked at his battered face, and saw . . . lightness. It made no sense, but there it was.

Steve leaned in closer, his lips to her ear. "Blue, I saved your bag for you. Just the little one with your mom's stuff in it." A motion, his hands in his pants, and he pulled the bag free.

That quick, he was gone, shepherded away by the woman.

She curled up tight under the blanket and cried. The tears were made of that night, and Rat's hands on her throat, his mouth on hers, the sound of the chain against Steve's face, the swinging of the lamp. All of it and more still—Mama, and Cass, and the cold, the endless cold, and not knowing where she was going. And she cried for her voice, her name.

Her name. She looked up for a clock, found a grandfather one on the far wall. 10:25.

Next to it sat a man. He was dressed in jeans and a loose denim shirt, with short brown hair and gold hoops in his ears. Javier, she guessed.

"Hey, don't be scared." He had an accent, a soft one that hid between his vowels, swallowed his "h." "It's okay. I'm not getting any closer unless you ask me to."

She pulled her blanket tighter. The room had faded gold wall-paper, and that grandfather clock, and a fireplace with a bouquet of flowers where the fire should have been. In the middle stood a plain table—the kind you'd find in a classroom—surrounded by chairs, and an upright piano.

Piano. She looked at the man again and mimed hands on a keyboard. He nodded.

"I was playing. Do you?"

She shook her head. The guitar—she reached for the handle, her heart slowing as she found it.

"Take it you're more of a strings kind of girl?"

She nodded.

"How'd you two know to come here? Right place, but we're hard to find at night."

She pointed to the piano.

"You followed the music? That's an unusual path to Nellie's Place."

This needed more than she could provide with gestures.

What's Nellie's Place? We needed someplace safe. I heard the music +.

She paused, feeling very young.

I thought that since I played guitar you would help us.

The man gave her a curious look. "You weren't trying to come here? Tonight—the meeting and all?"

Meeting?

"The Transgender Alliance. Liza and I run it."

She gave him another look. A man, stubble on his face, a shirt that draped smoothly down his chest. The kind of man Steve might grow up to be.

"You're not trans," he stated.

Blue shook her head. He leaned forward, resting forearms on his knees. "But your friend is. Can we maybe start from the beginning, so I can see what's going on?"

So she wrote it out. Not all of it, of course. Enough that he could understand. It took a couple of pages in the notebook, but he was patient. She sat while he read, letting the blanket droop from her shoulders as she warmed up.

"Bad news, huh?" He held a hand out to her. She took it tentatively. "I'm Javier. That was Liza who took your friend"—he glanced at the paper—"Steve, to get his face looked at." He paused, rubbing his jaw as he studied her. "Listen, you maybe should think about talking to the cops. The two of you got worked over pretty good."

She shook her head and retrieved the notebook from his grasp.

We can't! I can't.

He read, then raised one hand. "It's okay. I understand. The police can feel like a bad idea. I just think that maybe this"—he pointed at her neck—"deserves some attention." Staring straight at her, his eyes dark and steady, until she needed to look down.

Chimes began to ring: the grandfather clock turning over the hour. Eleven. Steve knew her name. He'd been with her for days already. They were running out of time.

Maybe the only right answer was the one she didn't want.

She stood up. Javier did as well, graceful as a dancer.

I have to go.

"Go where?"

Now. Leave before they get back.

It hurt to say it. All this time she'd been thinking that people who left didn't hurt when they went away. It wasn't true at all. It felt like an earthquake inside her, things being forced apart.

"Whoa, what's going on?"

I can't explain. You have to trust me.

He shook his head, slow and sad. "There's nothing I can do to help? Life doesn't have to be like this. Families can be worked out, and if they can't, well, families can be made. Romantic love isn't the only kind of love people can find."

I can't. It's not like that for me. Steve?

"We got his back, you understand? He'll be okay. We've seen kids come in in worse shape, real bad, and they do okay. We've got a pretty good network here. Places to stay, school, doctors—lots of trans kids need help somewhere along the way. We're here to give it to them. The question is: What do you need?"

Her boots. She couldn't leave without her boots. Crap. She rolled her head back, looked up at the ceiling, where, unexpectedly, a small bluebird was flying, painted with care on the tin work.

My boots. Steve took them.

Javier shook his head. "He refused to leave with them on. We gave him sneakers from the closet. Good footwear's gold when you're on the street."

Steve. He'd believed her, and he'd known she'd leave before he got back. He'd left the boots.

Either that, or he was afraid of what wearing them might mean.

"We've got other stuff in the closet, too. It makes sense to keep what we can on hand. Let's see what we can do for you."

She kept the blanket around her as they went to the closet. Not just to keep off the cold, though that was part of the reason. It wasn't so much that she was afraid of Javier . . . it was more that she couldn't stop seeing Rat in his place.

Javier dug through boxes and hangers, holding up things from time to time. She chose without thought. It wasn't until the end that she understood the pattern.

Javier did, too. "Might be safer that way. Depends. People catch on, they can be mean. Worse than mean. Your voice won't give you away, but the hair . . . That's gonna make it harder."

She ran a hand over her hair. She'd worn it the same way for years. A little longer than chin length, most of it turning to corkscrews as soon as she brushed it out.

Do you have clippers? Scissors?

Javier vanished into the bathroom, waved her in after him. She hesitated in the doorway. He said nothing, just waited. Behind her the clock chimed the half hour. *Time to go.* She walked in.

The mirror had lights around the border—soft, glowing ones. "Lots of kids want the chance to practice makeup somewhere safe. Liza set this up to help them."

Even under the soft light, she looked terrible. The bruises were coming out around her neck like a collar of dust. The whites of her eyes were bloodshot, everything puffy and dark with lack of sleep and crying. She twisted a strand of her hair, tugged.

"You ready?" He'd plugged a pair of clippers into the wall and stood, arm raised. She nodded.

It didn't feel like much of anything. A little tickly, here and there. A little weird to watch the hair drop from her head in great bunches, falling like leaves around her. *A tree*, she thought, *that's all it is. I'm a tree headed into winter, and my leaves will come again in the spring.*

"You okay?" Javier asked, resting one hand on her shoulder. She shrugged it off, nodded again. He kept going.

Once he was done, she changed into the clothes she'd chosen. Two tees, one tight, one loose; a long-sleeved crew; a worn flannel shirt; a plain green sweater a few sizes too big. Men's jeans, a little loose, hanging a little low. She held them up with one hand, ran her other hand over her shaved head. Without hair, she looked paler, her eyes wider, her bruises more obvious. The unfamiliar clothes, the smell of them—some detergent she didn't recognize—the way everything padded out her shoulders . . . For a moment, she could see a boy, some tired, scared boy who could have been a cousin, a friend.

Javier made a few adjustments when she came out. He took off his belt, warning her first—"You need something to hold up your pants"—and she tightened it around her own waist. "What you really need is a good coat, and I'm not sure what to give you."

He went to the closet again, searched, finally pulled something out. A navy blue peacoat, heavy, thick. He took keys out of one pocket, a wallet from the other.

She pointed at him. He nodded. She shook her head.

"I was thinking I wanted a new coat, anyway. Time to redo the image, you know? Something a little sportier, a little less old-man. You're just giving me an excuse."

Blue tried to refuse again, but he insisted. With the coat on, she looked almost completely unlike herself.

"And a hat. You're going to freeze to death without one."

For no reason came a vision of Rat's dungeon, and the blood, and his hands, and the feel of the lamp hitting him. She pressed one hand over her mouth.

Javier reached for her, stopped short. "Listen, there's nothing you can tell me that will be too shocking for me to handle. Bad things happen sometimes. I know all about it. I'm worried about you. What if you stay tonight, sleep safe, and we figure things out in the morning?"

Almost midnight. Time to move on.

She had nothing to take but her guitar and her keepsake bag. She stuffed the bag in the guitar case. The one thing they hadn't found in the closet was a pair of gloves, but her fingerless gloves were in the case and she put them on, figuring they were better than nothing. Her boots she laced quickly, the familiar ache settling in at once. Javier handed her a hand-knitted hat, blue, cabled, thick. She put it on.

Thank you.

She looked at Javier, the concern in his eyes.

I'll be OK. Plz take care of Steve. I need to know he'll be OK. Tell him—

Tell him what, exactly? She didn't have any sense at all of what she was doing anymore, beyond trying to keep moving, trying not to hurt anyone else. She needed a plan. More important, she needed to leave before he came back.

—that I'll check back here once I get things fixed. Make sure he knows that, OK? And I meant what I said by the lake. Tell him

But really there was nothing more. Nothing beyond the fact that leaving people sucked just as much as being left, that now she could see that maybe it hadn't been life Mama had clung to for so long, but her and Cass, that maybe Cass had missed her even as she walked out Lynne's door and into whatever future she'd chosen.

Thank you.

She touched Javier's hand, quickly, lightly. Then, guitar in hand, she went back into the cold.

OUTSIDE THE SNOW FELL THICK AND FAST, BLUNTING THE
lines of the buildings. Down the back of her neck the snowflakes
flew, landing in the space between coat collar and hat that her hair
should have covered. She shivered.

Come on, boots. Where do I go? Her only answer was the ache.
She turned left, took three steps. Somewhere a clock started to toll
the hour. She looked down the street to the corner of the block. No
traffic, just snow and the chiming.

She ran down the sidewalk, pausing at the edge of the cross-
walk, then into the middle of the intersection, the white below her
feet lit by the flash of the red stoplight above.

*I'm here! What now? Give me some sort of frigging sign, because I
don't have a clue. I can't just walk across Chicago and hope for the best.*

She looked in all four directions but saw nothing. The air
smelled only of snow. Head back, she opened her eyes wide, blinking away the snowflakes.

A honk. She spun, jumped back as a car slowed and slid past
her. The door flew open and a woman jumped out.

"Oh my God, are you okay. I didn't bump you, right?" She kept
the car between them, as if afraid of Blue.

Blue shook her head and reached into her pocket for the unicorn notebook. The woman gripped the door, her fear more obvious. Blue held the notebook up, the pen, wrote quickly.

I'm fine, you didn't bump me. I can't speak.

She leaned over the car to show the woman the page. The woman read it, examined her. Blue pulled the coat collar up, uncomfortably, aware of the bruises.

"What are you doing out in the snow with a guitar?"

The woman looked young. College age, maybe. Short hair, dyed red and cut as ragged as if she'd done it herself in front of a mirror. A nice ski jacket, but the car she was driving was an old, beat-up sedan. A little kid stared out at Blue from the backseat.

Leaving town.

The woman studied her again, as if she knew something about Blue, some secret they shared, some underground river they'd seen and sworn to keep hidden.

"Where are you going?" The woman had come around the car.

Blue looked down, brushed the snow off her notebook. What was the next stop along the Gully? The paper had gotten wet, and the ink stuck and sputtered, and it took her a while to remember how to spell the name.

Minneapolis.

"Me too." Up close, the woman definitely looked young. Also sad, and lonely, and more than a little cautious.

"Is there really a guitar in that case?"

Blue nodded. What did she think, that Blue was smuggling guns in it? And didn't the woman have something better to be doing than standing in the intersection talking with a stranger?

"Do you want a ride? It's a long drive in the snow. You can help me stay awake." She looked as far from sleep as Blue was from home. A ride was a ride, unless the woman turned out to be like

Florida and Rat. Only . . . Blue looked at the kid's little face, the uneven cut of the pale bangs. Something felt off, but not like with Florida.

Blue nodded. The woman opened the back door, then turned back to Blue.

"What's your name?"

Blue thought for a moment.

Interstate.

The woman gave her a funny look but returned to the child. "Lacey, Interstate's gonna get a ride with us. His guitar can't fit in the trunk, so you need to lift your feet and let me slide it in front of you. Okay?"

His? Blue's hand went to her shaved scalp. She was a boy; or at least she was playing one, for now. How could she have forgotten?

Lacey obliged, silent, little feet raised and lowered, shod in pink boots with butterflies on them. The kind Blue would have wanted when she was four—the kind Mama would have looked for in every thrift store they passed.

Behind them came headlights, and the woman flinched. A sedan rolled up, silver, a man at the wheel. The driver leaned toward them as he slowed to a stop, snow catching in his graying crew cut. With a gravelly voice he asked, "Everything okay here?"

"Yes, thanks, just moving stuff." Speaking loudly, a little too much force, a little too much cheer.

But it wasn't her the man was staring at. It was Blue, as if he knew her, as if she knew him. Cold chased its way down her spine.

"Okay, then. You all be careful." Window back up, the man shifting in his seat, the car sliding on by, the license plate obscured with mud.

Blue got in. The car swiveled a bit before picking up speed. The snow blew at the headlights, fluttered, and bounced off the windshield, the tops of the passing buildings invisible to her. *Good-bye, Chicago,* she thought, wondering whether Steve was back, whether he was okay. *Good-bye, everything here. Hello, whatever is coming.*

30

THE WOMAN DROVE IN GRIM SILENCE, HANDS TIGHT ON the steering wheel. The weather was making her tense, sure, but something else was, too. After all, who left Chicago in the middle of the night, in a snowstorm, with a little girl in tow?

"Mama?" Lacey said, a hint of fear in her voice.

"It's okay. You just try and sleep, sweetie." The woman glanced at Blue.

For that matter, who picked up a mute teenage boy they met in an intersection while leaving Chicago in the middle of the night? Blue turned that puzzle over and over as she watched the wipers rock back and forth, her head bouncing lower and lower on her chest until she dissolved into sleep.

"I'm Andrea."

They were parked outside a rest stop. It was early morning, and the snow had begun to let up, and the black had lightened to gray. Blue's stomach rumbled incessantly.

"Listen, do you actually have a place to go?" Andrea looked in the rearview mirror as she spoke.

Blue hesitated. How much did she really want to tell this woman, who still hadn't given a reason for the late-night trip?

"I'm just thinking . . . If you don't have someplace, I might be able to help."

Again, the feeling of something being not right. There was something tough about Andrea, something in the sharp way she watched Blue. But beneath that . . . there was something in the way she broke off eye contact more quickly than Blue expected, as though hiding herself away.

Not sure. You have room?

That quick glance toward her, then down again. "Yeah. Sort of."

"I gotta pee, Mama," Lacey called from the back.

"Of course, sweetie. Let's go."

Blue had a brief moment of confusion inside, almost following Andrea into the women's restroom. She turned at the last second and went into the men's. Empty, at least when she went into the stall. When she came out, a cleaning woman stood by the sink, one hand on the handle of a mop. The same burnt smell, only was it? Something in it reminded her just a little of Christmas. Oranges filled with cloves, a little sweeter, a little less decay.

What? She didn't bother writing. *It's been one day, and I didn't give my name, and if you're going to change the rules again, I'm going to tell you to give me my voice back.*

The janitor said nothing, just watched her. She was a small woman, dark-skinned, wearing a light blue uniform with a name tag pinned over her left breast. Blue read the name there.

What about it, Gabriela? What do you have to say now?

"Is that what you're going to do, Bluebird? Demand? From me?" She didn't sound scary, or mean. Just tired, if that were possible.

As if she could, as if she had the power to demand her voice back, not ask, demand. *I don't want you to change the rules again.*

I want to play things out the way you said. She swallowed hard. *You know what happened, right? I did something terrible. Not just what we did to Rat, but I told him my name. I wanted, I wanted you to hurt him, kill him maybe. And he did terrible things to us, me and Steve, and I had to leave Steve behind.*

I want this game to be over. I want to find Cass and be done.

The woman shifted her mop handle, leaned it against the wall. Up close, she only came to Blue's chest. She drew one finger along Blue's throat, tracing the bruises there.

"We all enter into bargains not knowing the true cost. All of us, every day."

Even you?

"Even me. All you can do is follow your path, do your best."

I thought you controlled everything.

"No one controls everything, Bluebird."

Can you—

But the woman was already going, slipping into her mop bucket, and then the bucket itself slipping into the floor, like a pocket being turned inside out. The floor sealed neatly behind her.

If no one controlled everything, where did that leave her?

Lacey settled down after she'd had the soggy muffin Andrea had bought her at the rest stop. She surprised Blue with one, too, but it did little for her hunger. If she'd had money, she would have packed her guitar case full of potato chips, crackers, anything that came cheap and portable.

Andrea just had coffee, sipping it as she drove. "I can't believe it snowed. I had everything planned out."

She glanced at Blue, lowered her voice. "I'm guessing you didn't have a plan. Sometimes you just have to run, right?"

'Cause sometimes the devil was on your trail. No, that wasn't what Andrea was talking about. Whatever she was leaving behind, she kept checking for it in the rearview mirror.

"I want out!" Lacey began to kick the seats with the tips of her boots.

"Not yet. I told you it would take a long time. Tell me what you can see instead of fussing."

But there was nothing to see beyond a steady landscape of fresh white. Lacey quickly resumed her kicking. Andrea's face hardened as she gripped the wheel more tightly.

Blue reached behind her for the guitar. It took a lot of work to free it from the case, more to bring it forward without hitting anyone in the head. It worked magic on Lacey, though, from the moment she touched the case. She didn't know kids' songs, but that didn't seem to make a difference. The little girl used verses she knew and simply pushed them into the spaces the music made.

By the time Blue was ready to stop, Lacey had dropped off into sleep. She rested the guitar between her knees, picking strings softly.

"Those were Dry Gully songs."

Warmth filled her chest. She couldn't help but smile.

"I saw them once. In the winter. My mom had their record, listened to it all the time. She drove us in a snowstorm when they came to Chicago. I was little, like ten, maybe. They were so good, and my mom was so happy. She sang along with every song."

A single tear trickled down Andrea's cheek. Following an urge, Blue reached up to brush it away. Andrea flinched. Then she laughed as though it were nothing, though the sad stayed in her eyes.

"The guitarist was so sweet. I think my mom wished they were best friends."

Because that's the way Mama was. What she gave at the mic, what people loved, was simply part of what she gave everywhere else.

"The other one, the fiddler? She was intense. I drew vines all over my arms with markers the next day."

They must have played Chicago when Blue was as little as the girl in the backseat. She and Cass had probably been in the dressing room while Mama and Tish played. Her life and Andrea's had brushed past each other on some snowy night.

"Anyway, thanks for helping with Lacey. With any luck, she'll sleep the rest of the way."

Blue cradled her guitar close and thought about the music it had played. If the woman in the red dress was right, then every Dry Gully concert still echoed inside. Blue pressed her ear against it and listened as the miles rolled by.

THEY STOPPED IN A PARKING LOT SOMEWHERE OUTSIDE
of Minneapolis, buildings suddenly appearing after what felt like
endless rolling fields of snow. A mall. She'd come all the way from
Maine to hang out in a mall, without any money.

Andrea looked around. She seemed fidgety, as if something
dangerous lurked among the shoppers heading in and out of the
stores. She hushed Lacey when the girl tried to ask her a question,
and urged her back into her seat. Finally, she looked at Blue.

"Can we talk outside for a minute?"

Outside, it was cold, gusty, the air filled with the sound of plows,
the damp chill scent of snow.

Andrea came around to Blue's side of the car. "Listen," she said.
"We've both got our . . . things going on, right?" She pointed at
Blue's neck and the bruises there. "Lacey and me, we're going to a
place I found out about. Not a shelter. At least, not the kind people
think of."

Blue just looked at her. She knew what her "thing" was. She
needed to know about Andrea's. Andrea didn't feel dangerous, but
whatever she was dragging behind her did.

"Shit. Listen, he'll have people after us already. He's a cop,

Interstate. His dad's a cop. His brother's a cop. You think any of them would take my side over his?"

Blue opened her notebook.

He? Your boyfriend?

Andrea looked at the page. She swallowed before speaking. "Husband. I got pregnant when I was seventeen. It seemed like a good idea, the getting married part. Just the rest sucked. But you know about that. Who was it that hurt you? Dad?"

Blue shrugged. Inside, she was doing a double take of Andrea. Cop? If she was running away with her kid, it wasn't like they just didn't get along. It had to be worse, right? She wasn't sure if the feeling in the pit of her stomach was pity or fear.

"Anyway, I thought you could come with us. You need a place. You could be like my backup. In case things are weird."

With me, things are guaranteed to be weird. Not that she was about to explain any of her life to Andrea. Go with her and hide from the police, or hang out here and hope that a warm place to stay fell into her lap. It wasn't a no-brainer as much as it was the best of bad options. She nodded.

Andrea took Lacey out and the three of them went inside the mall. There weren't many shoppers there. *Digging out*, Blue guessed, *Or happy for an excuse to stay home.* Andrea led them to a bench and sat down, Lacey in her lap. Like that, Blue could see the relationship, Lacey's big brown eyes twins to her mother's. The little girl nestled against Andrea's neck, Andrea's hand on her back.

Blue stood. The ache in her feet sent tendrils like ivy up her legs. She didn't know if staying was the right thing to do. Cass was waiting for her somewhere. The only way to find her was to keep moving. Tomorrow, though. One night in a bed while she made a plan.

A small woman approached them. She glanced at Blue warily, looked at Lacey, Andrea. "You all look tired," she said, with an accent Blue recognized as Minnesotan from watching *Fargo* with Beck. "Don't suppose you're friends of Ruth Kenally."

"Yes, ma'am, we are." Andrea's voice was confident, though her skin had gone pale.

"Well, hey now, that's an okay thing to be." The woman looked at the little girl again, met Blue's eyes on a second sweep of her face. "Your family here, they must be tired of traveling. We got, what, a brother, too?" Andrea nodded before Blue could even react. "Want to come with me, find a place to rest?"

Andrea stood, took Lacey's hand. She looked at Blue as well, a guarded glance that said *This is it, be quiet, be someone I can trust.*

The other woman waited. Blue looked at her, at the puffy blue coat zipped almost to her chin, at the thin skin pleated at the corners of her eyes and the gray streaks in the dull brown of her hair. She'd know the monsters; that was what Lou had said.

But she'd missed Florida.

No, she hadn't. She'd walked away from her, not for any clear reason, but that didn't matter. She'd walked away. She'd known.

Blue impulsively touched Andrea's arm, slid her hand down to cover where Andrea's fingers wrapped around Lacey's. The muscles trembled beneath her touch, Andrea, looking past her and still somehow into her, their secrets reaching for one another.

"That sounds like a great idea. Thanks."

The woman led them to a battered minivan driven by a boy. A boy maybe a bit older than Blue. Longish black hair in a ponytail, dark brown eyes, and a real smile, big as all get-out, as Teena's mom would have said.

Andrea hesitated at the sight of him. The woman waved them forward. "This here's Dill," she said. "He's been helping us out. We don't want too much traffic, you know. Draws attention. Dill does some driving, drops us off so there aren't no cars left around."

"Hey," he said. His accent was different, subtler, unrecognizable to her.

"How old are you?" Andrea stood by the door, skeptical.

"Nineteen." Another shot of that smile, bold and gentle at the same time. "I'm traveling, studying up on communities, seeing how different types work, structure and stuff. I try to be useful when I can."

It was enough to coax them inside. Blue loaded their bags and the guitar in back while Andrea fastened Lacey's car seat. Lacey sat farthest back, Andrea and Blue in the middle, the woman in the front passenger seat. The boy turned on the radio, tapping his fingers in time to the honky-tonk that played.

"Traveling," Andrea said. "This is your van?"

He glanced in the rearview, his eyes meeting Blue's for a moment. "Nope. I don't have a car."

"So how are you traveling? Train? Bus?"

"Train mostly. I hop freight as much as I can. Hitch the rest. Hiked a little."

"Hop freight?" Andrea's thoughts seemed to run a parallel track to Blue's. "Like a hobo?"

"Yup. There isn't anything quite like it. This time of year, in the north, not quite as awesome. Kind of cold. That's why I'm here for a stretch." Eyes in the mirror again. Blue looked down. A real live hobo driving them around. She thought about the librarian's father.

"What about your parents?"

"They're in Washington State."

"And school?"

It wasn't as though any of this made a difference to where they were headed. It seemed more like chatter to pass the time. To cover up whatever Andrea was trying not to think about, just like the things Blue didn't want to remember about last night. Something squeezed inside her, a organ constructed of sadness and worry and isolation.

Dill cleared his throat. "I finished up my homeschooling. I haven't decided yet whether I want to go to college."

"You can go to college if you've been homeschooled?"

A glance at traffic merging in from the right. "Sure. I was offered a free ride at a couple of schools when I applied. I wasn't ready, though. Felt like I had other things to do."

"Like this?" Andrea gestured at the car interior, the snow outside, disbelief on her face.

"Exactly. Like this."

With that, Andrea stopped her questioning. Dill seemed content to drive in silence. Blue hunched down in her seat, feeling unbearably old, terribly young, completely and utterly lost. All she had left was her guitar. She had no real home. No way to stop moving, not really, not if she didn't want to end up like Amy, or destroying everyone around her.

She shivered and closed her eyes.

THEY GLIDED PAST THE CITY AND AWAY, IN AND OUT OF fields and forests. No pine, not like Eliotville. Leafless, gray, and somber. They finally turned down a narrow road and bumped along on the plow-packed snow. She watched eagerly for the house, ready to be out of the car.

There wasn't one. Just snow and trees and sky.

"How—" Andrea began once they stopped; but the woman cut her off.

"The snow makes it hard. We've got to do a bit of walking, so's not to leave tracks right to where we're going."

Andrea looked far from certain. There, with the sun bouncing off the pristine snow, she looked as pale as a person could get, her sunglasses dwarfing her face. Blue wanted to reassure her—would have, had she known anything about what was going on.

"This is safe?"

"Whole lot safer than staying out in the cold. Ain't no one gonna see you out here, either. Gives you space to get things figured out and all. That's what you're looking for, right?"

A slight nod. A glance down at her feet, shod in the kind of trendy hikers that Blue saw on a lot of tourists' feet, nothing like the sturdy leather she'd slipped back on as they'd come to a stop.

"Okay, Lacey, let's go."

The snow came up to the tops of the little girl's boots, threatening to fill them with each step. Andrea, carrying two duffel bags, started to kneel down by her. Dill stopped her, taking both bags from her. "I got these if you've got her."

That same look from Andrea—part hard, part scared. Blue moved closer and, gripping her guitar in one hand, took one bag in the other. She was pretty sure Dill wouldn't run off with a bag full of little girl clothes, but if it helped Andrea feel safer, she could carry it. Andrea smiled and lifted Lacey to her hip.

Dill looked at Blue. Close up, his eyes were velvety dark, his skin with a hint of rust to it. He offered up that giant smile. "Thanks. I can take it back if you get tired."

The paths they traveled through the snow twisted back and forth on each other in snaky coils, around and around, crossing here and there. The scent of wood smoke blew past her, off and on, and she imagined things cooking on a fire—bacon, eggs, potatoes, toast cooked on a fork, s'mores even. Her stomach rumbled.

Dill stopped in a small clearing. The woods weren't dense the way they were in Maine. The snow in the clearing was churned up, footprints everywhere. Away from the center, five wooden frames rested on the ground, leaves and sticks piled inside them. A damp fire circle sat in the middle, a few stray wisps of smoke blowing upward.

So much for bacon and eggs. She looked around at the snow, the trees, the lack of anything like a building, or even a tent. So much for a bed and a place to stay as well.

"It's cool, isn't it?" Dill waited for her response.

She couldn't think of an honest one that had anything to do with cool. If she'd wanted to hike around in the snow in the woods, she could have stayed at home, with the promise of hot chocolate and cookies.

She shrugged.

"I mean, screw waiting around for someone else to fix things. Just make it happen yourself, right?"

She stared at him.

"Um, sorry. I guess it's not really what you're thinking about right now, huh?"

She reached for her notebook but stopped cold.

One of the frames moved. More than moved. It flipped back, revealing a hole, a face peering out at them. A pale woman's face, pinched tight with worry. The woman relaxed when she saw Dill.

"It's okay," she called back down into the hole. "It's just Dill and the new folks."

She crouched, swung a leg up, and stepped out. Behind her came a boy who looked to be ten or so.

Another frame moved. Another face emerged, this one a girl who looked Blue's age, her hair braided tight away from her face. She stared at Blue, studied her up and down. "Didn't know there was a boy coming."

A boy. She was pretending, and the trouble with pretending was that unless you did it constantly, unless you dedicated yourself to it, it didn't stick. She held the guitar a little more tightly and tried to imagine Teena's cousins, greasy rags in their hands as they leaned over a car engine. How would they stand? What would they do?

"He's part of the new family. The mama's little brother," the woman from the mall said.

"Whatever." The girl flicked her hand at Blue, dismissing her.

"Mama?" Lacey clung to Andrea's side. Her lower lip stuck out, and she rubbed at the hem of her jacket.

"It's okay, baby. It'll be like camping. Just for a little while."
The little girl began to cry, and Andrea hugged her tighter, the tiny
booted feet swinging.

Other people emerged as well. Women, young children, one
gangly boy who looked thirteen or so. All of them studied the newcomers with wary eyes.

Blue took her notebook out, crouched to balance the guitar on
her knees as a table.

Underground?

She held it up to Dill.

"Whoa," he said. "Can't you talk?"

She shook her head.

"No sign language, either?"

Another shake, the missing brush of hair on the nape of her
neck.

"That's rough." He studied her for a minute, as if he hadn't
really seen her before. "Yeah, so, this is literally an underground
shelter. They started digging it in the spring. One of the former
members here had some experience with building, and they found
stuff online."

Doesn't anyone notice?

Dill sucked on his lower lip. He thought before he talked, slow
and careful. "This is a wildlife sanctuary, so there's no hunting. That
was the biggest concern. But there's lots of land out here for hiking and stuff, so they just chose a place without trails, and without anything really special that would draw people to it. So far, so
good."

No way. She tried to understand what exactly she'd walked into.
Not scary, but really weird. Tunnel dwellers.

Why not regular shelters?

Surely kids didn't need to be living underground. Well, little kids. Kids who had moms.

He gave her an odd look. "What did your sister tell you?"

Right. Her sister. She looked at Andrea, wondered what she'd known in advance. More than that, wondered how Andrea had even connected with these people.

"Shelters are okay for some people. But, well, you wouldn't be able to stay with your sister in most of them. You're what, like fourteen?" She remembered all the things that made her think Steve was younger than he was, and nodded. "You'd probably be in a men's space. Unfortunately, shelters can be dangerous, too. And most of these women have other reasons to stay clear of social workers or police. They stay here and can keep their kids with them, and they share everything, and kind of police each other."

Stay clear of the police. That was why Andrea was here. For her, the chance to live underground was better than what she'd left behind.

THEY WERE ASSIGNED A HOLE. THE OTHERS CALLED IT A
unit, but she couldn't think of it as anything but a hole. The wooden
frames on the ground had canvas screens over them, and the leaves
and twigs were attached to the canvas to disguise it. Beneath lay a
tunnel that went downward at a long slow angle, eventually opening
into a wider room.

The room—it was a room, even if it had curved dirt walls and
smelled of soil, and even if the ceiling was scarcely higher than
Blue's head—had two nooks carved in the walls, with bedding laid
atop sheets of plastic. A flashlight on a length of twine hung from
the ceiling, the light shifting as it slowly revolved. Here and there
were holes, plastic tubing set at sharp angles, heading upward.

"Ventilation," Dill said. He stood close behind her. "They were
worried about the air getting stale without any exchange."

She nodded.

"See, Lacey?" Andrea, sounding the way mothers do when they
want things to seem better than they are. "It's a hobbit hole. We're
gonna be hobbits."

Lacey sniffed. "Hobbit houses don't smell like worms. And
they're warm."

"It doesn't smell like worms. And it's warm enough in here."

"It's not warm." The girl pouted.

"We'll be warm enough." Andrea sounded less than certain about that fact.

"You have the space to yourselves." The woman from the mall had followed them down. "It's below the frost line, so it stays manageably warm, and no one comes out here to bother us, long as we don't call attention. We share meals, so you got to do your part, like we talked about. And when you make plans to move on, you got to promise not to say anything about us."

Andrea nodded along. She looked like the squirrel that had once fallen from a tree onto the hood of Teena's truck: dazed, anxious, and clueless, the difference being that the squirrel had stared through the window for a moment, shaken its head, shaken its tail, and then leaped off the hood to vanish into the woods. Andrea just kept shifting and making quick little glances around them at the dirt, the plastic that hung from beneath the bedding, the imprint of a foot in the wall.

The entire space suddenly felt too small, too close, too likely to collapse on their heads. Blue pushed past everyone, headed back up the tunnel, hunched over to keep from brushing against the ceiling.

Back outside, the cold was noticeable. She kept on going, through the trees, kicking at the snow as she went. She couldn't stay underground, waiting for the next bad thing to find her in a dead-end tunnel with a little girl.

She finally stopped by a large bare tree. She knew better than to punch it. Tish had once punched a wall, and Dry Gully had sat out four weeks of shows. Hands were precious, more so when you couldn't speak.

Toes, on the other hand . . . It hurt to kick the trunk, but she didn't do any real damage to her foot or the tree. Just hard enough to knock a pile of snow down on her head.

Blue shook her head, tried to rub the snow off the back of her neck. The meltwater ran a cold river down her back.

"Snowballs are better." Dill squinted in the bright light. He held out a pair of red knit mittens. "Hands'll get cold fast, though, and it's hard to warm them up again."

She thought about the fingerless gloves, about Steve and the church basement, about playing in the park. That was what she wanted. To play. Not just to play, though. To sing.

Her guitar. She'd left it back in the room. Stupid—some lessons were impossible for her to grasp, apparently. She stepped back toward her trail.

"Sorry, did I scare you?" He held his hands up, flat, the universal symbol for *I am not going to hit you.*

She shook her head, made a strumming motion. That was probably stupid, too, to show him what she cared about. Then again, who would carry a guitar along with her everywhere if she didn't care about it?

"You really have a guitar in the case?" He followed her as she headed back.

She strummed again. To write would slow things down. *Had she set it down on the ground? Was it getting wet?*

"Cool. Hey, I have a real question for you. Can you hold up a minute?"

She didn't exactly stop, just slowed a little.

"What's your name?"

She didn't know how to mime that one out. She took out her notebook.

Interstate.

"Interstate? Cool. That's a road name. Is Andrea really your sister?"

Of course he would have noticed. Probably everyone else, too. Probably by the time she got there, they'd have thrown her guitar out in the snow.

"It's okay if she's not, at least with me. On the road, families can be all kinds of things." He sounded like Javier. It was true that she'd felt closer to Steve in just a few days than she'd felt to anyone at home for a long time. "I'm curious about your story, if you're willing to share."

She stopped walking, took her paper out.

It's a long thing. Plz don't tell anyone that Andrea's not my sis. K? Not for me, for her. Don't want her in trouble.

"No big deal. I'm just a curious guy. I like to hear stories. Like yours. Tell me something about yourself."

You 1st. The real one.

He tilted his head, considered the tree branches above him. "The one I told in the car is real."

She wiggled her fingers in a gimme sign.

"Really. Um, I'm here because I've been studying communities. People taking care of each other. Things are getting bad for folks without homes, without money. Really bad."

You have a home?

"I do. Doesn't mean I can't imagine . . ."

She stared at him, watching his face shift, twist, open.

"I have three sisters. My oldest one ended up with a bad guy, for a while. She didn't tell us, and she didn't have much help. She's okay now, but . . . I want to know what to do, you know? Plus, I don't know, last year was pretty tough, and I felt like I needed room to breathe."

She did, though. She wanted to hear everything, and not think about going back and sleeping in the ground.

Hopping trains?

He grinned. "So good. You have to try it someday. It can be dangerous, but if you're sober and careful, know what you're doing, it's more a question of watching out for people looking to mess with you. It's like being free, really free. Bothers my folks a bit, but we've talked it through. They get that I'm not buying into much of this stuff pushed on us by society."

There was something about Dill—half mysterious and half sweet—that made her want to be around him. Only she didn't really know him at all. He was just some guy who had driven her and Andrea and Lacey to the middle of nowhere and tried to get her to start a snowball fight.

Plus . . .

How old are you?

He glanced at the words sideways. "Nineteen. Why?"

No reason.

He wasn't all that old. Not that it made a difference. She didn't have time for . . . That was what she was doing, wasn't it? Almost flirting. She didn't have time to be almost flirting with an almost stranger. That was the sort of thing you did when you had a home and a family and a friend to giggle with it all about.

That was what she was doing, though.

Almost flirting.

Her guitar was where she'd left it. Not wet, not opened, not damaged in any way. Lacey perked up to see her open it, and Dill poked her again. "Come on, Interstate. Let's hear what you can do."

This time, holding the guitar felt different. Not like wood and strings. More like lips and tongue and vocal cords and air. She couldn't use her voice, and she couldn't use ASL, but she could still use her fingers to speak. Blue played a few of her usual tunes, then tried something she hardly ever did, a song her mom had written.

Soft as silence, here it comes, it went. She could hear Mama's voice, the way it caught a little on *silence. We've finally started our downhill run.*

She couldn't think about the song without remembering how, toward the end, Tish sometimes stumbled on the stage. How what had been a drink with friends became drinking after everyone else left. How she stopped staying over, sometimes stayed away for days; and how, when she was there, she and Mama fought more often than not.

Strange pick to play in her dirt home, to a little girl and a boy she secretly wanted to impress. Only, she didn't want to impress him, she wanted to speak to him, and this was the best way she could do it.

Dill sat next to Lacey on the bed, watching quietly. When Blue finished, Lacey said, somberly, "My dad isn't here."

"Nope," said Dill.

"He doesn't know where we are. It's a secret."

"Yeah, sometimes it's like that, isn't it?" Dill nudged the girl with his elbow. "What did you think about Interstate's song?"

"I think it was made out of feathers."

"Feathers, huh?"

She didn't continue, and Dill didn't push. Blue tried to imagine what a song made out of feathers meant. Was it light? Soft? Fluffy?

She didn't think so. She thought that a song made of feathers would be more like a swan—fighting to lift its body up out of the water on long, fierce wings.

DILL LEFT BEFORE DINNER. WITH HIM GONE, THE GRAY
felt grayer. Night would come, and more cold, and Blue would be
underground with her pretend family. Like moles. Or roots. Stuck
there.

In truth, the hole was better than she expected. It did smell of
earth, but it was warmer down here than above ground. And the
mat was more comfortable than sleeping on the ground. Well, tech-
nically it was *in* the ground.

It didn't matter. This was a hole, and she was there with Andrea
and Lacey, who'd started to cry at the slightest thing. She hated the
hole more than Blue did, and she hated the cold, and she hated her
mother for bringing her, and the bed for not having ladybug sheets.
Andrea waffled between forced cheer and edgy frustration, smiling
one minute and growling the next.

By the time they entered their hole for the night, Blue was
ready for sleep. They took off their coats, but left everything else on.
Andrea told Lacey a story, something about a cloud princess, and
when she finished, she got up and turned the flashlight off.

The dark swallowed them whole. Blue couldn't have found her
way out of bed, let alone out of the tunnel. Lacey whimpered.

"I'm right here," Andrea said. "Interstate's over there. He'd say hi if his throat didn't hurt. Just go to sleep, and when we wake up it will be morning and everything will be fine."

Everything wouldn't be fine. It would still be dark there, underground. They still wouldn't be home. Blue wouldn't have said that, even if she could. No reason to make things worse. That didn't mean she couldn't think it.

After a while, Andrea spoke. "I'm gonna turn the light back on for a few. She's out. Nothing wakes her when she's this tired."

A rustling noise and the sound of feet moving across the ground, slowly, carefully. Then a bright flash as she flipped the flashlight on. In the unforgiving glow, she looked tired and young. Pregnant and married when she was seventeen. Blue thought of Beck and shuddered.

Andrea came over close to Blue's bed. "You worried at all? You know, about people looking for you?"

People, no. The woman in the red dress? Yes. Then she thought of Rat, of his hands around her neck. He'd hurt her and Steve, and they'd run away. Together. This close, she could see a faint scar on Andrea's right cheek, another at the corner of her eye.

Andrea caught her look. For an instant, she looked even younger, like a child in need of a mother. Then, it was gone. "It just gets so you don't know what to do. It's not like I wanted it, you know?"

Blue shook her head, reached for her notebook.

"But, well, my mom was—" She circled her finger in the air by her ear. "Sick, you know. She, uh, so, she killed herself. After Lacey was born. So he said that it was just a matter of time. That everyone knew I'd be crazy, too."

Would she? For a moment, Blue wondered whether it was all a story Andrea made up. She could have stolen Lacey from someone.

Only, there was how Lacey rested her head against Andrea's neck, and the scars on Andrea's face, and the certainty, the absolute certainty, inside Blue, that Andrea told her the truth. She could hear the flute that played within Andrea, and never once did its music falter as she spoke.

Blue held a finger up. Andrea watched while Blue took the guitar out, strummed it softly, then launched into "Avenue A." She played as quietly as she could, thinking the whole time of watching Mama from backstage, of Andrea at ten, watching while her mother sang along with every Dry Gully song.

A fight brewed up in the morning. It had something to do with Andrea coming up late, and something to do with Lacey playing around one of the ventilation pipes to her unit, and other things that Blue didn't follow at all. Arguments, at least the ones Blue knew, usually started about something like broccoli and ended up being about hurt feelings.

This argument started with what might happen if a vent was blocked, and moved on to whether it was right to take in a girl from Chicago when there was a girl living under a bridge nearby whose boyfriend had threatened her life twice and stabbed her once. It ended when Andrea lifted her shirt with her back to them, exposing fine white scars that spelled out MINE across her ribs.

Lacey had been stomping the snow into slush. Blue grabbed her hand and led her back into the tunnel, as Andrea, her face gone red, walked off into the trees. Once inside, Blue took out her guitar and tried to think of fun songs. Lacey listened for a while, eventually growing bored and heading out again.

Blue stayed behind. Something Lacey had said yesterday had stuck with her, rubbing against her thoughts. A song made of feathers. She didn't know anything that sounded like that, not to her, at least. No song of her mom's, or Tish's, or anyone else's. She kept playing around, trying to find a sound that worked.

The feeling was about more than just chords. The swan was in her, long feathers tickling at the tips of her fingers, muscles stirring along her back. She put the guitar down, picked up her notebook.

She'd seen her mom and Tish work on songs together, but it was just something they did, like dishes. She hadn't listened closely enough. They'd bounce music back and forth between them, or one of them would hum the tune, the other test out the words. Always together. But that had to be the end of the process, not the beginning. Where did it start?

She didn't even know what she wanted to write. There was just a line stuck in her head, and as silly as it felt, she wrote it down.

I got a dollar in my pocket, fifty cents of that is yours.

Okay. What now? She looked at the words for a few minutes. She felt like a fake, but also real, as if she had something true to say.

I got a dollar in my pocket, fifty cents of that is yours.

I got a sleeping bag in my pack with room for just one more.

By themselves, the words were lonely. They needed music to tell listeners how to hear them. But she didn't know how to write songs. When Cass made up songs, they were about the hot guy showing up at Ren's Pizza, and she sang them in that voice all the boys loved. What Blue heard inside sounded nothing like that.

It sounded like feathers growing through skin.

BLUE STAYED AWAY DURING LUNCH. SHE WALKED OUT
along the trail instead, took a turn out into the field, and wandered
for a while. Everywhere the landscape looked the same. Snow,
trees, flat open spaces with tufts of grass accenting the snow.
Clouds. Animal tracks here and there, tiny ones, mice or squir-
rels, and bigger ones, metronome steady, from a fox. She followed
the fox, clumsily sinking deep behind the dainty steps. Clumsy,
always, but alone, too, one more creature wandering toward its
solitary destination.

"Hey."

Or maybe not so solitary. She turned. Dill waved, his breath
cottony steam around his face. The snow hid no one's trails, the
fox's or hers.

He walked to her, steady on his feet despite the snow. His
cheeks were flushed, and he looked younger than he was, like one
of the little kids from the holes.

There had to be a different name for them than the holes. She
felt in her pocket, found nothing there. Her notebook was back with
her guitar. A moment or two of silent cursing, then she reached
down and began to make lines in the snow. He watched, silent,
intent, until she'd finished.

"The holes? It's called Beyond."

She raised her shoulders in a question.

"Like, going beyond where everyone else is? Americans have all these lines, like, all life takes place within certain boxes. And people who live beyond that, people who don't have homes, or who choose not to have homes, people who don't look or act or have the same things as we believe they should—well, they become invisible."

Blue pulled one glove off and splayed her fingers. Her skin was pale, the veins blue beneath, but solid nonetheless.

Dill nodded. "That's the thing. You know you're real. Everyone in Beyond is real. How do we make everyone see everyone else? 'Cause without that, we're never gonna figure things out."

The desire to talk came like a wave, swamping her, working through a thousand tiny cracks she never knew she had. So many things to say, and only her hands to use and the snow to write on.

"Listen." Dill's eyes were dark, his eyelashes darker, stretching out in fine black arcs. "I want to take you somewhere."

She must have frowned, because he studied her face, spoke slowly, trying to be offhand but deeply serious. "It's . . . Is it me? Did something happen? I'm not going to hurt you at all, but I know you don't have any reason to believe that. Except, well, I don't know what I could tell you that would make you trust me. My mom would say I'm ninety-nine percent curious and one percent stubborn, which is dangerous mostly to me."

What did he see when he looked at her? How she wasn't a boy, how bad things followed her, how the people she cared about left her, one way or another, and she had just one chance to change that?

Only, Steve hadn't left her. She'd left him.

"What do you think?"

She looked across the snow, the light hurting her eyes. She couldn't stay, not for long, not anywhere, not even in a hole. But Dill didn't feel dangerous. Not even a little.

"It involves music," he wheedled.

She stuck her finger in the snow, wrote with an icicle hand. *OK.*

Dill wouldn't tell her where they were going, just that she needed her guitar. They took a long route hiking through the snow, the minivan a welcome relief by the time it came into view.

Blue leaned to catch sight of herself in the side mirror as they drove. Someone else—a boy with a shorn head and long-lashed eyes and a pimple on his chin—stared back at her. It figured she could lose everything else and still have acne find her address.

They drove for a long time, long enough that she started to wonder whether Dill was like Florida, whether he was returning her to Rat on a route of all back roads. *She should have been more scared,* she thought. In books, in movies, bad things happened, and then you were scarred for life, always afraid, until someone good came along and took care of you.

But inside, she felt numb rather than scared. Not sad, not happy, just dull, like the walls of the tunnel—solid, brown, impervious to everything. She wasn't scared of Dill because she couldn't be. Aside from the desire to talk when he'd found her earlier, she hadn't really felt much since leaving Chicago.

They stopped at yet another middle-of-nowhere destination. They'd followed wheel ruts up to a farmhouse. A few other cars were parked there, and a large white van trimmed with rust, but the windows of the house were boarded shut and the front door was padlocked.

Exactly the kind of place you might bring someone to murder them. The fear still didn't come, though, and she got out of the car, guitar in hand, and followed him.

He didn't go to the house. Instead, he followed a path around the back. There, the footprints in the snow spread out, leading across a field. The sun was setting, and all Blue could make out was a large gray lump. Another minute of walking, and she recognized the outline of a large barn.

A barn full of people. Musicians, the air full of the twangs of tuning instruments. An old woodstove in the middle of the space, the stovepipe running up and out the roof, a pot of something on the cookplate, the area around the stove cordoned off with what looked like bits of chain-link fence and pieces of guardrail. A woman with cornrows and work boots and a calico skirt over jeans paced off a space that seemed meant for a dance floor, drawing lines in the dirt.

"I told you you'd like it." Dill grinned, as if the scene made immediate sense. She looked to her left as a man wearing a worn overcoat lit a lantern, the sudden glow illuminating a mouth mostly empty of teeth.

What is this?

Her pen caught a little, the ink not flowing smoothly. A pencil would be better, though she'd have to sharpen it all the time.

"Music. Dancing. Light." He pointed at the lantern, at the many lanterns hung from rafters. "Food. Company. Magic."

Not long after, the emcee took the floor. It was the same woman who'd marked out the dance floor. She had a deep voice, rich as a cup of melted butter, dark skin, topaz eyes.

"Welcome to Barn Magic," she said, glancing around the crowd that had gathered. "I could say a whole lotta things here, but this isn't the time, is it?"

A chorus of "Hell, no!" and "We're here to play!" greeted her. She grinned, widely enough to show she was missing teeth, too, a few along one side.

"Didn't think so, beauties, didn't think so at all. Just gonna run down the rules, though, case anyone's forgotten them. This is a squeaky clean event, my friends. What that means is, if y'all feel a need to do something to drown this here experience, you gotta go. No drink, no drugs, no disrespect to anyone you see here. Understand?"

More shouting, an ocean of good-natured joshing that the emcee smiled through. "Chili's here on the stove. You got something to share, something to add to the pot, you come right up here and add it. You been hungry, you come and take some. No one here gonna begrudge you any of it. We all been hungry, every single one of us." Her eyes lit on Blue for a moment, held her steady in their gaze. "We all know what it's like to need. And as for the rest," she said, turning a full 360 to look at her congregation, "those rules are simple. Play like this is the end, and like it's the beginning. Play your story, and don't leave out none of the pieces. Remember that the devil is the one who tells you to play a tune that's not your own, and you can drive him right on out into the cold by playing what's in your soul. Begin."

Blue felt as though someone had wrapped her in the warmest coat she'd ever worn, raised her right up into the summer sun. It didn't matter that she was a stranger here; she knew she belonged.

At first, the music was a little of everything, as individuals stood up and did short solos. Voice, fiddle, guitar, rhythm played on legs, on buckets, on spoons. Instruments—there were far fewer of them than of players—were passed freely through the crowd. Some players were more skilled than others, but everyone was applauded.

After a while, there were hands on Blue's back, urging her forward. She'd never played in front of a real crowd, especially not in front of musicians, and she hesitated, right up until the emcee crooked her finger at her.

"Here we have Little Boy Blue." Blue looked straight at her, a razor shot of fear zipping through her before she realized she had the blue peacoat on. "What you got inside you to show us?"

She had a glimpse of faces, of shadows stretching up the walls, of her own fingers trembling as she tried to tune the guitar. She tried to think of anything Mama might have said about playing for real, but she'd never given Blue any instructions about it. Tish, on the other hand, had told her that when she was starting out she'd coped by imagining she was playing for a candle flame. So that was what Blue thought of, the way a flame bends with a breeze, with breath, how the color changes from base to tip. *Candle, candle, candle,* she thought, until the guitar was ready.

She launched into "Bluebird" without even thinking. Every now and then she caught her lips moving, singing words that didn't come. All the way through, ending with a little flourish, something she'd made up.

Everyone clapped. She felt she'd never heard applause before, never understood it at all. It reverberated inside her, shook everything loose from the shelves she'd tucked it away on. It wasn't until she'd made her way back to Dill that she realized she was crying.

"Okay?" He touched the skin beneath her right eye, gentle as snow.

It made her cry more. She kept on crying, through the rest of the talent show, right on into the break as people ate chili from paper cups, and a band formed at the front of the barn. Dill didn't say more. He just stood beside her, his hand brushing hers, almost like he was holding it. She didn't want anything more, just the bump of his skin against hers from time to time.

She finally took her notebook back out of her pocket.

Weirdest date ever, right? ☺

He read the words, looked at her, puzzled. Not puzzled like someone trying to understand something theoretical; more, he seemed confused right down deep inside. She remembered who she was supposed to be, who he really was.

"Interstate, I . . . I . . . This . . ." Before he could go further, a banjo kicked into high gear. The emcee was fronting the band, her hands bringing the banjo to life. The crowd pushed out toward the walls as dancers took to the floor.

Why had she said date? She knew it wasn't like that. Homeless kids drifting along didn't have dates. Or did they? Being lost, being scared, that didn't make everything else go away. Even Anne Frank, locked up in those secret rooms somewhere, had had a crush, had been kissed. Not having an address didn't take away your right to want to be in love.

An older woman came by and took Dill's hand; off they went, dancing some country step that Blue didn't know. Same with the next dance, and the next, and soon Blue settled back into the shadows and watched.

After a while, a new group arrived. Two women and two men, all nicely dressed. The banjo woman nodded when she saw them, played through to the end of the song, and then stopped. "We're gonna break for a few and let our good friends from Emmie's do their work."

One of the newcomers moved forward, up to the spot the band had vacated. She cleared her throat, the sound lost amid the conversations and restless feet. The banjo woman reappeared, put two fingers in her mouth, and gave a piercing whistle. The other woman smiled at her.

"I think most of you know us and are familiar with the resources in the area." She was tall, straight-backed, hands moving as she spoke. "Those of you here tonight must not be staying in shelters, because you've all missed curfew."

A few boos, a few hoots. She studied the crowd before continuing. "We've been working on some of the issues brought up in our meeting. Bedbugs are better in some facilities—"

"It's not just bedbugs," a woman shouted from the back of the room. "You try getting rid of lice if you got no space to call your own."

"Not just that," a man chimed in. "Try getting anyone to take you in for a night or two if you got bugs. Just not happening."

A buzz of agreement. The woman at the front nodded. "We understand that. That's why we're trying to address your concerns everywhere, not just with one or two locations. In the meantime, we're concerned about the number of you who are staying out in the cold. Winter's come early, and hard. Snow tonight, snow tomorrow, big storm coming."

"Ain't snowing in here. Downright hot," someone shouted, and the applause spread through the barn.

"Can't stay here permanently," the banjo woman called. "Barn Magic works because we come and go."

"It's a crime, though, leaving these houses to fall apart, when we could be living in them."

The long-haired woman smiled again. "The politics need to hold off for now. We're focused on keeping everyone warm and alive through the winter."

"Ain't politics when you're the one without," corrected the banjo woman. "It's life."

The long-haired woman nodded. "You're right. Bad choice of words."

The banjo woman spoke again. "Emmie's House does good work, folks. Y'all know that. We gotta correct them when they're wrong, but we do it with love."

Then Dill was at Blue's shoulder, leading her to the line for food. Some people had brought cups of their own; some had plastic spoons with their name written on the handle. Blue took a paper cup from a woman with a ladle and ate the chili quickly, wolfishly hungry.

The music began again, a new song, sweet and slow, starting up. She took Dill's hand.

"Um, listen, you're a lot younger and—"

She pulled him, ignoring the words, thinking instead about the feel of his palm on hers. The air around the dancers smelled of bodies, of smoke, of earth and dust and snow. She put Dill's hand on her hip, ignoring everything but what she could feel: the solidity of his back under her touch, the quick breath he took when she rested her head against his shoulder, when she leaned close. The music within him, like bagpipes over hills, calling, searching.

"Interstate?"

She didn't lift her head. There was no time for everything that would have to happen if they talked. Instead, there was now, this moment, the music and the warmth and being alive, so alive that her entire body sang, too, a song she was sure he could hear.

BLUE AND DILL DANCED TO EVERY SONG FROM THAT POINT on, winging arms, wiggling hips, laughing at each other. Finally, as more and more people settled into the old horse stalls, bundled together in groups of three to four, they held hands and made for the door.

A hand on Blue's arm stopped her in her tracks. The banjo woman's topaz eyes were even paler in the waning light as the lanterns were turned down.

"You two gonna take care, right? You know about the roads, about the Traveler, know not to take rides with anyone you don't know?"

A swirl of air brought with it the smell of smoke, of heat, of sweetness and loss. Blue stared at the woman, not sure how she'd missed it before. Was this a threat or a warning? Had the woman in the red dress been here all along, or had she simply taken control of the emcee in the same way she'd taken Blue's voice?

Dill answered her. "We're fine. I'm driving. We're safe."

Someone called to the emcee and she turned away. Blue looked at Dill, eyebrows raised.

"The word is that there's someone killing street kids. It's been happening for years, but it's getting worse. They call him the

Traveler cause he passes through a lot of places." He glanced back. "Hang on a minute. I'll be right back."

Blue stood by the door. Someone killing street kids. When she left Maine, she wouldn't have thought twice about that. Now, it raised the hair on her arms.

She looked back toward the dance floor. What light remained shone on a small group of musicians. None looked familiar. They must have all come late, and they played quietly now, people walking past them. A little man strummed guitar, his build as wiry as his hair. Something was painted on his instrument. She moved a few steps closer to see.

"This Machine Kills Fascists." It was a weird thing to paint on a guitar, but she kind of liked it. It made the music feel tough, like Rosie the Riveter flexing her muscles in that old poster.

Dill reappeared and led her out the door. Blue wanted more light, some way to communicate. Up in the sky stretched a band of stars like a crack in the night; and for a moment, her voice showed through there. She almost believed that if she could reach high enough, hold on hard enough, she could drag it back through to her. She held one hand up, but saw only her fingers.

She played with the radio as they drove back, looking for a song that summed things up, only she'd never heard a song that encompassed "the night you thought I was a fifteen-year-old boy hitting on you and I turned out to be a seventeen-year-old girl." It wasn't until they reached the parking spot for Beyond that she pushed away her jitters and touched his wrist.

He turned slowly. "Listen, Interstate—"

She leaned over, bumped against his shoulder, managed to get her lips half on his cheek, half on his mouth. He didn't move either closer or away—just held steady until she pulled back.

"Crap," he said at last.

She opened the door and stepped out. She didn't know what she was doing. Better to get back to Andrea, scurry down into the hole, hide there until it was time to leave.

"Wait."

She paused.

"I . . . This is really confusing. And wrong, wrong is the biggest thing. You're a lot younger than I am, and you're in a bad place. I guess I've been making things worse. I brought you tonight because . . . I think I'm as confused as you. You keep feeling different to me. Like someone older. I should probably just go."

She hadn't expected Dill to be the one fumbling for words. For once the lack of a voice appealed to her. She could think about what to say, rather than charge in.

She went back to the car, opened a door for some light, wrote quickly.

I'm a girl. 17. Thought it would be safer to travel like this.

He ran his hand through his hair. "Um. Well. Do you have a real name, too?"

It's a secret. Someday, if you're lucky.

More important, if she was.

"Okay. Okay, this night has been—" He stopped talking and took a step toward her. "Can we try this all again? Starting right about the point where you asked me to dance?"

She cupped her ear.

"No music? That's easy enough." Dill hummed at first, then started to sing. "Waltzing Matilda"—a little weird, but that was okay. He put his hand on her back, the other on her hip, and moved them through the snow. His voice vanished as he leaned close and touched his lips to hers, warm and cold all at once.

No, it didn't matter if you had an address, a name, anything. You didn't need anything but another person to feel love.

The next morning she woke, groggy and grumpy, then remembered dancing with Dill.

"You were out late" was all Andrea said as she helped Lacey get her boots on before heading up.

Blue nodded. She took out her guitar, her mind on Dill and Barn Magic. Lacey was fussing for the outside, and Andrea nudged her toward the door.

Blue plucked a string or two. A kiss. Just one kiss, one simple little thing, but it made her feel different. Her lips tightened into a smile as she strummed. He'd be back in the afternoon, and she had something she wanted to play for him. Time to practice. First, she needed a capo.

She opened the little box inside the case. The capo was there. Her keepsake bag wasn't.

Fuck. If she could have screamed it, she would have. Was it at the barn? Had it fallen out there? Or while she was dancing—had someone stolen it out of the case? It wasn't as though anything in it was of importance to anyone other than her.

It was hers, though. Her past. Her things. Her only means of identifying herself.

The license.

If someone had stolen the bag, then someone knew her name. She put the guitar down, reached for a boot. She'd put them on, go up, figure out whether there was some way to contact Dill, get him to take her back to the barn.

As she tightened the laces, she glanced at her pillow. A fine line of red velvet showed like blood beneath it. Her bag.

She grabbed it and dumped the contents out. Everything was

there. All of it. It must have fallen out yesterday, before she left, and she just hadn't noticed it. Andrea had picked it up and put it under her pillow.

Right?

Only, inside something gnawed at her, something with the soft clicking teeth of the man in the blue shirt. Had Andrea looked inside? Fury hit Blue like a storm channeled straight into the hole. One kiss. It wasn't fair. She'd gotten one kiss and now she'd have to leave, because of Andrea's snooping.

The anger pulsed through her, head to toe, as she left the tunnel. Andrea, digging into things when she shouldn't, being nosy. She had no right to do that.

Andrea was heating water on the little cookstove outside. Blue balanced her guitar on her toes while she wrote.

You looked in my bag?

Andrea looked hurt. "No. Lacey found it, and we put it on your bed."

You sure?

"No. It belongs to you."

Just as fast, the relief came. She picked up her guitar, a little light-headed as she bent over. Dill would come, and she still had weeks, and everything would be fine.

"But . . . the first day, when you were asleep in the car." Not anger this time. Dread. "I looked at your license. It was sticking out of your pocket, and I was curious. I know who you are, Blue."

Too many days. Too many, she didn't even need to count. She could feel it the way dogs feel thunder coming, the way leaves feel the winter's approach.

She ran. She didn't even know where, just ran, hitting a tree as she went. Andrea yelled behind her, and the guitar bounced in its case, and she just kept going. *I'm leaving, I'm leaving, let them be.*

She bounced into someone. The woman from the mall called out, startled, as Blue continued past. Running on and on before finally pausing to lean against a tree as she tried to catch her breath.

Then the crunch of feet in crusty snow. Voices. Men, uniforms, a group, almost to the camp. Her with no voice to scream, to warn. One male voice carried loud through the cold, followed by a wail: the sort of sound that surrounds a heart and stops it, even if you don't know the source of the pain.

And if you do?

Blue ran again. Away, through the trees, out into the snowfield. Her fault. She'd brought this on them. Lacey would be returned to her father. Andrea would go to jail, because who would believe the daughter of a crazy woman against a family of cops.

And it was her fault. Blue's. The one who'd left her license where it could be seen. The one who'd stayed when she should have gone.

By the time she reached the road, her lungs burned. She knelt in the snow, coughing. Her knees were wet when she stood, the wind cutting through the damp patches as if she wore nothing.

She wanted to run back, do something, but what? She couldn't stop what was happening. In fact, she could only make it worse. The woman in the red dress would destroy them all.

She'd lost everything that mattered. Mama. Cass. Home. Her voice. More, too—Steve, she'd lost him, and Dill, and Tish long ago. Lost, over and over. All she'd wanted was the chance to see Cass again, to hear her say *I missed you, I forgive you.*

Cass had left because Blue found the letters, read through them all. Blue had run into their room with them, told Cass that her father was Rick Rafael, lead singer for Device. He was the epitome of a rock star—and as unlike Mama as Blue could imagine. Only, Cass had wanted to see the letters, had latched on to what Blue had overlooked.

"He said he'd pay for everything. He said he'd take her on the road with Device." Fury had made Cass red, her makeup obvious on the scarlet sea. "But she talked it over with Tish and they'd decided together. Fucking Tish. We could have had anything we wanted if Mama hadn't been selfish and stupid in every way, if she hadn't picked Tish over my father . . ."

Father. That was the word that had broken Cass's voice, the one that had made her lock Blue out of the bedroom for the rest of the day. If Blue hadn't opened the sealed envelope, if she hadn't wanted to show off, hadn't wanted to make a crack in the glossy surface of her sister—if she hadn't done it, Cass would never have left.

An oil slick of disaster trailed behind her. It had to stop. She had to stop. Inside her was a road map: every wrong turn she'd made in life highlighted in red; every person she'd hurt, or who had left her, lit like stoplights she'd ignored. She wanted to peel her skin away, open herself up to the elements until she was nothing more than bones by the side of the road. Bones couldn't hurt, could they?

She didn't hold a thumb out to the first two cars that passed. She didn't need to. Her ride was coming. She could feel it.

The third car drove slowly. The silver sedan was piloted by an older man with a graying crew cut who looked her over as he pulled to a stop.

"Where you headed?"

Above her, a wall of clouds was spreading across the blue. More snow coming. She balanced the notebook on her knee, wrote quickly, the only possible answer.

Wyoming.

37

HE SAID NOTHING WHEN SHE SHOWED HIM THE NOTE explaining that she couldn't talk. He just kept the radio on, tuned to Christian music. Not pop, like what Cynthia had listened to on the drive to Chicago. No, this was hard-core, hymns sung by choirs, sometimes by soloists, often sounding as though they'd been recorded with a tape recorder set up in a basement. He shook his head when the DJs broke in, though they were less like announcers and more like preachers, talking about God and hell and the wages of sin.

The wages of sin fit perfectly with her mind-set. She kept hearing Andrea's scream, thinking about Lacey in her mother's arms, the scars on Andrea's face. She could write sorry endlessly, in blood, and never even come close to what she was feeling.

The man stopped for gas in the afternoon. She left the guitar in his car while she went into the rest-stop bathroom, ignored her hunger as she passed the racks of candy and chips in the store. Hunger had become part of her penance. If she shed everything, every little piece of herself, maybe the woman in the red dress would show Andrea mercy.

On the way out, she took her license out of her pocket and dropped it in the trash. No one would learn her name again, not without her giving it.

Somewhere in South Dakota it started to snow. Not hard, just steady, white flakes flying against the window. They stopped again, another gas station, and she watched the man eat a hamburger from a paper bag.

"Guess you don't need anything," he said after his first bite. "What I've seen is that the Lord provides for those who need it. If you don't have anything, that generally means you don't need it, or you don't deserve it. You understand that fact?"

She nodded. It made perfect sense. She didn't have anything because she didn't deserve it.

By that logic, Steve didn't deserve a home, and Andrea didn't deserve to love her daughter and be safe. Mama didn't deserve her life.

Blue shook her head. No thinking. Thinking meant asking him where they were going, piecing things together, getting out of the car with her guitar and figuring out what to do. She didn't want to.

She fell asleep with her cheek pressed against the window. By the time she woke, it was dark. The snow was coming much thicker, a solid sheet rather than individual stars. The headlights didn't illuminate much ahead of them, and the car shimmied as it went.

"It's not the way people think," the man said abruptly.

She rubbed her eyes and looked into the night, at the clock on the dashboard. They'd been traveling nearly twelve hours. A highway sign, barely visible through the blur, alerted her that they'd left South Dakota behind and were now in Wyoming.

"People always get things wrong. They think they know, and they never do. You understand that, don't you?"

Usually Blue woke slowly, her head fogged in until she'd been up for a bit. Not now. The world seemed much clearer, more focused, than it had been earlier. Her feet throbbed in her boots, and her stomach growled, and the blanket of self-pity she'd settled under had shrunk to the size of a place mat.

"They think it's about punishment. That's just plain wrong. It's about freedom from punishment."

It sounded as though he'd been talking for a while. The fear she should have felt back when he stopped for her, the fear Lou the truck driver had told her about, that she had felt at Barn Magic when she heard about the Traveler—now she could feel it. Loud and clear.

"That's the thing. When I first heard the call, I said it was too much. It wasn't right to ask me to do it. Then I realized it wasn't my right to choose or not choose. He'd tapped my shoulder and asked me to help, and I had to do his bidding."

Blue scrawled a note out, held it up. He paid her no mind. "It's the children, you see. Children like you. They want to find their way to Him, only they can't. The world's so full of the devil that it blinds them, makes it so they can't see the road signs. That's what I can do. I can open the way for them. It's like the light comes all the way down, deep inside me, and I show them. I free them."

The wind spun the snow around them, drove it against the windows, horizontally over the road. She didn't even know for sure they were on a road anymore. Snow in the headlights, snow stretching flat before them.

As if he were listening to her thoughts, he nodded. "Hard to tell where we're going. I can make the path clear for you, though. I'm here to help you find your way home."

The blinker ticked. Turning where, into what? The snow swirled, pulling back long enough to expose a sign, but not long enough to let her read it. The car bumped along for another ten minutes or so. The man continued to talk, rambling around and around the same points while her skin crawled with the sensation of a thousand millipedes.

Finally, the car came to a stop. She could see nothing but snow from the windows, the dark close around them, the headlights showing only white.

"I can see you understand. Maybe not totally, but enough that I can help you. I felt the light inside of me as soon as I saw you. Can you feel it, too? Can you?"

He leaned toward her. She recoiled, a thud as her head hit the window behind her. He didn't touch her. Instead, he opened the glove compartment and took a cloth bundle out.

"You're a lamb in a den of wolves," he said. His eyes were wide open, not cold, not cruel, not really even there. "Years ago, God asked that I find the lambs and free them from the evil of this world. God's work. If it weren't, I wouldn't have been able to keep doing it, would I?"

She shook her head. He seemed so calm. That was good, it had to be. Calm people didn't do terrible things. Her gut was quick to call that a lie. Creepy overrode calm every time.

He reached one hand out and touched her cheek gently, as though afraid of leaving a stain. She felt as though she were watching the two of them from some other place—above, outside the car.

"Lamb, I can help you. I can make the suffering go." As he spoke, he began to unravel the cloth from the object he held. She couldn't look away. The wind howled outside the car, shaking it.

"You've been born into a world of sin and you don't deserve it. I can lift you right out. I've got the light. Can you see it?" He opened his eyes a little wider, leaned forward. The odor of hamburger and ketchup drifted by, but no light shone from him.

He sat back up. The cloth fell away. She almost didn't recognize what she saw. A hunting knife, clean, the handle worn.

"We can pray together."

She heard a click, like two ends of a wire meeting. She leaned back, kicked out with one booted foot. His head thudded back against the glass, the knife blade catching the fabric of her pants. He moved slowly, free hand reaching toward the back of his head, as she threw open her door. She grabbed the guitar, the case catching on the seat until she yanked it free.

The snow reached above her knees. She ran as well as she could; it was like sprinting through ocean waves, only the wind screamed over this ocean and there was no way to swim.

"Come back!" he screamed into the wind. "Let me free you."

She believed she could hear him behind her, his breath as loud as the wind. She kept going, hoping that he was far away from her, that it was her own breath sounding in her ears.

She stumbled and fell twice. Each time she jumped up again, kept moving. *Run, just keep running.* Now and then she thought she saw a light. She would have run toward it, but she thought about how he said a light shone through him, and she kept moving, away.

She fell again, flat out. Pain flared in her ankle. She opened her mouth to cry out and instead inhaled a mouthful of snow.

From somewhere to her left she heard him call: "Come, lamb, come to me. Let me end your suffering."

She sank into the snow. It melted around her, cool and then cold, her heat dissipating in it. Waiting, waiting, the wind, the snow, the silence, somewhere his footsteps coming toward her? Away? At one point she heard his voice again, muffled this time, as if spoken through a scarf wound several layers thick. She couldn't understand the words, couldn't even tell whether they were words or merely sounds spewed out into the dark. Perhaps what she heard was not even a voice; perhaps it was the sound of the wind playing a human body like a harp.

Eventually there was no sound at all beyond the rise and fall of the wind. She'd been cold, but the heat started returning to her. She felt cozy, even, as though this were a place she could curl up in and rest.

Lying still was good. Lying still kept her out of the wind.

But lying still also meant letting the snow steal all her warmth. She had to move.

Blue stood, with effort. The wind bit into her instantly, hungry, relentless. It hurt to be upright.

But it didn't matter that the woman in the red dress was out there, or that the man in the blue shirt was. It didn't matter if all she had left of life was months. She wanted it.

Move. Her brain was thick as her fingers. She had to move, but where? Snow surrounded her, and somewhere out there was a man with a knife. She held the guitar case against her body, where it blocked the wind. Somewhere ahead was light. It flickered in the storm. At first, she thought it was the crew-cut man's headlights, but it was too high.

She shook her head. *Think clearly. Walk toward the light.*

Move. She forced one leg after the other toward the light. Once she reached it, she could sleep.

She managed to continue until she hit something that didn't move. Not a wall. More like seaweed. Its tendrils wrapping around her, pulling her down. She fell forward, one hand out, felt something tear at her palm.

Up. Relax her hand, hold it to her face. She could taste blood on her lips. She reached out gingerly and touched barbed wire. A fence, a light—she had to be headed toward a house. To reach it she had to get by the fence, though. Over or around—which would it be?

Around it was. One hand out, she began to walk along the fence. She'd made it only four steps when something grabbed her ankle.

She swung her leg. "Lamb," came the voice from below her. "Come, lamb, do not fight. Do you see the light, see it inside me? It's not too late, not yet." She could hear struggle in the words, as if he were drowning in the snow.

She saw nothing. She gave another swift kick, then raised her other leg and pushed down on the hand.

"Lamb," he said again, gurgling as if waves filled his mouth.

She could feel his fingers peeling away beneath her foot. She swung the other leg again, and it came free. She ran: stumbling, wading, listening. Again: "Lamb." This time it was faint, barely audible above the wind.

She had to keep moving. She pressed along the fence, to where the top strand dipped a little. Climbing over felt impossible, but she pressed on, dragging one foot and then the other over the top. From there, all that was left was to find the source of the light.

She knew after a while that she wouldn't make it. It was too far, too cold, she was too weak. Better to lie down at last and relax in the drifts. She came to believe there were others in the snow with her. Girls she didn't know, and boys, wearing ragged clothes; in their eyes, she could see light. She knew they wanted her to find her way.

Eventually even they faded from view. The world became a tunnel with salvation at one end and her at the other. It never came any closer, no matter how she tried. She sang, or it seemed she sang, "Bluebird" tumbling from her lips like water. The snow bounced off her eyes, fell into her mouth, consumed her with unabated glee.

She shattered when she hit the wall. She'd watched Beck clean fish before, the knife separating the meat from the bones, leaving only raggedness behind. That was how it felt—as though her flesh were coming away, with only torn pieces remaining.

A wall meant the possibility of a door, of heat and light and safety. She punched the wood, only capable of a dull thud. *I give up.* There was nothing to be done. It was too much, had been all along. The woman in the red dress had known that when she sent Blue out.

One thought bubbled up from the wasteland within: *Fuck the woman in the red dress.* She wanted her life, all of it. She wanted her voice, to use however she chose. She wanted to see Steve again, and Cass, and Dill. She wanted to ride trains across country the way Dill had. She wanted to see everything turn from snow to sun.

She inched along the wall. Something rattled by her shoulder, wood bumping against wood as the wind howled. She rubbed her numb hands across it, found a handle, and pulled. It opened, and she toppled inside.

It was dark but dry, and it smelled of hay. As she leaned back against another wall, she felt the tickle of whiskers on the back of her neck. She couldn't jump—couldn't really move at all—just reached with one hand to touch the soft muzzle.

Please, she thought, and sank to the floor.

BLUE AWOKE TO SUNLIGHT, A DOOR SWINGING OPEN, AND
the wet press of a dog's nose against her face. She raised an arm to
protect herself, then let it fall from fatigue.

A body crouched beside hers. She smelled something familiar.

"Who the hell are you?" She'd know that voice anywhere—the
rasp that followed her from turntable to YouTube to here, wherever
here was.

She lifted her hand again, trying to reach for the face she couldn't
open her eyes to see. It was captured by gloved hands—then, gloves
gone, by warm skin. The fingers probed carefully, examining the
ring on her finger.

"Jesus Christ," the voice said. "Blue?"

For a moment, as she woke, she believed it had all been a dream.
It had to have been, for she lay in a warm bed, not out in the snow.

Then she saw the woman in the rocking chair beside the bed.

Tish's short hair was shot through with gray, and she seemed
smaller than Blue remembered, but there was no doubt. Especially
once she spoke.

"I think you've thawed out enough to survive. That's a hell of
an entrance."

She stood, leaned over Blue. There were fine lines in the creases around her eyes, in the skin on her neck. "I'll bring you some tea in a bit. Go back to sleep if you can."

The next time she woke, Tish was reading in the chair. When Blue moved, she looked up. "You ready to tell me how you turned up in my barn in the middle of a blizzard?"

How had she? The snow had been a monster, holding her in its palm, trying to crush her. Only, no, it hadn't been the snow. It had been . . . Blue touched her throat with one hand, mimed writing.

"Since when can't you talk?"

There wasn't time for questions. The man was still out there somewhere. Blue clasped her hands together, then pretended to write again. Tish shrugged.

"You have a hell of a lot of explaining to do. Lynne know where you are?" Tish took a pen and paper from a desk at the far end of the room. She handed them to Blue.

Where to start? With the most urgent, she supposed. She scribbled out a few lines about hitching a ride with a man who'd tried to kill her.

Tish read it and raised an eyebrow. Blue waited for the words to sink in.

Apparently there was nowhere for them to sink. Tish shook her head. "Kid, take a look out there." She rose, pulled the curtains back on the window. It was hard to make anything out at first. The light seared her eyes, fell from the sky and rose from the snow in equal measure. When she was able to see clearly, all there was was snow: drifted, unbroken white for as far as she could see.

"A storm like that is rare around here. It's hard to survive it. Not sure how you did."

Blue gripped her pen more tightly.

Has she been here?

Tish tilted her head. "Her? Who?"

She hadn't. There wouldn't be a question if she had. The Gully ended here, where Tish had started. Blue had traveled all the space between Mama and Tish and hadn't found Cass anywhere.

"Who, Blue?" A little more force now.

Cass.

It wasn't easy to explain Cass, or to summarize nine years of life. Especially with a mind too tired to spell, let alone arrange words in recognizable patterns. Blue left out almost everything, except that she was looking for Cass, that she'd run away from an old man into the snow and found her way to the barn.

By the end, she was falling asleep. Tish pulled the blankets up higher, paused, patted them. "Sleep, kid. There'll be plenty of time to talk."

By the time she had the energy to move around the house, four days had passed. She celebrated by showering. It felt like washing off more than just dirt. The peace she'd found in Tish's bed, the dreams she'd had—they swirled down the drain with the water. By the time she exited the bathroom, dressed in Tish's sweats, and joined her in the sunlit kitchen, she knew she had to start dealing with things.

Tish had given her an accounting pad to use. Blue stared at it. She'd slept her way through four days. Tish knew her name. How was it that she hadn't suffered the wrath of the woman in the red dress? The right thing to do would be to thank Tish for the shelter, pick up her guitar, and head on out the door.

But she didn't want to go. She had no money, no clothes, no

ride. She wasn't even sure where the road was. And she was still tired, even after all that sleep. All she wanted was to go back upstairs and nestle down into the bed and close her eyes.

Instead, she sat at the table. Tish was already there. A pair of reading glasses was perched on her nose, and she sipped coffee from a mug streaked with the rosy colors of a sunset. How had she become old? She was just another woman with short graying hair and glasses.

How had she gotten to be old when Mama hadn't? How was that possibly fair?

"The police stopped by, Blue." She said *police* as if it were two words, emphasis on *po*. "Apparently there was a dead man in one of my snowbanks. An old guy who parked his car and got out while wearing the wrong clothes for a blizzard. He got snagged on a fence and froze up."

The Traveler. She'd kept going, but he hadn't. She thought of the faces that had lit the snow as she ran. The kids he'd murdered, she believed, there to see her to safety. He was done; he'd never kill another person. For once, she was grateful for the storm.

"You're safe, Blue. No one's gonna bother you here. I promise."

I may be safe, but you're not. She looked at Tish, solid, not dead, not hurt, not even looking regretful. *No one around me is.*

THAT AFTERNOON TISH HANDED BLUE A DIRTY BARN COAT
and a pair of work gloves and told her to come out to the barn. She
didn't want to—didn't want to ever go outside again—but she did.

Outside smelled so clean. The sky stretched forever, blue and
perfect, the snow brilliant beneath it. The snow-covered land looked
like the ocean, with crests and valleys formed by the wind that had
driven it this way and that. The red of the barn cut stern and sturdy
lines through it all.

The air inside the barn was sweet with hay, horse, and grain.
Blue didn't know much about horses, but her guess was that the two
there were old. The white one in the closest stall had huge pits above
its eyes, and long whiskers off its nose, and it nodded, watching
them with curiosity. The other one, a somber dark brown, stared
stoically, as if hoping for food but expecting disappointment.

"Old man," Tish said, rubbing the white one's face. He shook
his head, his long mane flopping from side to side.

Blue took her gloves off, pulled out her notebook.

Names?

Tish kept scratching his neck, letting him rest his head against
her chest. "No names. Old Man, Old Lady."

Really?

Tish moved on to the other. "They just arrived a few years back. Dumped, I guess. They were old then, they're older now."

Teena's family often had cats dumped on their farm. Dogs, occasionally. Never a horse.

"Hard times make for hard choices. I'm guessing someone couldn't feed them but wasn't ready to sell them for dog food. Lucky for them, I had the space."

Tish walked down the aisle, past other empty stalls. Blue followed. In the back was a small room with a woodstove, a counter, a sink, and a coffee pot. Tish pointed at the pot. "Heat up some water. I'll take care of the stove."

Blue did as she was told. As much as she wanted to hit Tish, to yell at her for being there and unapologetic, part of her wanted to cling to her. She was almost eighteen, and she was nine, too, wanting Tish to hold her, wanting to smell home on her, wanting to follow her into a room where Mama and Cass were waiting. She settled for following Tish everywhere, alert for all the ways in which the woman in the red dress could steal her away.

Tish had other ideas. "I got this. You go into the loft and feed the cat. Crunchies are under the seat. There's a bowl up there."

She went back out, past the stalls and the horses, up the stairs by the door. The hayloft had almost no hay in it. One or two bales in a corner, a collection of faded green twine hanging from a nail, cobwebs draped across the corners. A ceramic bowl in the middle of the floor, with DOG painted on the front.

Really, Tish? The cat can't just be a cat? She opened the bag, poured the crunchies in. From behind a bale came a tiny calico cat, tiptoeing along on four white feet. Older, Blue guessed, than the horses, at least in cat years. The cat gave a yawn that exposed a mouth of yellowed teeth.

Blue crouched down and rubbed her fingers together. The cat walked beneath her hand, then settled to lick her feet clean.

Fussy princess of a cat. You need a gold collar to go with that attitude.

"You find the bowl, or what?"

She thudded back down the stairs. Tish showed her how to pour something that looked like soup made of swamp grass into the shallow rubber pans belonging to the two old horses.

"Clary would have loved these two." She gave Blue a look that reverberated in some secret space between her ribs and her lungs, then gently tugged the bit of mane hanging between Old Man's ears. "Here's the deal, Old Man. This girl shows up here in the middle of the night, in a blizzard, says she's looking for her sister who's been gone for two years. And she claims she can't talk. Rather than have her lying on the couch all day, every day, when the couch is mine to lie on, I figure I'll have her look after you. But first, I need to show her a few things."

So Tish did. She showed Blue things like where to stand around a horse, and what to watch for, and what not to do. The itchy spots that Old Man liked to have scratched, and the way he stretched his neck out and wiggled his nose when they were scratched right. Tish did the same with Old Lady. By the time they were done, Blue didn't want to leave. The horses were honest and warm and didn't care what her name was or how she'd arrived in their home, just that she was there.

"This is the deal between you and me." Tish touched her face, turned her so their eyes met. "Tomorrow I'll teach you to brush them. You can do that, and feed them. In exchange, you can stay here and I won't sic Lynne on you."

Blue looked away. Too many things to think about. Too many questions to ask. It felt better not to have to try to talk.

"But, and this is a really big thing, Blue. I expect that you're going to tell me the rest of the story. Doesn't have to be today, or this week, but I expect it. If not, at some point I'm going to have to get other people involved. You understand?"

Sort of. Not really. Tish owed her something, owed Mama and Cass something, too, but Blue was the only one there. Did everything in life require deals, and Blue had just never noticed? If Tish required a story for her deal, she'd figure one out. It couldn't be that hard.

Blue had taken over the guest room, which was less like a guest room and more like the room that time forgot. The rest of the house had walls painted pale yellow with natural wood trim. When the sun shone in, the spaces felt bigger, like cathedrals, even though Blue could reach the ceiling with her hands.

The guest room had wallpaper, though, with tiny roses all over. The bedspread was black, and the roses struggled to be seen beneath posters of musicians—Chrissie Hynde and Patti Smith and other women Blue didn't recognize—and Van Gogh paintings, and concerts thirty years gone. On the wall next to the bed, the roses had been carefully filled in with black marker, a climbing vine of decay.

Blue took out the guitar that night. She hadn't before, except to peek in and make sure it had survived unscathed. Now she opened the case, laid one hand on the neck, and traced the body. She used to think that Mama had had the guitar stained to match the rich color of her hair, the Guild emblem pinned at the top like a jewel. She hadn't, of course. She'd bought it used with money she'd saved from babysitting.

It was such a simple thing: veneer, thin wood, metal strings. There was wear on the neck where Mama's, and now Blue's, thumb had rubbed while playing. She leaned down, held her ear over the hole. Had it all been a dream? Had there never been a woman in a red dress singing in Mama's voice, or a man in a blue shirt tearing Amy's soul away? Had Andrea and Lacey been found because the world was a bitter place, and not because the devil had made Blue pay?

The only proof she had of anything was her missing voice and a pair of boots that made her feet sore. But feet got tired when they were stuck in boots all day. And sometimes people lost their voices or just stopped speaking.

She lifted the guitar out of the case and tuned it. The urge to sing as she began to play was so strong it made her cry. She remembered being six and holding this guitar, hands too small to press the strings down, trying anyway as she sang as loudly as she could. Mama had clapped, and Blue had been embarrassed, because she hadn't meant to be heard, and proud, because she had been heard. Mama had lifted her into her lap, placed Blue's hands over her own, played for her, their voices winding together.

She didn't notice Tish until she'd finished the song.

"You look close enough to her that it takes my breath away, but you don't play like her."

No, she didn't. Somehow the chords were different in her head, the speed slower, or faster. It was like the urge to keep hiking a trail in order to see around the next corner, only she knew where these corners went. She just wanted to change them. Stretch them a bit.

And how could Tish say she looked like Mama, when Blue was inches taller, when she had no hair.

When she had no hair, just like Mama hadn't.

She ducked her head down to study the strings. Hurt didn't go away; it just lurked around corners in disguise. Tish came closer.

"There was one point, after we'd made the record and we were feeling flush. I asked her if she wanted to trade it in, you know, get something a little flashier. She insisted that everything she'd ever played was stored up in there, and that's what made her sound real." A shrug.

Ice grew through the room. Not sheets of it; strands, threads, everything touched by it. All Blue had to do was move and it would break, and she might break with it. Not moving, not changing, that was how you held on to things. Only she had changed. She wasn't nine anymore.

You still play?

Such a simple line, and it still took her a minute to write it, crafting each word with care.

"Play in what way?" For a moment, she saw something of the old Tish there, making a joke that she was finally old enough to get. "Not like that. There won't be anything like Dry Gully again for me." A pause. She could almost see Tish's dark hair on Mama's knee, both of them on the couch. "I play at a bar with some friends a couple nights a month. Kind of country, kind of fun, kind of me. We're called Pour Me Another."

Of course they were. Tish reached out. "May I?"

Blue didn't want to give up the guitar, but she did, too. She wanted to hear what would come out of it under Tish's hands.

But Tish didn't play. She stroked the sides, strummed once, held the body to hers. Her eyes were red as she handed it back.

"It wasn't just me, Blue," she said before turning to leave.

Blue flipped her middle finger at Tish's retreating back.

THE NEXT DAY, AFTER FEEDING THE HORSES, BLUE WENT for a walk down the drive, figuring she'd follow the road a stretch. She never reached the road. The driveway just went on and on like a road itself, one that ended at Tish's and probably began somewhere in the Atlantic. Sure, her boots liked the movement; but the truth was that they also liked the movement back toward the house after she turned around.

A terrible thought took root in her. At first, she'd believed the lack of direction meant Cass was near. Now, she felt a growing certainty that the boots gave no indication because there was no Cass to find. She touched her throat, remembering the pressure of Rat's hands there, and thought about Halloween, about waiting for a call that didn't come.

Blue walked faster and faster, finally breaking into a run. She thudded along in her boots to the house, snow-blind and heart pounding, and ran straight into Tish at the door.

She pushed her way past and knelt on the floor, ripping at her laces until she could get the boots off. It was only then that she realized she'd been crying.

"Time to tell me what's going on?" Tish leaned against the counter, watching her.

Blue shook her head.

"Listen, I'm sticking to my end of the bargain, but I need a few answers. Do you need to see a doctor?"

A shrink, yeah. That wasn't what Tish meant, though. She wanted to know whether Blue had been raped, whether she might be pregnant, all those things that people believe are the very worst things that can happen to girls.

She shook her head.

"Is anyone looking for you for any reason other than that you ran away from Lynne's?"

She shook her head again.

"I'll keep waiting, then. Just not forever."

After dinner, Tish played for her. Not Dry Gully songs. Ones you might hear joined by a steel guitar or a banjo. Some songs Blue was sure she'd heard at Barn Magic.

Gentler, that was how Tish sounded now. Not that she couldn't still have been what one reviewer had named her—"the dark angel of alt country"—but that fierceness was held in reserve, replaced with a wry humor.

"Now you play for me," she said as she laid the fiddle on the couch.

Blue shook her head.

"No, really, I want to hear you. You owe me for dinner, right?"

If she'd played for strangers, she could play for Tish. Only, the logic was flawed, because who cared what strangers thought? She'd have to face Tish every morning until she moved on.

She got the guitar anyway. She didn't know what to play, so she played a couple of Dry Gully songs: one of Mama's and one of Tish's.

Tish listened carefully, her head resting in the palm of her hand. "Which do you like better?"

Blue froze. An impossible question if there ever was one. She loved the one Mama wrote because it sounded like Mama. She loved Tish's because it felt like thunder.

Both are cool, just different. Like the two of you—different but right together.

Tish didn't speak for a few minutes, enough time for Blue to wonder whether she'd said something really wrong.

"That was us. Totally different and right together. We used to have a joke, Clary and me. You know Woody Guthrie and Pete Seeger, right?"

Blue shook her head. She sort of knew, just that one of them had written "This Land Is Your Land," and one of them played the banjo, and maybe something about the Dust Bowl. Nothing she'd want to be quizzed on.

"What the hell are they teaching kids these days?" Tish asked. "The two of them were in a band called the Almanac Singers. Radical shit, kid, folk tunes and political words. Woody played a guitar, and Pete played a banjo. Woody's guitar had a very simple message painted on it: 'This Machine Kills Fascists.' The kind of thing you want from an instrument, that spit-in-your-eye attitude.

"Pete, his banjo had a message on it, too. His said 'This Machine Surrounds Hate and Forces It to Surrender.' Had to take a pretty steady hand to get that on a banjo, that's what I always thought.

"Clary and me, she used to say that was us. I wanted my fiddle to destroy. She wanted her guitar to spread love. But we wanted the same thing, just had our own ideas about how to get there."

What would you write on your fiddle?

She expected a Tish answer, something flip and a little lewd. What she got instead was a pucker of the lips, lines above her eyebrows.

"I don't know," she said at last. "'Open to Do-Overs,' I suppose."

It figured. If anyone needed a do-over, it had to be Tish.

"Do you write anything of your own?"

Whole notebooks of stuff. Haven't you noticed? Blue shrugged, not sure how to answer.

"Those songs are fifteen, twenty years old. You must have some things of your own to say."

Oh. Songs. She thought of what she'd scribbled down at Beyond and blushed a little.

"Pony up, little girl. What are you keeping secret?" Tish leaned toward her.

She couldn't share it. Instead, she took the capo out of the case, put it on, and played the little music-box tune that she'd made up.

It hurt to play it. Not in her fingers, not through her calluses, but inside, in secret spaces in her joints, swollen with what she'd had, what was gone. Losing Teena had seemed terrible, back in Eliotville. Here, after everything else, it was nothing. Almost nothing. She'd be lying to say it didn't hurt some to remember watching fireworks from the bed of Teena's pickup on the Fourth of July, talking about nothing while feeling it was everything. Being friends.

Tish had dumped Mama as a friend the same way Teena had dumped her, only she hadn't even had a reason. Blue ended the song abruptly and carried the guitar back to her room, leaving the case behind.

As she lay in bed after Tish turned the lights out, a memory nudged its way into her mind. Toward the end of the night at Barn Magic, there had been a wiry guy playing guitar. The words painted on the body of his guitar had read: "This Machine Kills Fascists."

She crept out of the room, down the hall to where Tish's computer sat. Turned it on, waited while it whirred to life, waited more while the modem slowly connected. Searched for Woody Guthrie.

It was him. The guitar, the hair, the body. She looked to see whether he lived anywhere near Minneapolis.

No. He didn't live anywhere. He'd been dead a long, long time. She'd been watching a ghost in the barn.

If she was seeing ghosts, that had to mean the game was still on.

BLUE WAS WALKING THE DRIVEWAY WHEN THE WEATHER
changed. Surely the snow had been used up in the storm that tried
to destroy her, she thought, but the wind stung her cheeks raw as
the gray spread like oil across the sky. By the time she turned back,
the first few flakes had begun to fall.

Tish had a newspaper laid out on the kitchen table when she
came in. "Look here. Seems our human Popsicle had a past."

Blue kept her face neutral as she read. The Traveler had a
name—Robert Francis Smith—and a sales job with a feed distribu-
tor that kept him on the road. A former wife and a child who'd run
away when she was fifteen and was never seen again. There was, the
state police said, some suggestion that he might have been involved
in the disappearance of several prostitutes, to judge by items found
in his car, but the nature of the lives of such individuals made it
difficult to keep track of their whereabouts.

Blue curled her fingers inward as she read. By the time she'd
finished, she could feel the bite of nails against her palms. *Such
individuals.* Had she read an article like this last year, she would
have imagined tough women wearing fake leopard-skin jackets and
short leather skirts.

Whom was she kidding? She wouldn't have thought of them

at all. Calling them prostitutes made it easier, didn't it? It made it okay that the police hadn't noticed them go missing, because they'd chosen their lives, hadn't been driven into them.

"Ready to talk now?" Tish must have had a guidance system alerting her when to attack, because Blue took out her notebook instead of walking away.

When she started to write, she was just going to tell about the Traveler. But then she continued with Andrea, and Beyond, and further back to Rat and Steve. And then it seemed silly not to keep going all the way back to Maine, leaving out only the woman in the red dress. She wrote, and Tish waited, and it was only when Blue had finished and handed the notebook over that she realized what she'd done.

"Jesus, Blue. You've been running through all kinds of trouble. Why didn't you call Lynne for help?"

I couldn't.

And I can't explain why.

"'Couldn't' isn't a good enough answer. What did you do that was so unforgivable that Lynne wouldn't take you home again? You were searching for Cass."

Sometimes the best defense was a good offense. Teena had taught her that.

Unforgivable? What about my mom? What about never coming to see her, not even coming to her funeral, not even calling us? Explain that.

The lines went deep in the paper, channels for the ink to run. Tish looked . . . angry? Not really. Sort of angry, sort of sad, sort of defeated.

"I wasn't the one who made that call."

What do you mean?

Something sticky and unpleasant opened inside her.

"I didn't decide, Blue. That was Clary's choice."

She needed help. We needed help. No way would she send you away.

Tish stood abruptly and walked to the counter. The glass of water she poured herself trembled a little, enough to make the fluid slosh within.

"I'm not lying. I may not like everything I've done in my life, but I'm grown-up enough to accept responsibility for it. Before she told you about the diagnosis, she told me she wanted me gone."

Blue couldn't even write the word, just mouth it. *Why?*

"Oh, Blue, she said a lot of things, and I don't know what was fear and what was real. She had you and Cass, and she'd raised you traveling with the idea that she'd always be there, and suddenly she wouldn't. I think she called a retreat. Take you back home, stay with Lynne, be safe."

What did she say?

"She said I wasn't stable enough. She said a hedonist wasn't what she needed, and she didn't trust me to change. She said she couldn't have her girls depending on someone undependable." She spoke as if she'd told this story a million times. "I told her that wasn't fair, but she said life wasn't fair and I needed to accept it. She told me not to say good-bye, just to leave. She thought it would be harder, more confusing, for you and Cass if I stayed in touch. So I left."

No way. Mama would never have done that. She loved Tish.

"I stayed with some friends. I bummed around for a while, picking up work here and there. I drank. I used people to try to fill that hole you all left. Then my dad had a second heart attack, and I came home. He died. I kept the ranch. I play with Pour Me Another, and I go out with my gal, and I don't drink anymore. There aren't many days that I don't miss your mom, though. What we had, what we were, was special."

But maybe she changed her mind. If you'd tried . . .

Tish gave a gruff laugh. "You think I didn't try? I mean, no, not at first. I was too angry. But later I started calling Lynne's and writing letters. Near the end, she let me come and visit."

Visit? Blue didn't remember any visit.

Again with the mind reading. "She set it up for a school day, and I had to promise to be gone before you were home. I went thinking I could get her to change her mind. Then I got there and realized she was dying. She was so thin, like birch bark and twigs."

Then. Near the end, when her mother's eyes had grown bigger and everything else smaller, when she smelled not of Mama, but of poison and decay.

"I asked to take you and Cass, the way things were supposed to be. She said no. She said you needed to grow up normal, because she wouldn't be there to help you figure out the best way to be different."

Tish gave her a wry smile. "I told her that I was a pretty good role model for being different, and she said she didn't want you growing up like me. I can't pretend that didn't hurt. A lot." She shook her head. "Anyway, I couldn't challenge her. I didn't have any legal right. I told her that I loved her, but I didn't think her decision was a good one. It didn't matter to her."

Mama sent Tish away. Tish didn't run. Mama had taken the one person they'd known, the only other person who felt like home, and sent her away.

Outside, the sky had turned dark and the window howled, but she no longer cared about the snow.

I don't understand. If she wasn't going to stay with you, why not stay with Cass's father?

"Rick? What are you talking about? How do you even know about him?"

The letters.

"What letters, Blue?"

She ran to her room. Into the keepsake bag, out with the letters, and back to the table.

Here. He was going to help + bring her on tour.

Tish looked over the pile quickly, then back at her. "She never wanted you to see these."

A slow sear rose up Blue's face.

I found them in Lynne's storage.

Tish shook her head. "These weren't for either of you to read."

How could it hurt? She'd been dead for years.

The heat continued to spread across her cheeks. She didn't need Tish to tell her how wrong she had been.

"Even dead people deserve some privacy. You read those letters— tell me what they mean."

Blue hadn't been totally sure when she read them. That was another part of the reason she'd shown them to Cass.

We figured he'd offered to take care of Mama and Cass + you'd talked her out of it.

Tish pinched the bridge of her nose. "And why, exactly, would I do that?"

In for a penny, in for a pound.

Cass said you were selfish. Mama meant more to you than you did to her + you hung on + kept her from going.

Tish shook her head. "We weren't even together then, other than the music. Give your mother some credit for making her own decisions. The letters from Rick were because he wanted her to abort. He offered to cover the expenses, and then bring her on tour with him as a backup singer. It was better money than what Dry Gully was making; but in exchange, she'd become one of those nameless women who makes the band sound great and doesn't get the credit she deserves. She was old enough to know what she wanted. It wasn't that. Plus, she was worried her chances at being a mom were vanishing."

Tish went to the woodstove, poker in hand. "I didn't talk her out of anything. I told her that if she wanted a baby, we'd have it together."

How do I know you're not lying?

The anger slid across Tish's face and was replaced again by that unfamiliar patience. "Call Lynne."

Right. Nice try. She pointed at her throat.

"Blue, you were born with working vocal cords. I know; I was there. You still haven't told me everything. What happened to your voice?"

All she had to do was explain this one last piece. It would start something like *I kissed a woman in a red dress in the middle of the night and she sucked my voice out. No, I'm totally sane.*

No way. Some stories she couldn't tell.

42

THE LIGHTS STARTED TO FLICKER A FEW HOURS INTO THE
storm. Tish made them noodles with peanut sauce and broccoli, and
they lit a candle on the table, just in case the power went out. She
didn't push Blue for more and didn't offer more herself. Instead,
they took turns playing, then played one song together. Tish raised
an eyebrow when Blue chose it.

"'Avenue A' feels a little dark for a seventeen-year-old."

It was weird playing together, in so many ways. The obvious
ones: playing with someone, when she almost always played alone;
playing with a fiddler, which she'd never done. Then the others:
the way the music brought memories up, things she'd forgotten.
The flash of the copper clasp Mama wore around her wrist when
she played, how Cass used to lean forward, elbows on her knees,
to watch, the side glances Tish and Mama gave each other, as if
they played only for each other. Now, playing with Tish, Blue kept
looking at her, too, because playing together was about following
and leading, exploring, trusting.

Eyes closed, Blue could remember Mama backstage somewhere
that reeked of cigarette smoke and the smell of beer. She watched
her laughing as she caught Tish's shoulder, turned her, and kissed
her. Happy.

She stopped midsong. Tish stopped, too.

"What is it?"

Blue stood up, left the guitar against the couch. Mama had kicked Tish out. Mama had agreed to raise her and Cass with Tish, and then told Tish to leave. *She wanted you to grow up normal . . .*

Tish touched her wrist. "Blue, what's going on?"

She couldn't even write. How could she explain? Tish was the bad one. Tish was trouble, she was a black eye, she was drinking and late nights, but she was also laughter and bad movies and help with homework. She was home, and Mama had left her.

Mama had chosen to leave them without a parent instead of risking that they would grow up . . . like her? On the road, playing music with someone she loved?

Why leave? Was she ashamed of being a musician?

Before Tish could answer, the lights went out.

In the dark, with only the flicker of the candlelight to combat it, the noise of the storm seemed much worse. Even so, it was softer than it would have been at home. No trees bending and groaning beneath the snow, so much less for the wind to whip through. The darkness swallowed everything.

"I should get the generator going. Storm like this means no power crews working for a while."

No way to respond without light. Except . . . She played the first few lines again. Waited.

"It's not that easy to explain, Blue. When we first met, we both wanted everything. We were sure we were going to be famous, because we were so good. It's what you learn—if you work hard, if you have talent, you'll make it big. Only then you don't. Eventually you find yourself somewhere you didn't expect—with two kids and hair turning gray and no money—and being on the road can feel . . .

foolish. Because if you were good, you'd be playing stadiums, you'd be on the radio."

The wind groaned against the house. "Clary wasn't embarrassed to be a musician. She was embarrassed that she'd left home sure she could make it, and then ended up where she did. Rick offered her the chance to at least be on the stage she'd dreamed of, but she couldn't take that last step. Sell herself out."

But she sold the two of you out. And me and Cass. She sold us out, too. Mama might have known fame wasn't everything, but the alternative she'd picked had left all of them alone.

Blue wanted to apologize. For Cass's anger. For Mama saying she wanted her kids to be normal. For believing it had been Tish who walked out, left them all behind.

Sorry. How could a five-letter word ever contain all that regret?

BLUE BEGAN TO LOSE TRACK OF TIME. DAY AND NIGHT
tumbled together, almost meaningless. Tish had a few rules, like
having to get up every morning, having to wear clean clothes, and
having to do the barn chores and eat. Aside from that, she could
do as she wanted. She walked up and down the endless driveway
in boots that seemed as lost as she felt. Why didn't they give her a
direction? Why hadn't the woman in the red dress done anything
to Tish?

With no way to answer her questions, Blue retreated. She slept
and she read books she found on the shelves. And she played guitar—sometimes alone, sometimes with Tish.

She'd known she had a lot to learn, but Tish managed to show
her things without making her feel like a beginner. They tried out
all sorts of songs—lots of Dry Gully, but others as well, including
ones from Tish's new band. The new ones weren't melancholy or
angry. Instead, they were wickedly funny, the sort of humor that
made her embarrassed and laugh at the same time.

"So you have Clary's ear, which is good. You pick things up
quickly. You don't play like her, though, and I think you're not
being fair to yourself to keep trying to."

She wanted to argue that she wasn't trying to play like her
mother, but fatigue kept her hand still.

"Have you tried writing anything of your own?"

The thought of sharing the song she'd scribbled down in Beyond made Blue's insides curl. She had felt good while writing it, but the magic had vanished somewhere on the page. Now it seemed foolish.

Tish studied her. "You have, haven't you? Show me?"

She shook her head.

"Show me. Trust me, the first things I wrote were worse than you can imagine."

She opened her notebook and handed it over.

Tish bobbed her head as she read. Not a wobble, a bob, as if she were hearing something. It wasn't until she started to produce a few notes that Blue realized she was imagining music.

"Do you have music for it already?"

Another shake of the head.

"So this is kind of what I get from it." She took the guitar from Blue.

She tried to listen instead. It wasn't quite right. It sounded a bit like Dry Gully, lacking . . . It was an itch she couldn't reach. She put one hand over the strings.

"Okay, let me hear what you have."

It was like trying to raise a sunken log in a river. Blue grabbed for it anyway, the music slippery in her hands and the tune she made sputtering before finally catching.

She caught Tish watching her fingers the way Blue remembered her focusing on Mama's hands. She said nothing, though, just watched. Then when Blue tried it again, she joined in. The fiddle made it fuller, realer.

"Now, if only you'd speak, we could hear how this song might sound."

If only.

Days and weeks passed, the time stretching further and further. Around and around the thoughts went in Blue's head. Tish had been part of their home no matter where they had lived. Mama had stolen that from them and then walked out on the conversation completely by dying.

Mama had died.

Superman's Fortress of Solitude had nothing on hers. No one could find her, not even the woman in the red dress or the man in the blue shirt. As long as she abided by Tish's rules, her world was snow, horses, music, and sleep. The woman in the red dress was a nightmare. Beyond, Barn Magic, Steve . . . They were simply dreams of another kind.

SOMEHOW IT BECAME LATE JANUARY. SHE KNEW ONLY because Tish made a point of telling her, laying a calendar out on the table.

"This is when you arrived." Her finger tapped on a page. "This is where we are now." She turned the pages and selected a day. "A long time without you explaining much, Blue. I'm thinking we've almost reached the point where I need to call in some help."

Blue shrugged. She hadn't thought about travel in . . . she had no idea how long. Everything was fuzzy, even how she'd ended up there.

I can go.

Tish shook her head. "Wrong answer. I don't want you gone. I want you *here*. Really here, kid, not off in some hell of your own."

It wasn't hell. It wasn't anything, and that was exactly what she wanted.

"I can help you. We can try to find Cass together."

No need. If the boots didn't know where to find Cass, how could Tish?

The next day, Tish gave her a bag of cowgirl clothes, stiff and smelling of a store, and told her to be ready to go at 5:30.

She spent the day feeling as though the floor had been electrified, every step carrying the danger of pain. She didn't want to leave the ranch. Outside, the world was cold and deadly. The librarian had been wrong. Kindness didn't matter. This was the kind of world where someone could die in a ditch, unnoticed.

Still, she put the clothes on and met Tish by the door with her guitar at the appointed hour. Tish had dressed up, too—a long black skirt, a black silk tank, some kind of woven turquoise-and-green jacket over it. She wore makeup—smoky smudges around her eyes—and silver earrings, and the scoop of her tank exposed the tattooed eye at the base of her throat. Over it all, she wore a long black coat, and she carried her fiddle case in one hand and spun the car keys around on the other.

The driveway—the one that stretched forever when Blue walked it—took no time at all to travel. The road beyond was a canyon with walls built of snow. As they picked up speed, she could have sworn something moved by the side, a figure reaching out and then gone.

They drove to a bar whose windows were lit with red and green lights left over from Christmas. Blue followed Tish inside, carrying her guitar. Every table was full, with more than a few people standing along the back wall. Older folks: men with slicked-back gray hair, dry-bleached blondes; cowboy boots and lariat ties. The bartender—a weathered woman with hair dyed fire-engine red—handed Tish a bottled water.

"You been M.I.A.," she said. Her voice was exactly what Blue expected, the kind that belonged to a woman named Marge. "Folks started to think you pulled a runner. Again."

Tish laughed. "Not likely. I got nowhere to run to, not anymore."

The woman waved her hand. "Whatever. The girls are waiting in back."

Tish kept moving, drink in her free hand. Blue tagged after, trying hard not to knock anyone in the head with her guitar.

The back turned out to be a little room off a low platform set up as a stage. A guitar waited in a stand, and a bass and three mics lined up in the front. The *girls* were all women at least as old as Tish.

"JFC, Tish, cutting it a little close, aren't ya?" The speaker had long blond hair pulled back with a large turquoise clip, and bangs that rested neatly across her forehead.

"Sharlene, abbreviating the words doesn't cancel out the fact that you're swearing. Women, this is Blue. Blue, these are Pour Me Another."

"You always did have the manners of a ranch hand, Tish." The blonde approached Blue. "Hon, I'm Sharlene. Tish and I go way back."

"As in, they used to hate each other's guts in high school." The new speaker had gray hair cut in a bob, and a mole above her upper lip. "Louise."

She held out her hand. Blue shook it, conscious of the doughy weight of it and the tang of the woman's perfume.

"And that's Lana. She don't talk much, but she knows her way around a mandolin."

The last woman—lean and dark-skinned, with fingers covered in silver rings—shook her head. "No reason to talk to y'all. Not if I expect anything resembling common sense."

The others laughed. All but Tish, who was busy warming up her fiddle. The bartender poked her head in, and Sharlene nodded. "We're coming, we're coming. Just give the Gypsy here a chance to get herself organized."

Just like that they were headed out on stage, leaving Blue on her own. She walked out, still carrying her guitar, and leaned against the corner of the bar. Someone had always made a nest for her in a backstage corner whenever Dry Gully had played—a little swirl of blankets somewhere people wouldn't trip over her.

Tish stood to one side on stage, fiddle in hand. To see her there, so different from how she used to be, and so much the same—it hurt in Blue's throat, made her eyes sting. Had Mama been there, she would have been different, too, in ways no one would ever know now.

There were hoots from the crowd as the band launched into its first tune, one Blue recognized from the songs Tish had taught her. Sharlene belted it out with Tish and Lana on backup. *The creek ain't dry / Just climb a little higher / The wood looks bad / But beneath there's a fire.*

The bartender came over, offered her a water bottle.

"I know you're not legal, so don't try to convince me otherwise."

Blue held up one hand. The woman eyed her as if Blue were making a play for her job. "How come you're with Tish?"

She put down the guitar, fumbled for her notebook. The woman watched, one elbow down on the bar, while she scribbled out an answer.

"Niece, huh? Not by blood, you're not. Tish hasn't got any siblings."

Sometimes it doesn't matter if it's blood.

The woman shrugged. "Fair enough. What do you think of your aunt?"

She's always been the best.

There was an intermission eventually. Blue went back into the little room with them, listened to their private jokes, stood awkward and alone. Tish looked happy. Not the way she had after a Dry Gully concert, fever-flushed and a little dangerous.

This was her life. She'd had Dry Gully, she'd loved Mama, and then she'd moved on. Life did that, moved on. Cass, wherever she was, she'd be different now, too.

Mama shouldn't have changed, couldn't, but it felt as if she had. She'd become thoughtless, cruel, even. All those memories, every one now lit by an unfriendly light. Mama hadn't considered anything but her own regrets when she decided to leave Tish and take them to Maine. How could she have done that, never giving any of them a choice?

Then the band was going back out, and Blue was following again, this time leaving the guitar behind. She didn't know why Tish had made her bring it, didn't know how any of this fit with her threat of calling for help. No one in the bar looked like a psychiatrist waiting for a patient.

She'd gone all the way to the back this time, near the door, when she heard her name. "Sapphire Blue, where's Sadie?"

Like an arrow, straight through her and out the other side. Sadie, Mama's name for the guitar. Blue shrugged, trying to look nonchalant as everyone turned toward her.

Tish gave her a no-arguments look. "Go get her and come up here."

Up there? No frigging way. This wasn't Barn Magic, this wasn't trying to get warm and being thankful for a few lanterns and some chili. They were getting paid for their music, and she didn't know most of it, and they already had a guitar.

But Tish stared her down, one finger tapping ever so lightly on the body of her fiddle. This wasn't a fight Blue would win.

And maybe she didn't want to win.

Guitar in hand, she stepped onstage. The other three women moved back, leaving her alone with Tish. "Plug in," Tish said. Hands shaking a little, Blue took the cord Lana handed her and plugged it into the bottom of the guitar.

"This, dear barflies, is Blue. She's underage and harder than a railroad tie, and she's got me looking out for her, so none of you even think of trying to buy her a drink later on."

Laughter from all sides, the sound buffeting her as she stood mute.

"This is also her first time onstage, even on a pissant stage like this one, so you'll forgive her if she stands here like a statue instead of tuning her guitar like a real musician."

More laughter. Blue played a few chords, conscious of everyone watching her.

"'Avenue A,'" Tish said out of the corner of her mouth before returning to the patter. "We're going to play something from my past," she told the audience. "Something about the roads love travels when it ends."

The guitar led in "Avenue A." The song was Blue's to start, and everyone was waiting. She began to play.

It was as if time were an accordion, the pleats of it—lengthened by years—suddenly pulled close. Mama's guitar, her own hands, Tish's fiddle crying, then Tish's voice taking its place, rough and lonely. It was who she had been, who she was now. In that moment, she knew what it meant to tell your life to strangers in three-minute bites of music. She knew why people did it, no matter what it cost them.

Then it was over, and the applause poured through and around her. Tish whispered something to her, too soft to hear, like a feather stroking her ear, and kissed her cheek. The other women patted her on the shoulder, and Sharlene helped her unplug the guitar. She watched the rest of the show feeling as though the music were a river flowing through them all.

When the music ended, Blue went outside. She wanted the fresh air. The stars stretched forever across the sky, the land as flat and open as the ocean. She tilted her head back and breathed deep.

The smell reached her at the same time as the voice. It wasn't quite the same: sweeter, softer, fresher, a wood fire with cider brewing on top, just a touch of rot thrown in.

"Bluebird, you've been hiding." Like silk, like skin. Not one single voice she knew, but more familiar than any.

How could I be hiding? Can't you see me everywhere?

She was wearing the red dress again. Her long black hair blew loose around her shoulders. Her black coat was open in the front, her feet shod in high black boots. The night wrapped around her like folds of velvet.

"Interesting question." It didn't sound interesting. It sounded more like puzzlement, like uncertainty. "Sometimes life puddles, Bluebird. Sometimes you throw a stick into the water upstream and wait and wait, and it doesn't come, because it's lost in an eddy somewhere."

So I'm a stick?

She could feel the amusement ripple toward her.

Wait. Now that you've found me, promise me that you won't hurt Tish.

She had been hiding, and now she was being pulled from her burrow by a creature with teeth and claws, and she couldn't let the same happen to Tish.

"Tish." The woman drew it out, like the slip of water over sand. "Tell me—does she know you? Does she know you as well as I know you? Does she know all your secrets?"

Does it make a difference what she knows? She knows me. She took care of me. She's—

"She's what? Tell me what she is to you and I'll tell you what I'm going to do."

The rattle of a door came from behind them, the sound of voices spilling from the open door. Tish and Sharlene paused there, Tish laughing as Sharlene touched her cheek, kissed her. Then Tish walked across the lot toward them.

She's . . . she's . . . just her. That's all. I'm going to leave, once things are set. I just haven't yet.

The woman in the red dress smoothed her coat, tied the sash. "Nice evening," she said as Tish neared.

"So it is. You ready?" Tish asked, one hand on Blue's shoulder. Blue nodded. Together they turned, left the woman behind them.

She fought the urge to turn back to see whether they were being pursued. Instead, she walked close to Tish, their arms touching, until Tish put one arm around her.

"Good job, kid. You made me proud tonight."

BLUE WALKED DOWN THE DRIVE, NOW KEEPING TRACK OF the time with a watch swiped from Tish's desk. Five minutes, ten, fifteen, twenty, and there was still no end in sight. After the first five minutes, the house looked no farther away, the road no closer.

She used to cover the two miles through the woods to Teena's house in a half hour. When they'd driven out last night, it had taken no time at all. Blue took one last look, and turned back.

A puddle. Somehow in the middle of Nowhere, Wyoming, a puddle had formed around Tish. Stay in the puddle, she was safe. But the thing about puddles was that they could dry up, or come undammed, and then there would be nothing to protect her anymore. Or Tish.

Tish was in her office with the door closed when Blue came in. She found her notebook, wrote quickly, and knocked at Tish's door.

Tish scanned the note. "Leave. Blue? You still haven't told me what's going on, and it's winter. There's no way I'm just going to put you on the road somewhere."

You have to.

She paused, thought.

It's life or death.

Wrong thing. She should have known better. Tish pointed to

the rocking chair in the corner of the room. "Sit. Tell me what's going on. All of it."

If Tish wouldn't take her, maybe she could leave another way. Hike out the way she'd come, through the snow, with no idea where she was going. Maybe her boots would tell her. Then again, maybe the puddle was the reason they hadn't known where to go.

"I'm serious. You've told me a collection of events, but not why they happened. Not why you won't talk."

I CAN'T TALK!!!

She thumped the table with her fist. More than that, opened her mouth, tried to yell, strained until her throat seemed to be tearing open. Silence. Air, moving without vibration.

Tish held up both hands. "Okay, you can't talk. Tell me why. Healthy young women don't suddenly lose their voices. What happened at Lynne's?"

Sometimes distance made it easier to see. She touched her throat.

Last spring, I broke up with my BF, and then Teena, my BFF, dumped me.

That wasn't right. She tried again.

Cassie left. It was just me and Lynne, and

Further back still. Didn't her story really need to begin *Mama was dying and I could see it coming and couldn't stand it.* Wasn't that the place where everything else started?

Loss grows like poisoned brambles. It takes the good spaces and the bad, it creeps into everything, until you look down and realize that every step is surrounded.

It all poured off Blue's pencil tip onto the paper. What happened before, what happened at the crossroads, the woman and the kiss and the feel of her voice being sucked away. Amy and the man in the blue shirt; the church, the driver's license, Andrea and Lacey and the police coming to Beyond. Everything.

When Tish finished reading, she set down the paper and touched Blue's cheek.

"Baby girl, you've had it tough."

She had to write, couldn't wait any longer.

I'm crazy, right?

Tish pulled away, looked at her own hand as if something might be waiting in it. "*Crazy*'s a mean word. People use it to hurt themselves, hurt others. Not all that many years ago, I would have been called crazy for being who I am. So let's set that word aside.

"This world, we see it through all kinds of peepholes. Microscopes, telescopes, binoculars turned backward." Laughter echoed in Blue's head, a memory of all four of them playing with a pair of binoculars. "Sometimes we see things one way, sometimes another; some of them are never recognizable again. It's the magic of being alive."

You're not answering.

"I believe you made a deal in November, Blue. I believe that deal has driven you away from home, into some god-awful places as well as some incredible ones. I believe that trip isn't done yet."

Blue felt as though her body had laces running through it, just like a pair of boots, and they'd been tied so tight for so long that she'd forgotten about them, and now, suddenly, they were cut free and there was nothing to bind her breath, to hold her in. Free, too free, no longer knowing how to be.

"The thing is, Blue, I don't know if you really know who you made your deal with."

A sucker punch, knocking her flat.

What do you mean?

"The rules may be different than you think. You've been running so hard that you have no idea where you're going, what's driving you."

Trying to keep everyone.

Tish took the paper from her.

"No, listen. You believe you're trying to save people from you. You believe this woman has your voice and she chooses when to give it back. You've given up every bit of power you have; and Jesus, Blue, you have a lot. I understand you feel you need to move on, and I'll help you with that. But you need to think about where you're going, not just what you're running from."

46

THE DEAL THEY MADE WAS FOR HER TO STAY UNTIL THE
weather turned toward spring. In the meantime, Tish bought her
a sleeping bag and a new pack and clothes to fill it. Together they
looked over maps and talked about where musicians traveled and
where runaways did, and how those places overlapped. Cities where
Cass might be, things she might be doing.

Blue kept returning to the idea of the puddle. If the puddle kept
the woman in the red dress from finding her, couldn't it also keep
her from finding Cass? It wasn't that Cass was dead, it was that the
boots were stranded. Once she stepped into the current again, she
would know where to go.

Only, she had been so sure she knew where to go when she first
set out.

*I thought it was the Gully. You know how you and Mama
found each other.*

Tish nodded. "That's the thing about journeys. Sometimes
you have to reach past everything you know. My journey and your
mom's aren't yours. Or Cass's."

"Songwriting's not for the meek." They were sitting at the table,
Blue's words laid out before them. "It means putting a piece of

yourself out there, in front of people. Your words, your music, no filter. Not that everyone does it that way. There's plenty of crap out there written by people who spent more time worrying about rhyme than they did about what their song actually said. I don't think that's what you're aiming for. Not if I go by what you've written here."

Tish ran an index finger down each page in turn. Finally, she stopped, tapping one verse.

> *I got a dollar in my pocket,*
> *Fifty cents of that is yours,*
> *I got a sleeping bag in my pack,*
> *With room for just one more,*
> *I got miles of road I've traveled*
> *And miles more to roam,*
> *And the only thing I know for sure*
> *Is as long as I'm with you, I'm home.*

"First of all, that's where it actually starts to sound like you. Not like me or Clary. Just you."

Blue ducked her head a bit. Tish was right. It was like letting someone peek inside her.

"Second, the last line loses it completely. Did you try to sing it to yourself?"

She pointed at her throat. Tish rolled her eyes.

"In your head. Jesus, Beethoven was deaf and still managed to write music that made sense."

Tish pushed away from the table a bit and began to clap, slow and steady. Instead of singing, she spoke the words to the rhythm of her clap. When she came to the last line, it all fell apart.

Blue studied her words while her cheeks burned flame-hot.

"Kid, that's the way it goes. No one stands up for the first time and goes out to do a world-record dash. I had notebooks of crap before I found the first few lines that worked."

Blue rubbed the eraser of the pencil against her lips for a moment. Then, heart fluttering as if she were cutting with a scalpel instead of drawing a line, she crossed out the problem words.

Now Tish sang, using the music they'd been toying with for weeks: *"And the only thing I know for sure / Is with you I'm home. Closer."*

It felt good. More than good, like sunshine, like a warm bed, like laughing. Like Barn Magic.

She found the phone number online and copied it into her notebook carefully, then set it on the table in front of Tish.

Tish's half of the conversation gave little away. "My niece," she said, and "sometime in November," and "hospital." She nodded, doodled on the page. "I understand, and if she could talk for herself, she would. Since she can't, I'm acting as intermediary."

More nodding. Her hand over the mouthpiece. "Is there anything personal that you can tell me that will help them know it's you?"

She thought about Nellie's Place, the piano, the warmth.

Javier shaved my head. He gave me his coat, too, and a hat. He said families could be made, that romance wasn't the only kind of ♥.

Tish paused, gripped Blue's hand in hers before continuing. After she shared everything Blue had told her, she nodded, said, "Hold on, you can say it to her."

She handed the receiver over. Blue clutched it to her ear.

"Interstate, right?" The voice on the phone was deep, lush.

"This is Liza. I took Steve to the hospital the night you were here. I'm so glad to hear from you, darling. Can you give me some kind of sign, tap or something, to let me know you're okay?"

She tapped her nails against the phone, as hard as she could.

"Okay. Well, Steve's just fine, too. He's staying with Javier for now. You two took such good care of each other. He told us all about it."

He was okay. He'd known her name, but she'd left quickly enough. Not everyone was lucky enough to live in a temporal puddle like Tish. Rat hadn't found him again, and Javier was taking care of him, and he was okay.

"He's doing really well, sweetheart. I wish he was here to talk to you, but he's not. He's got a job, just a little part-time thing until he's got a better idea of what he's doing. I'll tell him you called and that you're okay. He's been worried. You think you can call back later?"

She clicked off, quiet as she could. Steve was okay. Homes could be found. New families could be made. And girls who lost their voices would have the chance to find them again.

EXACTLY ONE WEEK INTO MARCH, BLUE WALKED OUT THE door into air that smelled of spring. She couldn't have described it any other way. Meltwater, maybe, and sunlight, and the hint of earth even through the blanket of snow.

That would have been enough to make up her mind, but when she walked down the drive, her footsteps sloshing in the soft snow, it took her no more than five minutes to reach the road, a minute longer for the implication to sink in. She stood there and watched a truck go by, its wheels throwing up water, then turned and ran.

Tish wasn't home. That made it easier.

She'd kept almost everything stored in her pack. Now, all that was left to do was to stuff a few more pairs of underwear in, a couple of peanut butter–and–jelly sandwiches, and she'd be ready to go.

Almost.

It was much harder to leave a note for Tish than it had been to leave one for Lynne. Again, she had that sense of not knowing how to make everything fit, only this time the optimism had been stripped from her. What do you say to someone when you know you might never see her again? What if you'd already been lost to her once?

Tish,

I don't understand why Mama did the things she did. I'm sorry. I wish you'd been with us. I wish you'd been with her. I ran away at the end because I was scared, and I wish I hadn't. I know you wouldn't have. You would have loved her then just like you loved her before, and that would have been the best thing for her.

If I make it to Cass, I'll come back here again.

Thank you.

♥

Blue

She started out walking. She'd told herself that hitching would be easy, but every passing car made her jump to the side. The Traveler's face looked out at her from the sun glinting off every window.

Walking felt good. She'd missed her boots, at least when she was moving. The clop of them against the pavement, their solidity, the height. She could walk forever, just keep on going.

She kept thinking about what Dill had said about hopping trains. Missoula: that name stuck with her from when he'd talked about freight yards. The workers would be okay, he'd said, most of them. Friendly, even. Everyone else, she needed to size up carefully. Some folks hopped because it was the way they lived, their own Beyond. Others were looking for a thrill, and some of those thrills involved hurting people.

She'd be okay, though. She wasn't Blue out here, she was Interstate. She'd survived Rat and the Traveler. She'd survived being left, by her mom, by Cass, by Teena. She'd survived leaving Steve and Dill, and now Tish.

She was through with all that. From this point on, she'd be arriving, and there wasn't a force anywhere that could stop her from surviving that.

She didn't choose the VW bus. It chose her. One second, it was speeding past; the next, it gave a loud bang and wiggled to the side of the road on a very flat tire. A woman got out, ran a hand through straggly bleached hair. "Do you know how to change a fucking flat?" she called into the bus. The answer was clear enough when she kicked the offending tire.

Blue paused, considered her options. Teena's dad had spent an afternoon teaching them to change flats. He didn't ever want his girls left on the side of the road, counting on the kindness of God knows who to help them out, he'd said. His girls. Teena and her.

Another woman got out, this one in ridiculous heels and a fur coat so fake it might have been made from skinned teddy bears. She gave a low whistle. One more minute, and a sailor emerged. At least, he was dressed as a sailor: white-and-blue uniform, hat in his hand. The sun glinted off his electric-blue hair.

The first woman lit into a string of profanity so detailed that Blue couldn't help but grin. Whatever they were doing, they hadn't blown their own tire just to try to get her in their car.

She hurried forward. The three of them looked at her expectantly. She set the guitar down on her feet and unzipped the pocket in her backpack that held her notebook.

"You think she's got a gun in there?" The second woman, High Heels, talked with an accent straight out of Boston.

Blue touched a finger to her lips, pulled out the notebook and held it up.

"Nah, she's gonna rob us with words." The sailor. The bright blue of his hair made the red freckles on his nose stand out even more. "Maybe she's got a bomb. Maybe she's practicing her bank robbery skills."

"Listen, babe, I can almost guarantee that whatever guitar you've got in that case is worth more than the piece-of-shit instruments we've got, so don't even bother trying to get something from us." The blonde had a Janis Joplin voice, so raspy that the inside of her throat had to be made of crushed glass.

Musicians. It was her duty to help them out, theirs to give her a ride. Right? That was what Lou had said all the way back in Maine.

Have a spare?

The blonde squinted at the note, one eye closed. "You know what to do with it?"

Blue nodded.

"Well, aren't you my brand-new very best friend?" The sailor and the woman in heels burst into applause.

The three of them gathered in a semicircle around her as she took off the old tire and put on the spare, the sailor holding her guitar for her. When she finished, they gave another round of applause, as hearty as what she'd received at the bar with Tish.

"Suppose you might need a lift, right?" The sailor held out her guitar. He had to be four inches shorter than Blue, but the lines on his face suggested he was older by a few decades. Good lines, the kind that pointed out where his eyes would crinkle with laughter.

Where ya headed?

Not that it made a difference. They'd been driving the same direction she was walking. That was enough for her.

"Missoula. Got a gig tonight."

"Speaking of which, we gotta motor." High Heels, flashing a gap-toothed smile. "You coming or not?"

She gave her best grin and climbed into the bus.

BY THE TIME THEY GOT TO MISSOULA, IT WAS DARK. THEY stopped on the outskirts of town, at a little roadhouse flanked on either side by old boxcars.

"Listen," the sailor said as he pulled a bass taller than he was out of the back and handed it to the blonde. "You can sleep in one of those cars if you don't have a place to go. No one'll bother you."

They left, hurrying through the door, the noise from inside loud and uninviting. Blue thought about following them, then thought about her empty pockets and her belongings and decided against it.

The interior of the boxcar was very dark. She turned on her flashlight and shone it across the empty floor, the walls mostly free of graffiti. The space was empty, aside from a couple of tin cans in the corner. She picked them up, looked inside at the smooth clean surfaces. Back outside, she collected gravel from the parking lot in the cans and poured it out on the lip of the boxcar doorway. It wasn't much, but it might warn her if someone came. Tin cans on a string would be better, but she didn't have any string, other than the ones on the guitar, and those were too precious to waste. She unrolled her sleeping bag in the corner, slithered into it, and propped herself up against the wall. The sounds of the bar—doors opening and closing, the faint music—soothed her. The way they had when she was little, listening to Mama and Tish talking between sets, everything warm, safe, and happy.

Blue woke with a start. The sunlight shone in from the crack of the door. There was frost on her sleeping bag, and her nose was cold; but the rest of her was warm. Too warm to want to get up. From somewhere farther off came the rumble of a train. She couldn't believe she'd actually slept in a boxcar outside a bar. Might as well sleep on a sidewalk, all her things laid out for people to take.

No one had taken anything, though. Blue rose from the sleeping bag into the cold with a rumbling stomach. The stream of sunlight drew her to the door. She rubbed her eyes and stared out.

Nothing.

The only things to break the surface of the snow were her tracks, the tips of grass, the corner of an old foundation. There was no parking lot. No roadhouse.

The band had driven her. She had been in their bus, had breathed in the scent of their perfume, heard the heater working overtime to warm all the way to the backseat.

Was their bus the same as the city bus in Chicago? Was the woman in the fake furs kin to the blues-singing bus driver?

Instruments, voices, musicians . . . *Musicians play in the midst of ghosts every day.* Did they travel with ghosts, as well? She looked around again, taking in snow, sun, a dark snake of a road farther away. A musician, then. That's what she had become.

Blue didn't have to walk long on the road before someone stopped for her. The weathered pickup that pulled over had two bumper stickers affixed to the back: "NDN Pride" and "My Heroes Have Always Killed Cowboys." Two teenage girls looked out at her.

"Need a lift?" the girl driving asked.

She nodded, dropped her gear in the truck bed, and climbed in. The passenger gave her a thorough once-over. Blue looked back. The driver had straight brown hair in a long braid, a thin, straight nose, dark eyes. The other girl had black hair, black eyes, dark skin.

"Where you headed?"

Blue opened her notebook.

This is Missoula, right? The Freight yard?

"What's he writing?" the driver asked, glancing over.

"He's looking for a train."

"Figures." She grinned. "No one wants to hang out in Missoula for long. What's your name, train guy?"

Interstate. You grow up here?

The passenger read the question out loud, and both of the girls giggled. Their closeness made her ache a little. She used to giggle with Teena in the same way. No need for words sometimes—they'd just look at each other and know what the other was thinking.

"On the rez. Evie's going to start school in the fall. Wildlife management." The driver sighed wistfully.

What about you?

Blue showed the question to the passenger, pointed to the driver. Instead of reading it, the girl answered. "She's going to be working with her auntie. They cut hair. She's really good at it."

How do you know each other?

More giggles. "We're cousins."

"Where were you coming from?" The passenger nudged her with her knee. "Not much out there for folks like you."

Like you. Girls pretending to be boys? Girls who left everything they knew and wandered through the country like water trying to find its way to the ocean? Children who weren't children anymore;

orphans looking for love; innocents robbed of their money, their certainty, sometimes their lives?

It wasn't the places where Blue didn't fit that were important anymore. It was the places she did. Traveler. Musician. Sister.

Sister. The boots were urging her forward again. She could feel the clock ticking: *Time to go, time to go.*

She drew a deep breath, listening for a moment. The music inside the girls flowed together. Drum and flute, sharing the beat. *Cass,* she thought. She and Cass shared music that no one else did.

Passing through. A friend told me Missoula was a good place to hop a train. ☺

"Sure . . . if you're nuts. You know people die and stuff when they do that, right?"

Not me. I'm pretty tough.

THEY DROPPED HER UP THE ROAD FROM THE FREIGHT
yard. Dill had told her not to walk straight through the middle carrying a pack. Best not to call attention to herself, not from the workers or anyone else traveling.

She'd thought it would be easy. Once there, though, she recognized her mistake. The trains were massive up close, the air smelled of iron and grease, and everything clanged and groaned. Nowhere were there signs pointing out which engines were headed east and which were headed west. As she stood there contemplating her options, a hand settled on her shoulder.

Fighting panic, she turned to find a gray wool hat with longish black hair sticking out from under it. She stared into brown eyes so brown they seemed like tunnels to another place—somewhere she wanted to be.

Dill.

"Thought roads were your thing, Interstate."

She couldn't tell if he looked happy or mad or just indifferent. It couldn't be the last. Not him. She fumbled for paper.

Thought you'd be gone already.

"I stayed to help through the winter. Now it's time to head home. My family's expecting me."

Beyond?

He shook his head. "All filled in. We got some of them places to stay."

Andrea?

She raised her eyes hesitantly.

Another shake. "Doesn't look good."

Blue tore the page from her notebook, crumpled it, blinking away the tears that pooled in her eyes. Her fault. All of it.

Dill touched her hand. He took the paper from it, smoothed it out. "It sucks. It's wrong, and I don't know what to do other than just keep telling people how wrong it is. Someone's gotta listen, right?"

She shrugged.

"Gonna hop a train, huh?" Dill's smile didn't just tell her life went on—it said life was beautiful. Was that true? Did life have enough room in it for broken hearts and magic both?

She knew the answer. All she had to do was remember the faces lit by lantern light at Barn Magic.

Thought so. Headed for the coast.

"Why the coast? What are you looking for?

Good question.

Family. Home. Same as you. Same as anyone, right?

He grinned, looked along the closest track. Somewhere farther off, a whistle sounded.

"Well I happen to be traveling to the coast, too, dear Interstate. I'd love your company. Would you do me the honor of traveling with me?" He gave a bow, his eyes never moving from her face.

She couldn't stop the grin that started near the middle of her mouth and spread outward. In case that wasn't answer enough, she took his hand in hers and squeezed it.

"Come on, then. We don't want to be late."

Dill had already picked out a car before he'd spotted her. It looked like a boxcar would if someone had sliced off its top half. They had to climb a ladder on the side to get up, and inside were a few boards and a rusty piece of metal.

"Come on," Dill said. "We'll be happier if we snuggle in a corner."

She gave him a look, wondering for a minute if he really thought she had come to Missoula and climbed on a train just to fool around with him. He raised his hands.

"It just gets really windy. Promise. You don't have to sit with me at all if you don't want."

She grinned. She hadn't been looking for him, but she was happy she'd found him. She followed him to a corner, settled in next to him, one hand on her guitar case.

The train started to move. It jerked at first, then picked up speed. The wind blew against her face and the sun shone down as the dirt and slush and noise of the train yard faded away into roads, then roads and trees, and then just trees.

Had someone told her back in Maine that they rode on freight trains, she would have thought they were freaks. Hoboes rode them: guys from the last century with dirty caps and dirty hands and nowhere special to go. Blue studied the chapped skin of her hands, the grease streaks from where she'd gripped the metal climbing on, and thought about her own lack of a destination.

Dill didn't say much as the hours tumbled by. Not that she could do much better. Still, it felt as if a conversation was going on around them, the clatter of the train speaking to the blue of the sky and the arc of the mountains. The air she breathed in continued through her, sweeping away everything but the things she could see, smell, taste, and hear right then.

Feel. Don't forget that one. Warmth flowed in the places where Dill's shoulder touched hers, where his hand rested next to her thigh. Dill felt different than Beck, like an adventure, not an obligation.

"Tunnel's coming." Dill shifted. "Oh, crap. Tunnel."

Ahead she could see the black mouth in the mountain. She shaped her shoulders into a question.

He answered by opening his bag and pulling out a mask. "Respirator."

She drew a question mark in the air with her finger.

"Longest train tunnel in the U.S.," he explained. "All that diesel exhaust gets trapped inside. There are giant fans to blow it out in between trains, but it can get tough in there." He hesitated. "Here. Maybe you should wear it."

She shook her head and pushed his hand back toward him.

He tugged a strap, back and forth. "Listen, we can share. I'll wear it for a bit, then you. Back and forth. If one of us gets dizzy, we'll swap for longer."

They have to be fitted, right? All that adjusting? You know more about trains than me. You need to keep us both safe, so you need the mask.

He gave in at the last minute, as the dark space grew larger, closer. She drew a couple of deep breaths, curling one arm around her face.

Then the tunnel engulfed them.

The only tunnels she'd ever been in had been on highways, none of them a length that took more than a minute or two to traverse, all brightly lit by streetlights. This was nothing like those. The dark grew as the mouth of the tunnel shrank behind them. Everything seemed smaller and tighter, until she was certain that the ceiling would close in and crush their car like a mosquito against a knee.

Dill's hand enclosed hers. He spoke loudly, hard to hear over the noise and the cover of his respirator.

"The first time I went through, I screamed. Just like a little kid, you know. I didn't wet my pants or anything, but I was freaked.

"I was by myself then. A friend had told me about riding, said it was like being God, going where there were no roads, no houses, just wilderness all around. He died before he could ride with me, so I figured out how to ride the section he loved and spread his ashes along the whole way. Even in this tunnel. Now I feel like he's here all the time, like somewhere there's this guy, this tall, skinny guy with red hair and bad teeth and long fingers, giving his hand to someone to help them on the train when they need it. That's who he was. Couldn't take care of himself, but he always wanted to help other people."

Blue would have asked lots of questions if she could have. Things like how Dill's friend died, and why he spent so much time on trains, and how Dill had met him. She thought of her mother then, of what it meant when people asked how she died, their faces pulled a little tight, as if it were something unpleasant. One mother, one cancer, one girl in a well-labeled box. There was so much more to Mama than cancer, or even than being Blue's mother. Maybe asking how someone lived was at least as important as asking how they died.

The air tasted of fumes, hot and foul, and her head began to spin a little. She gripped her guitar more tightly and started to count. *One, two, three, four* . . . Cough once, suck in a lungful of hot factory breath. *Twenty-one, twenty-two, twenty-three* . . . She held her eyes closed tightly for a moment, streaks of lightning flashing across them. *Fifty-seven, fifty-eight, fifty-nine* . . . Or had she counted those already?

She sucked in another deep breath, only to be overwhelmed by another bout of coughing. Nothing seemed clear. It was as if her brain had been wrapped in bubble wrap and packed away. Time was passing—it had to be—but she had no idea of how fast.

Then everything opened into daylight again. Dill's face hovered near hers, and his hands gripped her shoulders. "You okay? You okay?"

Blue felt as close to a bird as she believed it possible to be. The air rushing past smelled of melting water and pine, not just heat and exhaust. The sky was everywhere. She lifted one hand, waved her arm in the wind, and opened her mouth wide.

She pressed up against Dill the way they had before the tunnel, only this time she thought of how he had whispered to her in the dark. It made her feel alive, as though her feet reached down into soil like roots while her hands reached toward the sun. In that moment, there was only one right thing to do: turn her face toward him and touch her lips to his. And the most right thing he could do was kiss her back, touch his hand to the back of her neck, his fingers rising under her hat to slip through her hair.

BY THE TIME THEY REACHED THE CITY, NIGHT HAD
settled deep. Lights and highways spread out around them, the trees
replaced by buildings. Fog smoothed all the edges, making ghosts
of everything. The smell of the ocean was subtler but unmistak-
able—she felt as if years had passed since she'd last breathed in salt
air. Dill looked happy—thrilled, even—and she reminded herself
that he was returning home. Seattle was nearly the end of travel for
him, not merely another stop.

As soon as the train slowed to a halt, he pulled her down and off
the train, scooting past other cars, other tracks, and out to a road. As
they walked, Dill fished a phone out of his pocket. She stared at it
dumbly for a moment. He had a phone.

Why wouldn't he? She'd have one, too, if she hadn't left hers at
Lynne's. Now it seemed so odd. A phone meant people to call, other
people with phones. It meant money. It meant voices.

She suddenly felt tired. Hungry, too, and more than a little
dirty. She watched him text for a minute, trying to remember the
last message she'd sent. It must have been to Lynne, a day or two
before she left.

"My sister's partner's on the way," he said, tucking the phone
back in his pocket. "You can stay with us tonight, if you want. It's a
drive, but you'd love it there."

He talked quickly, a little self-consciously. The words didn't register at first. Stay at his sister's. Tonight. She'd kissed him, and now he felt he should bring her home with him. He knew nothing about her, though, except that she played guitar and didn't speak and had lived in a hole for a bit. And really, what did she know about him?

She trusted him, though, and staying with him sounded far better than searching for something alone. She nodded.

A station wagon pulled up soon after. An African American man wearing a hand-knit red sweater several sizes too large for him stepped out and hugged Dill. He paused to shake Blue's hand, then threw their bags in the back. Only when he tried to take the guitar did she move, gripping it more tightly and shaking her head.

"I just thought you'd like more room in the car," he said. "You can keep it with you in the backseat."

"Uh, Fray, this is Interstate. She doesn't speak, and she's been on the road awhile." There was a long pause. He would have mentioned all this in his text. This was for her sake, not Fray's—letting her know how he'd explained her to them. "She's a good friend of mine."

"That's what Yar said. Interstate, I'm very pleased to meet you." He held out his hand again. She took it, slowly. "Sorry if I moved too quick. It's that Yarrow needs me home. It's William's time—" He turned to Dill. "I've been away most of the day and we still have a long way to go."

She fished in her back pocket, took out notebook and pen, pausing to yawn.

No prob! Thx so much! ☺

The noise of the car doors woke her. The air smelled damp, the lights outside swaddled in fog. Blue could make out an open door to a house, a woman's voice. Dill's face swung into view in her window. "Come on," he said. "Come and meet Yarrow."

He vanished into the fog. She followed a moment later. Toward the door, toward lit windows and laughter. Dill and Fray had been joined by a woman who looked so much like Dill that she had to be his sister. She shared his black hair and dark eyes, but was smaller and curvy, as though shaped by a baker who delighted in her dough.

"Interstate," the woman said. She looked like the hugging type, but she merely shook Blue's hand. "I heard about you from Dill during the winter. I'm so glad you met up again. You're welcome here."

Here. A two-story house with a single-floor arm of an addition stretching to one side. Blue caught a brief glimpse inside before being led through a sitting room and a kitchen and out a back door. Dill followed, her bag resting on one of his shoulders. The guitar she'd held on to.

"You'll probably be happier out here—" Yarrow directed her across a grassy lawn and through another door. "Dill usually stays in the yurt when he's visiting. Right now Roe is in here, but she's happy to share. Do you mind an air mattress?"

Yarrow turned a battery-powered lantern on with a click. The room was round, maybe twenty feet across; and the walls were made of latticed wooden slats covered in canvas. An empty futon rested on a frame on one side. An air mattress lay on the other, made up with sheets and blankets. A drum kit stood in the middle.

"Roe probably won't be home for another hour or so, but she promised to be quiet coming in."

Dill laughed. "As if that's ever been a problem for her."

Yarrow laughed as well. They even laughed the same, their

noses wrinkling along the same lines. *Families,* Blue thought, and she gripped her guitar more tightly.

After a sandwich in the kitchen, she took a long shower in a very small shower stall situated in a bathroom off a long hall. Yarrow and Fray had vanished after making sandwiches, and Dill's gaze had kept sliding to the door until Blue said she was tired and wanted to go to bed. Clean and alone, she returned to the yurt. Someone had laid a nightgown on the air mattress: flannel made for someone shorter and wider than her. She put it on and slid beneath the covers. Everything had a faint bleach smell and felt stiff and clean as hotel linens.

Watching Dill and Yarrow had opened a spot inside her, sore and sweet and full of the things she'd misplaced over time. She tried to remember everything she could about her sister, good and bad. Cass had been good at making people laugh. She'd take things in directions people didn't expect—lewder, darker, more absurd—then ambush them into responding.

Blue had always assumed the humor was Cass's own, but now she recognized it as coming from Tish. So much of Cass seemed to stem from Tish, not looks as much as attitude. Mama had given birth to Cass, but Tish had been her parent, too, for longer than she had been Blue's. Where would Tish have gone, if she'd run away like Cass? As nice as it was here, she could still feel the tick of the clock beneath her ribs. Cass was a riddle whose answer she was running out of time to find. She couldn't stay, not for long.

She hadn't spent much time thinking about it before the door opened and closed. Rain had begun to fall, creating a soft, steady drumming on the membrane of the yurt, and the intruder's footsteps hidden beneath it. Blue fumbled for the lantern switch. The light revealed a girl with her shirt over her head and nothing on beneath.

"Uh . . ." The girl gave her a steady look, neither raising or lowering her shirt. "I'll assume you're the mute girl, because anyone else would be apologizing right now, and because you're wearing Yarrow's clothes."

The mute girl. Was that how Dill had introduced her to his family? Blue assumed this girl was part of his family, though she didn't look the same. She was tall and angular, with honey-colored eyes and chin-length hair the shade of a golden retriever. She unabashedly finished pulling her shirt off, then took a much longer one from under her pillow and put it on. Blue was too tired to even think to turn away.

"Yes? Go ahead and nod."

She did so, a little annoyed, a little too sleepy to care.

"Okay. I'm Roe. Yar probably told you, right?"

She nodded again.

"And I'm totally beat, so what about lights out now? We can play twenty silent questions in the morning. 'Kay?"

Blue turned off the light, listening to the rustle of Roe getting into her bed. Somewhere in the house a light still shone, casting a sliver of warmth on the lawn. Dill, maybe, still awake in bed, or Yar and Fray, talking about their guest, about the return of wandering siblings.

BLUE WOKE WITH A START FROM A DREAM OF FLASHING
lights and rushing traffic. The futon was empty, its blankets thrown
back. Either Roe was a stealth artist, or she'd slept like the dead.
Either way, she felt a little exposed. *That's me: Mute Girl, doesn't
speak a word and sleeps through anything.*

She dressed quickly and left the yurt. Dampness engulfed her.
It was like stepping into a sea of someone else's sweat. Tall ever-
greens formed a curtain of dark green around the yard. She hurried
to the house, guitar in hand, unwilling to leave it alone.

Last night she'd missed a lot of things. The dry-erase board
in the kitchen containing a list of names and numbers, for example. The pair of locked cabinets. The industrial-sized oven with six
burners.

Fray came in while she was paused in front of a typed phone
list that included not only hospitals and emergency services but also
funeral homes and churches. He wore the same large sweater as
last night, only now he also had a stethoscope looped around his
neck. He smiled.

"You're up early. Didn't expect you for hours yet." He took a
key ring from his pocket and opened one of the locked cabinets.
Inside were rows of pill jars, prescription pads, and a pile of files.

He pulled a small paper cup from a dispenser and in it placed two pills from a vial.

Is this a nursing home?

Only a few unused pages remained in the notebook. She'd need a new one soon.

Fray had moved on to filling a glass with water but stopped to read her note. "Didn't Dill explain it to you? I would have assumed—" He cocked his head at a sound from the hall, then continued. "No, I suppose it didn't come up, did it?

"This house is part of the Willow Wind community. We try to provide a safe place for those who choose to step outside of mainstream society, for those who are pushed out, for those with no one to depend on. Everyone needs a home, Interstate."

He glanced at his watch. "I need to bring these down the hall. Would you like to come with me?"

He was carrying pills and had a stethoscope around his neck . . .

You an MD?

"Yes. One who's about to be late with someone's meds. Are you coming?"

Blue nodded and followed. A hippie doctor who lived on a commune; a drummer; and a smiling woman—these people were Dill's family. She saw him in a whole new light.

The hall led into the single-story addition she'd noticed last night. It looked a lot like a nursing home, only nicer. It was clean but not sterile; Monet prints hung on the walls between doors. Most of the doors were closed; Blue stopped at one that was ajar. The noise coming from within was one she would have known anywhere. In an instant, she was back in Lynne's house, curled in a chair, listening to the agonizing rasp of her mother's faltering breath.

She stepped back, away from the door.

Fray stopped, looked at her. "You've seen someone die before."

Yes. No. What was the right answer to that question? She settled for nodding.

"William. We've been taking turns sitting with him. I'm sure Yarrow would welcome the company if you want to go in."

Go in and watch someone die? He couldn't possibly mean it. If she hadn't stayed with Mama, how could she possibly stay with a stranger?

She peeked around the corner. A withered old man lay in the bed. His dark skin was a grayish hue, and his lips had faded to blue. Yarrow smiled at her, holding up a vast expanse of cloth she was knitting out of maroon yarn. "Have you come to sit with us?"

Blue shook her head, backing rapidly away. The only place she knew to go was the kitchen, where she found Dill and Roe eating toast at the butcher-block table.

"Hey," Dill said. "Sit down. Let me make you some toast."

She shook her head again. Her hands were trembling so hard, she was afraid she might drop her guitar. If she had had any breakfast, it would have come back up again. He was just a man she didn't know, dying elsewhere in the house. She needed to get a grip.

Both Roe and Dill were watching her. Did it show—the fear that had sent her scurrying away?

"Dad's one hundred and fifty percent thrilled that you're back in time to help. It's like nothing quite so stellar has ever happened before," Roe said, shifting her gaze to Dill. "He said he'd be here by nine tomorrow morning."

"Yeah, well, when is he ever not that excited about things? Um, Interstate, are you okay?"

She wasn't getting a grip. If anything, it was getting worse. She took her notebook out.

You know that man in the other room?

"Man in the other room?" Dill repeated.

"William," Roe said. "She means William. Right?"

She nodded, feeling like a bobble-head doll.

"Sure I know him. He doesn't really go for William. Yarrow's the one that calls him that. Anyway, he prefers Willy."

Where's his family?

Dill answered. "Most of his friends have died. He never had a partner or kids. He was a musician—a bluesman."

"No *was* about it, bro. He'd be pissed as hell to hear you say that." Roe looked up at Blue. "He plays guitar, like you."

You never turn down a musician in need.

Only he wasn't in need, right? Yarrow was with him, and other people would take turns. She didn't owe anything to this little old man lying in a bed down the hall. There was nothing she could do for him that they couldn't.

Only there was. Her heart beat a little harder as she reached for the guitar case resting by her feet.

She couldn't find Cass, and she couldn't save herself, but she could sit next to Willy and talk to him in the language they shared. She could stay.

You think I could sit with him?

She almost changed her mind at the door, when she heard his rasping breath again. But Yarrow smiled, and Roe followed her in. Yarrow offered her chair to Blue, saying she needed a break.

An almost completely empty bookcase stood beneath the window beside her. The middle shelf held a glass of water, a washcloth, and a digital clock, its red numbers dim in the daylight. On the top was a single, framed, black-and-white photo of a man playing a guitar.

She looked at the man in front of her. He was so small now, except for his hands resting on top of the blanket. They were huge and rough and curved as though still cradling the neck of his guitar.

She opened her case and tuned up the guitar, strumming the first notes to "Bluebird." Somewhere in the strings she could hear her voice. It was different from the one she'd had—a realer one, made of train smoke and soil, snow and good-byes.

When Blue finished the song, Roe touched Willy's hand. "You can't know anything about him at this point except what someone else tells you, and that's a shame. He was a damn good guitar player, and he had a voice like . . . I don't know how to describe it. Huge and rough. He told me a thing or two about how I play my drums." She grinned. "He helped make me a better drummer."

She glanced at Blue. "And I can tell you that he probably never listened to Dry Gully, but I have. That's her guitar, isn't it? Clare Riley's? Let me guess. You're her daughter."

Lots of words floated around Blue's head, such as *How* and *You're kidding me.* Maybe they weren't floating so much as racing around and around, a little racetrack going nowhere. She'd have to leave. Roe couldn't know her name, but it didn't matter, did it? Knowing who she was had to count the same as knowing she was Blue Riley.

Roe continued. "They were killer. You sound more like the other one, Tish Bellamy."

It was one small step from knowing who her mother was to knowing what her name was. All it would take was five minutes online. She'd have to leave. She had to, anyway—she didn't have that much time left to find Cass. But right then staying by Willy's bedside seemed more important than anything else she might ever do.

She began to play again. Nothing of her mother's, nothing of Tish's or anyone else's. She played the music that had first come to her in Beyond. She could almost hear all the words, and they helped move her fingers, told her where the accent points fell and when to back off. She could hear everything in it: her entire story.

"Nice," Roe said at the end. "Better if you had a bit of backup. You ever play with a band?"

Blue shook her head. Beside her, Willy kept on breathing, softer, louder, sometimes stopping for an agonizing stretch before returning to his work. Lynne had told her and Cass that it was okay to talk when they sat with Mama, but they'd been too scared. Lynne had a friend who came to help, though, and the two of them did talk. Not about important things, even, just stories from when they were all younger, or what they'd been doing that week, or what the weather was like. She supposed she was doing that, only with fingers and strings.

She kept playing. Roe left after a while. Yarrow poked her head in at one point, but she didn't stay, either. There were just Blue and Willy and the guitar, and the rain that had started up again and streaked the windowpanes.

After a long time she wasn't even playing songs, just following chords around and around, her fingers wandering the strings. It wasn't until she heard the silence beyond the music that she stopped.

Willy wasn't breathing.

Finally, a breath came, slow and shuddering, sliding out like the sea on the sand.

Then a space, longer, longer, longer, before he breathed again.

Willy was dying, and there was nothing she could do to stop it.

Her hands stilled. Not her heart—it beat fast inside her. The urge to run was so strong, and yet . . . her boots said nothing. No ache, no pressure. This was where she was meant to be.

She watched Willy as if to blink would be a betrayal. The way she should have watched Mama. So intent that she didn't even notice the figure until the smell came to her. Oranges, whole, fresh, in the middle of winter; a warm fire on a cold day.

She was a tall woman. Beautiful—not like a model; like someone who had lived a long life, had seen everything there was to see and had found enough to make her happy. Her skin was darker than Willy's, her hair collected on top of her head by a deep red scarf. She bent beside the bed, never once looking at Blue.

Another breath, dragged up from the bottom of a very deep well. The woman touched his cheek. "I know," she said. "I've heard it all, Willy. I know you always stayed true."

She leaned over him and touched her lips to his. As she pulled back, something silver stretched between them.

No. Blue stared, afraid of teeth, afraid of tearing and chewing and suffering. Something different happened, though. The silver thread stretched, thinned, a water droplet between the two of them, until, with a final sigh, Willy's chest sank down completely. The thread vanished.

The woman stood. She laid one hand on Willy's chest and sighed out a long, slow breath. Guitar music shivered through the room. Blue could hear the squeak of strings as fingers ran along them. The song spiraled around her, around the bed and onward, past the room, dissolving into chords as it spun out into the world.

All the songs, even the forgotten ones, swirl in the air to become part of what's to come.

Willy's.

Mama's.

Even though they were gone.

Blue didn't start to cry until after Fray had come in and done what he needed to confirm what she already knew. Once the tears started, though, they didn't want to stop. It was as if she'd tapped into a secret well, and it might take the rest of her life to empty it. She refused to move from her spot, to do anything other than cry over a small, elderly man whom she'd never known, who'd died so quietly in front of her.

But she did know him. She knew what she'd heard—the song the woman in the red dress had drawn forth from him.

Tish was right. She'd never understood who her bargain was really with.

When Yarrow and another woman came in with washcloths and bowls of warm water, Blue returned the guitar to its case and stumbled out of the room. She ignored Yarrow's call, instead continuing down the hall until she came to another open door. This one led into a large room. Windows covered the far wall, looking out onto the yurt; the sky was already darkening again. Night had arrived so soon. Had she spent the whole day in Willy's room?

A series of mismatched couches made a horseshoe around a TV. Two women looked up as she entered, then returned their attention to the screen.

"Not sure our boy has a chance." One of the women shook her fist at the TV, exposing a hand with just three fingers. "He made it all the way to the finals, but these things are rigged."

Blue sank into the couch. She felt as though part of her had stayed in Willy's room, that even now she was sitting in the silence there. A familiar logo bounced in the corner of the TV screen: a hot pink musical note in a blue box. *Major Chord.* Jed and Jill belonged to another lifetime now—one where women didn't take their children to live in tunnels, where predators didn't lurk, feeding on the lost wandering the streets.

"You gotta admit, that boy and girl in that band, they're real cute together. She don't look stuck up, not at all. Can't imagine that Mr. Rick Rafael is gonna give them the time of day, though. No, not him."

Rick Rafael? She could see him in her mind, black leather and spiky hair and mascaraed eyes. She could imagine Mama, too, her bracelets jangling as she embraced him.

Where would Cass have gone?

Inside Blue was sinking and rising simultaneously, her heart beating out a rhythm that could have been fear or triumph as she stared at the TV, her feet beginning to ache in her boots. Three finalists: a short African American man with a shaved head and gold hoops in his ears; Lost Highway, Jed and Jill holding hands and looking at each other with fake devotion; and a woman, C. R. Smith—immaculate hair, deep red lips, mascaraed eyes so similar to her father's.

Cass.

I have to get to L.A.!

Dill stared at her blankly. Roe took the note from his hand, nodded her head. "Cool. How fast?"

The entertainment news had said the taping of the final show would be on Thursday. It was Tuesday evening already. She held up two fingers.

"Two days? Wait, Interstate, you're just going to take off? I thought," Dill paused, glanced at Roe. "I thought I was going to show you around."

Good-bye notes had become second nature. Leaving someone in person was so much harder.

I have to go. I can't explain it in a way you'd understand, but after I'm finished I'll tell you all about it. Or come with me.

Once finished, she'd have a home, a sister . . . a voice. No more notes, ever. She touched her throat.

"But—"

"Dude." Roe slid off the kitchen counter she'd been sitting on. "The girl needs to get to L.A. The only correct response to that is 'How fast?,' not all this 'But you promised' crap. Promises are stretchy. Not every train runs on the same schedule."

Dill looked back and forth between them. "I can't go. Dad's counting on me."

"It's okay. I can go. Haven't been to La-La Land in a while."

Blue could have argued. Would have, but for a clock ticking inside her. It wasn't herself she was saving now. Cass was the one who'd signed with the devil.

Dill borrowed Yarrow's aged Volvo to drive them to the highway early the next morning. He stopped on the side of the road and got out of the car with them. Roe had insisted he couldn't stay while they waited because no one would stop for the three of them. He'd reluctantly agreed. The sky overhead was heavy gray, but beside them stood a tree covered in the silver green of newly fledged leaves, and a bird sang from the top. Dill hugged Roe, then stopped in front of Blue.

"I'll see you again, right? This isn't just 'bye?'"

She was almost finished with good-byes. One quick touch—her fingertip on his cheek—before pressing her lips against his. It was the closest thing to an answer she could offer. Her boots were telling her it was time to go.

Roe had said that getting rides would be no problem, and she was right. Once Dill left, the second car to pass by stopped for them. The middle-aged man driving took them all the way to the California border. By the time he dropped them at a highway truck stop, it was midafternoon.

"It's not always easy to pick truckers," Roe said as they looked in the plate-glass window of the diner. "First of all, they're not supposed to pick up hitchers. Second, lots are either religious nuts or looking for sex. Third—"

Blue hit her arm and hurried for the front door. The hair on the woman's head wasn't black anymore, it was flamboyant red; but the face was the same.

Lou! ☺

She scrawled it quickly once she reached the booth, then held it out, sure the woman wouldn't recognize her. For a long minute she thought maybe she was wrong and it was just some other woman sitting by herself, cracking peanuts from a bowl and drinking bottled water.

But Lou's face broke out in a big grin. "How the heck are you? No way I expected to see you again, let alone all the way out here. Figured you'd settle yourself down in Massachusetts somewhere, get your life straightened out."

Nope. I'm here.

She felt inordinately pleased. Queen of the Roads, that was her.

How ya been?

"I've been just fine, thank you. I changed things up a little bit. New hair. New traveling companion. Took on some western runs for a bit. Felt like it was time to try out something new, you know. 'Course you know. You know all about it, don't you?" Blue nodded and allowed herself to return Lou's smile.

Her eyes shifted over Blue's shoulder, to where Roe stood. "Looks like you got a traveling companion of your own."

Just for now. Headed to L.A.

Lou looked concerned. "Now, hon, you're not doing something stupid, right? None of this 'I'm going to be a star' foolishness? I thought you'd know better than that."

No way. We're

. . . what? How could she explain it?

going to see my sister. She's a finalist in Major Chord.

"Is she now? Music runs in your family, I guess." A glance at her watch. "Look at the time. I need to get moving. Got to get this load all the way to the border."

"So you're going through L.A.?" Roe nudged Blue.

Lou studied Roe. She must have looked at Blue the same way, once upon a time. Blue had looked at others that way, too—watching for the little clues, the ones that didn't even register as thought but traveled as electrical impulses, raising the hair on her arms or easing the muscles in her shoulders.

Finally, she nodded. "Yes, I am. I take it you want a ride?"

"Yes, ma'am." Roe pressed her chin into Blue's shoulder.

"Come on, then."

Lou's new companion turned out to be a German shepherd. "Ladies, this is Lola. She's a good girl, long as no one bothers me. She's only got three legs, but she gets around just fine without the fourth."

Lola disappeared behind the seats, only a disdainful sniff in their direction to let them know she'd seen them. Roe and Blue followed her back, only to have her leap forward to claim the passenger seat.

"So you hitched with her before? Crazy kind of luck for you," Roe whispered. Lou had turned on a lecture, a man talking about the history of humans in the Arctic Circle, loud enough to drown them out.

Blue shrugged.

"That's what you're doing? Going to see your sister? She know you're coming?"

She shook her head before settling back, guitar between her knees. Only five unused pages remained in her notebook.

She ran away. I haven't seen her for two years. More like 2½.

"Sucks. Your parents no good or what?"

My mom died. No dad. My mom left Tish when she got sick.

"Why?"

That was the million-dollar question, wasn't it?

I think she felt like she'd made bad choices. She thought leaving would make us make better ones.

Roe laughed. "That worked out well."

It could have been funny, had it not been for the years without Mama or Tish. Or for all the ways she and Cass hadn't fit in Eliotville, no matter how they tried.

Dill's your brother?

Roe shrugged. "Yeah. Not by blood. I was adopted when I was two."

You remember your parents from before?

She didn't know if that was the wrong kind of question.

"My birth mom, yeah. She was on drugs, and she knew she was going to lose me, so she asked at Willow Wind if they would take me in. Natalie, our mom, said yes. When my birth mom got clean, finally, a few years back, we started meeting again."

What's that like?

"Okay. It's kind of tough. I was really angry at first, and she's HIV positive, which made me angrier. You kind of want a mom to be the person that does everything right by you, you know? But lately I've been thinking she did what she could at the time, held it together enough to put me someplace where I had the whole frigging village to raise me. I have a mom who loves me, and I have this other **woman,** who I'm learning to be friends with; and that's the way my **life looks."**

A memory came to her, of Mama and Tish, Mama's feet in

Tish's lap as they lounged on the couch. Happiness cocooned around them all, sturdy and safe and permanent.

At least, it had felt that way.

So what are you doing?

Roe gave her a funny look. "Going to L.A."

After that?

Another page gone. She needed to be more careful. With no money and time running out, finding a new one wasn't a priority.

"Who knows? I was trying to get my band hooked up again, but we pretty much define that whole 'irreconcilable differences' thing. Like, Lucy and Cam think we're way back in the nineties. Gotta take some time and think about that whole 'Who am I and where am I going?' piece."

How old are you?

"Eighteen."

At nineteen, Dill was traveling alone and studying communities and helping homeless families. At eighteen, Roe had already had one band and was thinking about what to do next. Their lives looked nothing like those of the kids Blue had gone to school with, the kids she would have been graduating with, had she not left Eliotville. There were so many more choices in the world than she'd ever realized. The trick was to know when you were running away from something, and when you were running to meet it. Telling people that Mama and Cass were the only real musicians in her family—that had been running away. Same with trying to keep everything the same with Beck and Teena, even though it felt like she'd been still. What kind of running was the deal she'd made at the crossroads?

Who was she?

Nine years ago, she'd been a scared little girl whose mother was dying. Nine years from now, she'd be twenty-six, old enough to have gone through college and graduated and found a job. Or not. She remembered the feeling of playing with Tish in the bar, of Barn Magic, of music and of feathers growing through skin, and the words that kept coming to her even when she tried to ignore them.

She scribbled the words down and held out her notebook to Roe.

Know anything about songwriting?

53

THEY REACHED L.A. CLOSE TO ELEVEN. LOU LOOKED THE two of them over again, shook her head a little. "You look a little harder than when I picked you up in Maine, but not mean. The road's just burned away your baby fat, hasn't it?"

Blue nodded. It was true in a literal way: Javier's belt was loose enough these days that she could slide it over her hips on the smallest hole. But the other way was right, too. The road had stripped away all her unnecessary pieces.

"You sure you're okay? I hate to leave you in this city without knowing where you're going."

We'll be OK. Thank you.

Blue wrote on the back cover of the notebook, every page filled. It was okay. If she was right, she wouldn't need it much longer.

"Okay, ladies. You be careful, then. I hope your sister does real well."

Lou honked as she pulled away, the dog smiling from the passenger's seat. The last time Blue had watched her go, she'd been scared. This time Blue felt like a torch: not yet lit, but so close to the flame and so ready to burn.

"What do we do now?" asked Roe.

Blue looked around her at the lights, the streets, the cars, so different from Maine. It didn't make a difference. All it took was the intersection of two paths.

We need a really good crossroads.

"You're crazy," Roe yelled.

Blue didn't look back. She'd told Roe to wait for her. Believing she knew what she was doing didn't mean nothing could go wrong, and she didn't want Roe with her if it did. She left her pack, too, and the guitar case, slinging the guitar by its strap across her back.

The city was all lights, sound, and traffic, even at three minutes to midnight. The hot air smelled of exhaust. The buildings were lower than she'd expected, and less dense, though spires rose in the distance. She could see "Hollywood" on the street sign across the road. A few drivers yelled at her as she strode out to the middle of the intersection. There was no island to stand on, just the pavement and lanes, with her in the middle.

Then the lights changed and Blue stood there, frozen, as the traffic rushed past. Somewhere she heard a clock begin to chime, or maybe it was only in her head. It didn't matter. She closed her eyes and thought, *Now.*

Nothing changed for a moment. Then the noise of the traffic lessened, smoothing away like paint gliding over a dirty wall. She opened her eyes.

Around her, the world zoomed by. Lights, cars, people, lives— she saw them as brilliant streaks flashing past. *Slow down*, she wanted to say, but they couldn't. In that space, she understood they couldn't, that everything passed by faster than you ever thought it would.

She wasn't alone. She could feel it in the electric spark that raced up her spine. She only took in pieces at first: the red dress blowing a little in the breeze, the tips of the long black hair rippling as well. Next came the smell, the sweet scent of meltwater and wood smoke as spring brought an end to winter.

"Interesting choice," the woman said. "You used to be able to hear the dreams whispering from the hopeful come to pay homage here. Now?" She shrugged. "One more set of streets."

Roe had told her this intersection used to be famous, still was in a kitschy way. The road names had meant nothing to her.

"Bluebird."

She'd left her notebook behind, as well. She thought, instead, of leaving Maine, of the librarian and her photos, of Steve and his courage, of Andrea and her daughter, of Tish, of music and faces and cruelty and kindness. Of herself.

It's time. It's mine. You have to give it back.

"Are you commanding me, Blue Riley?" The woman watched, intently.

I am.

The woman stepped forward. "Close your eyes."

Blue did. She could feel the woman come closer still, could feel the heat of her and the movement of the air. Even closer, her hand brushing against Blue's forehead, carrying with it the smell of diesel and dirt, of Mama, her skin, her soap. For a moment, Blue wavered, but she kept her eyes closed.

She felt lips touch her forehead as hands held her head. A rush-and-tumble traveled through her, like the filling of a cup beneath the spill of a waterfall. She heard bits of songs—so many, so different—their notes like the battering of butterfly wings against her.

"Open your eyes."

Still everything streaked past fast as starlight, only the woman in the red dress motionless before her.

"Do you know what you will do? He is stronger than you think, but so are you."

As if there was a question. The world may have been tipped toward the place where someone could die in a ditch without help. That didn't mean she wasn't going to do everything in her power to right the balance, starting with her own sister.

She nodded. The woman smiled. "You'll not share it with me, will you?"

Blue shook her head. Her voice. She'd given it away once; she never would again. Life took things from you: mothers, friends, sometimes even choices. But that wasn't the same as giving parts of yourself away. It was her voice to use: to say no and yes and "I love you" with, to sing with, even to hold silent. That night at the crossroads, her voice had meant little to her. Not just her voice. She'd ignored so many parts of herself, the ones that could be brave or loving, that could hurt and survive and become something more. The woman in the red dress had taken from her at the crossroads, but she'd given her the chance to become . . . herself.

The woman was gone. Around her the traffic stilled as the light changed. She ran across the road and back to Roe, who sat on her pack, drumming on her knees.

"That was one of the weirder things I've ever watched anyone do. Tell me we didn't come here just so you could play in traffic."

Blue looked up into the sky, the sooty gray sky, all the stars hidden from view.

"Hell no," she said. "It's time to find my sister."

ROE KNEW A PERSON WHO KNEW A PERSON WHO COULD
tell them all the ins and outs of filming *Major Chord*. Before she'd
talk to that person, though, she wanted to hear how Blue had walked
into the intersection and come back with a voice.

"Were you pretending all along?"

"No way." It felt funny to talk. She missed the writing a little.
No room remained in the notebook, though. It was full of magic.

"So what was going on?"

Blue told her everything. They sat on the curb at a bus stop; Roe
drummed on the soles of her sneakers with the drumsticks she'd
brought along, while Blue explained it all.

"So why *then*? Your sister had been gone for two years."

"We had a promise that we'd always be together on Mama's
birthday. The first year, she called. The second, she didn't." The
rest—Teena and Beck and all the things that had felt so important
in Eliotville—mattered so little now.

"Why'd she go?"

"I thought it was because I'd found these letters to my mom
from Cass's father. Cass got mad because she thought they meant
one thing, only they didn't. Anyway, I thought she left because she
was mad at me. Now I think she was looking for her father because

she thought he could fix things. She thought our lives would have been better if our mother had been famous."

Roe nodded. "So why *Major Chord*?"

Blue explained the rest, about the man in the blue shirt and Amy's soul and the contracts the others had signed. "The man in the blue shirt is using fame to get them to give up the truest part of them. 'Cause that's what a soul is, right? Like, Jed broke his promise to Bet, left her behind after she gave up her scholarship for him. I can stop it still, if I can get to them."

They spent the night on the living room floor of a crowded apartment. It belonged to Fray's nephew, who picked them up looking half asleep and vanished as soon as they reached the place.

Roe had answers for them by breakfast the next morning. "The deal is that tickets to the filming tonight are totally gone; but my friend has an idea. This story you have, the whole teenage-girl-travels-across-country-to-see-missing-sister thing? People watching would eat it up. So he has a friend who has a friend who works for Entertainment Express, and she can get you in to see a producer. They can probably get you to the show tonight."

The office building Roe's friend sent them to was deep in the city. Blue shivered as she looked up at the towers. It wasn't Chicago, and she wasn't who she'd been then. She touched her throat and hummed, just to hear the sound. The feeling passed, replaced by a sense of conspicuousness as she walked into the building, her jeans loose around her waist, her T-shirt faded. The thud of her boots sounded nothing like the clip of the receptionist's shoes; she felt like an elephant following a bird at a watering hole.

The producer listened as she told her story again, a version tailored to her goal. He went from bored to calculating as she watched. By the end, he was all but rubbing his hands together.

"So C. R. has no idea you've come to see her?"

"None."

"And do you have any musical talent yourself? Anything?"

She smiled. "I play guitar and sing."

"Spectacular. Let me make a few phone calls."

She and Roe waited under the receptionist's curious eye for ten minutes or so before the phone buzzed and the woman sent them back in.

"Well," said the man. "What do you think about joining your sister onstage tonight?"

"I'd love to." She rode the adrenaline wave like a surfer. "I have a question first, just so I don't mess up. Can you tell me about the rules of the contract for *Major Chord* contestants?"

THEY TRIED TO CONVINCE BLUE TO WEAR A DRESS, BUT
when she stepped out of the black SUV that evening, she was in
jeans. They were clean, fitted jeans, and the producers' stylist had
paired them with a green T-shirt that was crisp from its first wash.
The boots she'd offered no compromise on. They no longer made
her feet ache. She missed it a little—not the feeling as much as the
sense of purpose they'd given her. That was the point, though. She
understood it now. They never were telling her how to find Cass,
just reminding her to keep moving until she found herself.

She had Roe with her. Roe had her drumsticks. Blue had told
everyone that she was coming with her own band, but the truth was
that she had only the two of them, along with the song she'd written
out on sheets torn from the unicorn journal. It would have to be
enough.

A woman with a clipboard directed them through the back
door of the theater and on down a dimly lit hall to a small room.
Another woman bustled in behind them and approached Blue with
a makeup brush in hand. Blue shook her head.

"You'll look washed out. You want to look good onscreen."

"Not worried about that." Makeup wouldn't make a bit of difference to what she was about to do.

Everyone left but Roe, and Blue settled down to wait, her stomach tying itself in knots. She'd escaped Rat. She'd figured out the puzzle. She had lost people and survived. Why was the thought of stepping onto the *Major Chord* stage so hard?

Because this time she was playing for more than pocket change. This time she was playing for Cass, and she was doing it in front of an audience big enough to give almost anyone stage fright.

She sat hunched over the wastepaper basket, her stomach roiling. A knock at the door brought on dry heaves, and Roe left her spot rubbing Blue's back to answer it.

"Holy shit" was the first thing Blue heard. She raised her head.

Tish. Spiky hair, leather jacket, dark-rimmed eyes. Fiddle case under her arm. Battle gear.

"How did you know?" Blue's stomach lurched, then quieted for a moment.

"Hey, she speaks! Sharlene has a thing for these reality shows, and we were watching the other night together and I saw Cass. I knew who she was, and I knew you'd come for her. I figured you might need help. I thought I should be here." The look she gave Blue was full of so many things that were hard to say. "Anyway, I pulled a few very old strings. Rick and I were never on good terms, but this got his attention."

"He knows?"

"Now he does."

Her heart gave a lurch of its own. "Have you seen her? Does she know?"

"Not yet." Tish laid her fiddle case down on the table, opened it. "I assume you've got something of your own to play. You planning on sharing it with me?"

Blue raised her guitar, then lowered it again. Something else needed answering first. "Did you know who the woman in the red dress was?"

Tish studied her before speaking. "Blue, there's always a muse waiting. There's always a journey required. You can't play—can't sing or write for real—until you start finding your way."

"But she hurt people." Blue could still hear Andrea's scream as the police entered Beyond.

"The world hurts people. We hurt people. She just made you open your eyes. And now that you see, it's up to you to start making things better. Come on, kid, time to teach me your song."

She had only one chance, and it hinged on holding the audience long enough to bring Cass in. Cass had been told by the producers that they'd done some digging to find out more about her background and that they loved the angle of Mama and Dry Gully and a tragic death so much that they'd done a special arrangement of "Avenue A" to showcase her voice. Cass wouldn't like it, but she'd do it, because those were the rules of her contract. She had to sing what they told her to sing, had to dress how they told her to dress, had to be the person they decided she should be. In exchange, they'd fabricate fame for her.

To break the contract—to free Cass from the man in the blue shirt—Blue had to get her to be true onstage. She needed her to be the real Cass, not a doll with Cass's voice and Cass's hands and nothing of her own. And to do that, she needed her secret weapon.

Tish looked it over first. "Good work, kid," she said, and suggested a few minor changes, only one of which Blue used. When they played it through—Roe providing a beat on the table, Tish coming in on fiddle like a swallow soaring effortlessly above—Blue nearly couldn't sing. And when Tish joined her on the chorus, she missed a line as her throat closed around the words.

How had Mama given it up? How had she walked away from Tish who loved her, from the music that loved her even more, to return to Eliotville? Because she'd been scared. Because she'd seen what was coming, and she'd run back to the one place that had felt like safety, even though it didn't fit.

"It wasn't all her." Tish looked at Blue as if her secrets were paraded on her face.

"What do you mean?"

Roe coughed and knelt to examine her shoelace.

"I was stupid, Blue. I forgot that fame is something other people hand you, while success is what you define for yourself. I was chasing the wrong thing, and it made me angry at the world. I started drinking more than I should. I started to believe what people said about me, started acting like it. It was her; but it was me, too, and it was complicated. We were stuck with her regret and my anger, and then we just ran out of time and there was no way to make it right anymore."

A light gloss of sweat shone on Tish's neck, her arms. The lines around her eyes, her mouth, were deeper in the harsh light. They were lines shaped by laughter and tears, by mistakes and triumphs. By Mama, by all of them.

Blue understood.

WHEN THE NEXT KNOCK CAME, IT WAS TO LEAD THEM
backstage. The darkness there made the stage brilliant, like the sun
rested on it.

"Do you know what's up? Something, right?" A woman's voice,
close to her ear. Jill.

Blue got as far as "um" before Jill grabbed her.

"Blue Riley? How did you end up here? You were in Massachusetts last I knew. Wild!"

But Blue wasn't paying attention, because the woman ahead of
them had turned. Shorter hair, thinner face, same sly eyes, same
careless mouth. "Blue? Bluebird? Oh, my God." Everything vanished around them, just Cass holding Blue's shoulders, pulling her
so close that she could barely breathe.

There are things you can forget about someone gone away—
things you have no reason to remember: like how you're taller by
just a finger's width, and how it sounds when they say your name,
or how they bite their lower lip when they try not to cry. And then,
the moment you see them again, everything is there, as if you'd
covered up your hand with a towel, forgot about it for days, months,
years; until suddenly you found it again, working perfectly, and
unmistakably yours. Blue clung to Cass as if she might step into the

light and vanish again. It was that quick, that simple, that impossible to ever be without her again.

"What are you doing here? Did they find you? Is Lynne—" She broke off as she looked past Blue, into the shadows. "Tish?"

Tish didn't move.

"What are you doing here?" The anger that had eaten away at Cass in Eliotville twisted her face into something ugly. She stepped toward Tish, reached out, and shoved her.

"How can you be here? How can you even think of being here when you left us? You left me." In her sister's face, Blue could see how hurt hardens itself into armor, into fury.

Tish cleared her throat. "I'm so sorry, Cassie Bear. I let my hurt get in the way of taking care of you. I never should have done it."

"It's not that easy," Cass said. "You can't just say things and have it be done."

Suddenly there was a woman with a clipboard, and she collected Blue and Roe and Tish, leading them onto the stage. From beyond the curtain came a steady rumble, and Blue knew she couldn't face what was on the other side.

"I can't. There's no way—"

Roe answered. "This is nothing, Interstate. Badasses like you chew up crowds this size and spit them out before breakfast. You're not even going to see them when the curtain goes up. It'll be black out there, so you can pretend you're singing in the shower."

The woman with the clipboard was motioning with her fingers: five, four, three—Blue's mouth went dry, someone was at her elbow plugging the guitar in—two, one. She wasn't prepared—how could she be?—for the moment the curtain rose. *Don't look,* she thought, *even though it's black, don't try to look into it and see.* She glanced back for Tish and found the man in the blue shirt instead, grinning at her from the wings. Her voice retreated into her throat, wrapping itself up like a flower blooming in reverse. She couldn't sing. Not while she could remember Amy and the snick of teeth and her endless scream.

He patted his hands together in fake applause. He'd won. He knew it, she knew it. The only person who didn't know it was Cass, waiting in the wings to lose her soul.

Blue closed her eyes and saw the lanterns lighting the walls of the barn. She could almost feel the warmth of the woodstove. *Remember that the devil is the one who tells you to play a tune that's not your own, and you can drive him right on out into the cold by playing what's in your soul.*

She began. Together, they'd worked out an intro similar enough to "Avenue A" that no one would know the difference until she sang the first words. Then it was up to them to hold the audience, up to her to get the others to join in. It all started with the first words.

Cold starlight, dusty road . . .

She almost stumbled, but Roe was there, providing the pulse beneath. Then Tish came in, spiraling above. The music was more than just Roe and Tish, though, it was Steve, and Dill, and Andrea, and the clatter of the train. It was the woods of Maine and the earth of Minnesota. As she reached the chorus for the first time, she realized it was Amy, too, her soul taken by the man in the blue shirt; and Marcos and his drugs; and the hunger that hollowed them. *This world*, she sang—and it was the librarian, and her father, and her mother waiting, always waiting—*This world* . . . She turned toward the others offstage.

She sang to them, willed them to join her. *This world*, she told them, *is full of broken things, but together we can mend them.* She meant it, every word.

When it was time for the next verse, Blue turned forward. As she moved her head, she saw the man in the blue shirt, still grinning, and she sang even harder.

I got a dollar in my pocket, fifty cents of that is yours. / I got a sleeping bag in my pack, with room for just one more. Only it had room for so many more, for all of them.

They'd reached the chorus again. Blue motioned with her guitar. Why would any of them join her? Fame waited for them as long as they ignored her. *This world,* she sang, and she could see beyond the dark and into the empty spaces of the cities and boarded-up houses; then beyond those places, to where the invisible go. To abandoned barns filled with light and music for just one night, where musicians played what was in their hearts to save one another from the cold.

She heard Jill before she felt her. Jill's voice chased Tish's harmony, her hand on the small of Blue's back as she joined her at the mic.

Two verses gone, three to go, with Cass still in the wings.

They came before she'd even reached the end of the next verse— Jed, and the man the women had talked about at Yarrow's—and they joined the chorus from the start, delving deeper, their voices the shovels that broke the ground at Beyond. They were the men who were not Rat, or Andrea's husband, who came to help and not to destroy, and in doing so, saved themselves.

Another verse, another chorus, and still no Cass. If she didn't come, she'd win the show by default, because the other contracts were already broken. All Blue had was their mother's guitar and her own voice to call her.

But that wasn't true. Blue had the others onstage, and now, growing, the voices from the audience like the ocean rolling in.

For the first time, she tried to see them, the crowd hidden in the darkness before her.

At the final verse, *The light covers you, covers me,* Tish and Roe pulled back, letting Blue sing to Cass on her own. She could see Cass wavering when she turned, and she stepped toward her.

Around her, darkness crawled across the stage. The man in the blue shirt no longer lurked in the shadows. He stood between Blue and Cass. The darkness that came with him brought a chill that traveled into her. She'd never had the power to change anything, it told her, never had a chance.

"Buyer's market," the man in the blue shirt said. His teeth glistened as he spoke. "I told you that before. Everyone's selling so cheap. The few you've saved, they're nothing. A few pebbles on a gravel road. You make your stand here, and you'll be forgotten within days, if not hours."

Could be the end is coming, could be time to go, / Could also be change running, beside us on the road. Blue sang because there was nothing else to do, because the words were hers, and because she had no other way to reach Cass. She forced her fingers to keep going despite the cold; her lips to move despite the frost that grew on them; her heart to beat despite the fear that closed round it.

"Sing all you want, little girl; but you lost, long ago. This world dances to our tune these days—and face it." His grin stretched wider as the odor of decay wafted from his mouth. "One girl with an old guitar means nothing to anyone anymore."

The chorus. Around her came the voices of everyone, candle-light in the dark. *This world,* she began; but despair swept in as she turned back to face the audience.

Until she heard the voice that mirrored her own. She didn't

turn. The sensation of feathers spread over her skin, her hope rising like wings. The voice came closer, Cass pressing a shoulder against Blue as she leaned in to share the mic, singing the way they had as children. From somewhere far away, Blue heard a roar so huge it drowned out everything. At first, she thought it was the man in the blue shirt, come to destroy them all; but then someone swung a spotlight over the audience, and she could see hundreds of people on their feet, their applause shattering the ice inside her.

That night they waited until after the crowds had emptied out and the cameras had been packed away before trying to leave the building.

Jed and Jill left before them. "It was exciting, but it wasn't going to change things," Jill said. "Instead of the backup singer, I was the singing girlfriend. That's not what I'm looking for."

"And I'm totally not the guy they were selling," Jed said. "The thought of always living like that . . . no way."

"Where's Bet?" Blue asked.

Within Jed's face something trembled, a seismic shift that hurt her to see. "I thought she'd be here. I assumed, I guess. I haven't really talked to her in—"

"Way too fucking long," Jill finished for him. "We both screwed up on that one."

"Big time," Jed said.

Only then a noise came from the back of the theater, a door opening, and Blue could see Bet standing back there. Jed jumped down from the stage and ran toward the back. Jill picked up his guitar and hugged Blue before following him out. The last Blue saw of them, they'd each had an arm around Bet.

That left the four of them—Blue, Cass, Roe, and Tish—to meet Rick Rafael as he headed out to his limo. He studied Cass carefully before speaking.

"I don't see Clary much in you. I wouldn't have seen myself, either, without Tish pointing it out."

They stood there, Cass looking him over just as thoroughly. "I thought it would be different," she said finally. "Silly of me." She turned to walk away.

"Is that it?" he called after her.

"You were never my father, not in any real way. Not any more than Donor 707 is Blue's."

A lone woman approached, cutting through the tension. She wore a black blazer unbuttoned over a blue silk shirt, and she held out her hand to Blue.

"Let me congratulate you on one hell of a performance. You have real star quality, Miss Riley. Kind of rough in the presentation department, but with some coaching and a little wardrobe help, you could be big. I'd love to talk more with you. I think we could make a deal, get you recording soon."

Blue touched her throat and rocked a little in her boots. She thought about the feel of singing in front of the *Major Chord* audience, the moment when she'd heard their applause. Without help, she'd never get that back. Once in a lifetime, if that, you could steal onto someone else's stage and play. Perhaps this evening would always be the best, the brightest moment in her life, already gone by, unless she made a deal.

"Um, I'm not sure. Do you have a business card or something?"

"Yes, but I'd really love to talk with you soon."

"Not tonight," said Blue, taking the card from the woman's hand.

On a street corner ahead of them, a lone man began to play a banjo. She watched with curiosity as he started to sing. She knew the song in her bones, even if the words were unfamiliar.

"Just a minute," she said to the others; and she ran to him, feeling around in her pockets for change. But she saw no case or cup to drop money into. The man nodded at her. She tilted her head to read the words written on the body of the banjo: "This Machine Surrounds Hate and Forces It to Surrender." For a moment, the air was filled with the whispers of thousands of songs, voices, instruments played and gone, a river of echoes. Music made, lives lived: Mama's, Willy's, everyone's. Blue nodded in return.

If she closed her eyes, she could see the lanterns of Barn Magic and hear the music play as the chili heated on the woodstove. *Success is what you define for yourself.* If that was true, how did it look for her? What did she want from this life: what the woman had to offer her, or what she had yet to find on her own?

She looked at the card in her hand, then tore it neatly in two pieces, four, eight. She emptied the shreds into her pocket.

Maybe the answer was as simple as this: maybe every voice had a role to play, a song each could use, a way to keep making things better. Maybe what seemed like the best was only the beginning.

Acknowledgments

A BOOK, LIKE A WRITER, IS SHAPED BY A THOUSAND hands. While I'll mention individuals below, I'd like to provide a more general appreciation first. Every day we are offered so many ways to make a difference to someone else: to be generous even if it slows us down, to be gentle when we see fear, to be respectful when confronted with something outside the range of our experience, to be real when it is easier to pretend. Those kindnesses—the ones I've experienced or witnessed throughout my life—have paved the road for this book. Thank you all for them. You're spectacular.

My gratitude for my agent, Alice Speilburg, is limitless. The fact that I finished writing *Devil and the Bluebird* is due in no small part to her patience, support, and sheer enthusiasm. I count myself lucky to have her as adviser, cheerleader, and advocate.

Thank you to my editor, Anne Heltzel, for recognizing the heart of this story and believing in it. Her vision helped to clarify my own and made this a far better book. Thanks also to the whole team at Abrams and, in particular, Alyssa Nassner. They took my humble, double-spaced, Times New Roman manuscript and made it into a beautiful, well-designed book. I honor their hard work.

While it is possible to write without ever interacting with another human, the road toward publication is one best traveled with friends. I am deeply indebted to Christine, who reads with heart and mind and challenges me to write for both; to Abigail, who understands that there is dark and light in all journeys; to Nancy, without whom I might still be writing stories in secret; and to Jenna, who has listened and supported endlessly.

To Hilary and Stone Pony Farm, my gratitude for quiet space and a warm woodstove and the smell of horses and hay.

To Ed, many thanks for stories about trains and for thoughts on Blue's travels.

The support of my parents has been essential to me as a writer and a person both. Thank you for believing in your eccentric daughter. Likewise, thank you to my brothers and their families for their own unique brands of cheerleading.

I know of no words graceful and strong enough to explain what my children, Daniel and Acadia, mean to me as a writer or a mom. Without them, my stories and my life would be so much less.

And to Jonathan—my truest reader and dearest friend—so many thanks, so much love.